FROM FLORIDA WITH LOVE

Sunsets & Happy Endings

Karen Dean Benson
Patricia Campbell
Allan Dyen-Shapiro

Mariah Lynne
A Y Stratton
Diana Welker

M.A. Ellis
Sonja Gunter
M.L. Joy
Doris Lemcke

Southwest Florida Romance Writers

From Florida with Love
Sunsets & Happy Endings

by

Karen Dean Benson
Patricia Campbell
Allan Dyen-Shapiro
M. A. Ellis
Sonja Gunter
M. L. Joy
Doris Lemcke
Mariah Lynne
A. Y. Stratton
Diana Welker

Published by
Melange Books, LLC
White Bear Lake, MN 55110
www.melange-books.com

ISBN: 978-1-61235-902-1

Published in the United States of America.

Cover Art by Caroline Andrus

This book is dedicated to all writers working to achieve their dream of publication.

The Fishy Place

Karen Dean Benson

Frustration creeps up my bones like crawling ants and nips at my fingertips. I'm alone in this little apartment and feel the urge to lash out. Ranting on a blank page of my computer will have to be the balm for my inner savage beast rearing its ugly head. I'm a writer and my grandmother and mother's stories itch to be told. How to begin? All the social turmoil in this place keeps me from settling to the task.

A long life brings me, Erin O'Banyon, no satisfaction right now. I'm far too concerned with Phases I, II, III, and IV of the *Fish Tail Manor and Resort for the Elderly* to concentrate on anything productive, and certainly not writing.

About six months ago, my eldest, Patrick, dumped me in Phase II at the ripe age of eighty-five. Believe me; I've come to learn being the oldest in Phase II is an accomplishment. If I fought for my rights, I could probably go back to Phase 1, but I no longer hold the controls to my future. In a weak moment, I signed them off to Patrick. Heck, I think he belongs in Phase III, except they don't deal with alcoholics here.

I can't blame it all on Patrick, I confess Fish Tail Manor and Resort held an allure when I lived in my own home. Someone else to cook and clean, no bills to pay, no upkeep. Mowing four acres was a weekly chore that consumed what time I have left. I traded all that for 24 hours, seven days a week that are all mine. I could probably arrange to have my butt wiped if I asked.

Fishy business is what I call this place. I play euchre on Wednesday evenings. On Thursday, they carted my euchre partner off to Phase III. You just never know, do not see it coming. I sure didn't, we won the game largely due to her finessing.

Staff can be blindsided, also. We all know a *client* can unexpectedly bypass Phase I, II, III, and IV and head straight to the morgue.

Condo to casket, I say. Like playing Monopoly. Oops, she landed on death row, oh, no, it's only Phase IV. The reality is that this is the end of the road at Fishy place. Makes one wish the movie Cocoon wasn't fiction.

I never could win at Monopoly. Nevertheless, I've outlived three husbands, am as healthy as an ox, walk several miles a day, and can't seem to winch down my brain. This serves me well as I pour through more than one hundred years of letters and newspapers from Saginaw and Detroit, Michigan that I'm trying to put in book form.

Before moving here, when I still lived in my home, walls and shelves spilled over with books, artifacts and relics collected on world travels. Of all my possessions, my adult children packed letters my ancestors wrote. Paper sacks crinkled and fragile with age, stale with basement mildew, burst with memories of lives well lived. My children decided I would need a hobby; thus, the sacks accompanied me here, to fishy place. Apparently, they knew I'd have time a plenty on my hands.

The day I became aware that this written history existed was in the fall of 1985 when my mother delivered them to me. That same day, she also announced she was having a heart valve replaced and needed someone to drive her to U/M Hospital in Ann Arbor, Michigan. My two brothers and I scrambled to talk her out of it but she kept repeating she wanted *quality of life*.

Can you beat that? Quality of life? She was seventy-nine at the time and drove her own car, lived alone, smoked every day, and loved beer, though diabetes put a bit of a crimp in that activity. Poor thing, she made it through the surgery fine, but the valve they prepared for her was too big and they kept her on machines while they found one small enough. By the time they finished surgery and weaned her from the machines, her organs had lost their gusto. She never left the ICU ward and three months later died on St. Paddy's day, a wee colleen to the end.

I always intended to write her life story, but my six children and all those husbands got in the way. Unbelievably, it has taken incarceration in this place to settle me down long enough to read the letters.

You would think at my age most things wouldn't shock me. Better yet, I simply wouldn't give a hot dang. Nevertheless, reading the history and categorizing them into years is humbling. My mother's stamina and determination to overcome some of the worst life had to offer fills me with latent awe and respect.

I feel like a blundering idiot. Do I begin when she was the baby in the family, not yet five, and her father abandoned them, only to be found twenty years later with another wife and children? The desertion cost my mother plenty, emotionally. She traced his grave, in unconsecrated ground because he'd committed suicide, to St. Louis, Missouri.

Isn't that the berries? I finally get to a time where I'm sitting at my desk sorting out my thoughts and the dinner-gong bongs. I'll get back to this maybe tomorrow.

I hate that blasted gong. It makes me feel like a cow plodding to the trough. When I leave my apartment, I'll be in a herd of my dearest and best friends, all fifty of them who live on this floor. They'll fight for the elevator and wiggle in, elbowing each other. I can still take the stairs. Thank God Phase II has stairs. Had enough of that elevator my first day here.

Oops, I forgot I signed up for a bus trip to Corkscrew Nature Preserve. We leave after lunch.

It's evening now. I'm in a better frame of mind after the adventure to the nature preserve. Our outing held some unusual twists, even for me.

The bus was jammed with my nearest and dearest. Bobbing white heads and metal walkers and canes plunked down in the front of the bus. By the time I climbed on board, I gingerly edged my way to the very back.

Walter Mature, I laugh at his name, because he sure is all of that, wrinkled and near bald, sat next to me and didn't rest his jaws the entire ride. I've noticed him a time or two playing Euchre. He had the gall to ask if he could be my partner next Wednesday. It was almost as if he knew my other partner wouldn't be around anymore. I considered his offer in two ways; he was either insensitive as a mule to intrude on the loss of a friend of mine, or he had gumption.

I didn't answer him and scooted closer to the window. I hoped he might think my batteries blew out. A satchel I carried held some of the letters I intended to read as we whistled along forty-one to the swamp. Walter Mature scooted right with me and I felt his eyes scanning the letter in my hand. It was dated 1902 and my grandmother had written to her eldest daughter, my Aunt Lucille, who'd been sent to Detroit to live with an uncle now that the family was destitute after the father abandoned them. My grandmother lied to an insurance company and said he died so she could get the little bit of money. At that point, she didn't really lie, she hadn't a clue what happened to him. And, to ease the financial burden, the priest at St. Mary's hired her as housekeeper to tide her over. Ten years were to pass when a friend of grandmother's saw her husband coming out of a bank in St. Louis, Missouri.

Walter's breath was on my cheek. He had his nerve. I glared at him and he had the decency to unpeel his eyes from my letter and sit back against the black vinyl bench. I folded the letter, tucked it back in the satchel, and put my attention to the scrub landscape.

"You've kept that letter over one hundred years. May I ask who wrote it?" I glanced at him as he pushed his glasses back up his nose.

"My grandmother. My mother's mother."

"Are there any surprises?"

My hand caressed the canvas bag. I'd only brought five letters with me. Five out of probably two hundred. "Not yet. But I know enough of their history to know the likelihood."

"You've set yourself a noble project." He patted his baldhead with a kerchief. The air conditioning wasn't reaching the back of the bus.

The bus swerved with some construction and my shoulder punched Mr. Mature. I would have apologized, but at that moment he lifted his arm to put behind me and I cast him what I hoped was a don't-you-dare-trespass-on-my-person glare.

He flexed his fingers, placed both his hands on his knees, and stared straight ahead. His glasses slipped down his sweaty nose.

I hugged the uncomfortable metal wall of the bus and did my best to pretend he didn't exist. I spent the time thinking of my mother's and grandmother's letters, wondering if I did know their complete history. When we finally arrived at the swamp there was quite a commotion exiting the bus and entering the preserve. The burly bus driver hand delivered almost every occupant to the planked walkway and in many cases opened up the metal walkers. His face blotched with the humidity. A good-natured man, he laughed and smiled with his duties.

I scooted faster than most to a deck that hangs out over the lowland, saturated with water, where you can watch the ibis and heron feed. I've been to the swamp before but this is the first time I see a flamingo. A gawky kind of bird, they usually fly in groups, this one was a loner. I read a book by the famous birder John Audubon. He was a painter and naturalist, he noted a flock of flamingo in the Florida Keys in 1832. Having read that, most folks don't realize the flamingo is not natural to Florida.

Like a gaggle of geese, gray heads bobbed along with metal walkers and canes and clanked their way up the boardwalk to the deck, pushing and shoving their way to the railing. My sandaled feet were in peril so I moved aside. A whole flock of Rosette Spoonbills winged in, a beautiful cloud of pale pink spluttered into the pond, reed thin legs settling into the scum. Their bills flat like paddles.

We're in a drought right now in southwest Florida, so this pond, which is designated a lake, has shrunk. In Michigan where I lived a good portion of my life, this is a puddle. Not much room for the heron now. He poked his tiny beaked head into the air and flapped his wings at the intrusion of the spoonbills settling to feed. They'd obviously scattered his lunch.

The scene reminds me of a diorama teaming with life. I stretched my neck to see to the far side of the pond. Spaniards beard flapped in the breeze, cutting a clear view of a gator. They always remind me of a discarded, blown-out tire until they move.

By golly, the gator's eyes shifted, indicating he searched for a snack. Did he eye the flamingo? His patience was impressive. Not so the metal canes and walkers. One thing about aging folks, they all seem to be short and require the need to be upfront, first at the railing. My ankles protected, I edged to the corner of the deck and hung on. Unlike the seniors maneuvering for space, the gator didn't make a ripple.

A brown water snake coiled along a branch on the other side of the pond, his forked tongue slicing the air. Knowing they feed on frogs and fish, he probably finished with lunch or he'd be slithering along the edge of the filmy layer of pond scum.

The scent of the pond, smoldering in the heat, calls to mind a powerful musky aroma stirring memories of places I've been; a gothic library with a dungeon-like basement in Detroit that I frequented as a young girl. A special favorite was a used bookstore in Dinky Town situated just off the campus of the University of Minnesota. The shelves teamed with the incense of who we are and from where we come. A thick molder reminded me I'm alive.

As a young girl, I used to visit the cave-like structures beneath cathedrals with my grandmother. We called them grottos. The mystery and lure of the darkened corners, filled with the incense of melted candle wax, was perfume for my young soul. Now, with my eyes closed, I take a deep breath of the life and death here in the jungle like atmosphere of Corkscrew preserve. Disparate as they are, the grottos and this preserve give me a sense of reason for being, makes me feel part of the structure.

A sudden splash, and my eyes spring wide chasing the memories back into their corner. The water show is over in a split second. Like the red velvet curtain on a drama, the gator snapped his mouth on a spoonbill, the snake slithered to another branch, the heron pointed his beak and took wing, and a cloud of pink followed in his wake.

The flamingo could have been a plastic lawn ornament, one leg bent upward, its concentration on a meal never wavered, even when ripples swept the surface of the pond.

OOhhs and aahhs rose from the grey-haired canes and walkers. Mr. Mature, unbeknownst to me, stood close behind. He placed his hand atop mine as it rested on the railing and said, "That we could fly away, too."

It was nearing sunset over the swamp, blistering rays of light beamed through the palm fronds and aged cedar and oaks. A patch of sandy beach, on the far edge of the pond, etched with the prints of wildlife.

I looked at the gnarled hand atop mine, then upward at Mr. Mature's watery eyes wondering what was on his mind. I asked, "How are you at finessing tricks?"

If his bushy eyebrows didn't instantly flag in the air, I'm not an aging crab. To what did he think I was referring? Men! I lifted his hand off mine and let it drop back to the railing, turned on my heel and walked away. I made darn sure to sit between two women on the ride back to Fishy Haven.

Three days later, I rode the elevator up to the tenth floor rather than take the stairs. My arthritis in my left knee was bothering me a bit. There is only one elevator and fourteen floors. This used to be a Hyatt rising like a Phoenix on the edge of the Caloosahatchee. A stucco building, pink like the flamingo. Driving across the bridge into North Fort Myers, you can't miss this aging relic.

In order to get to my apartment in less than an hour from the common dining room, I have to be quick like a jackrabbit after mealtime. The Otis is as slow as a tortoise. Folks get off one floor at time, up it vibrates until it finally empties. As we make our way upward, I visualize the waiting line in the lobby, winding like a snake about the marble floor. The metal walkers and canes baby step toward the shiny metal doors. Full up, the twin doors slowly close and once again, it shimmies upward floor by floor. The metal walkers, especially, take up so much room; five folks are a packed ride. I could suggest an organizational plan, but I'd rather complain.

I managed to be the first on and because I live on the tenth floor, scooted to the back. Nine of us without metal walkers got on, and wouldn't you know Mr. Mature was the tenth. He either didn't see me or was ignoring me, which suited me just fine. Tonight was euchre night and I hadn't decided what to do. He'd been the only one to ask about being my partner. As far as I am concerned, he can keep his bushy, testosterone brows to himself.

Slowly the Otis emptied and, by the time we arrived at my floor, there were six of us, counting Mr. Mature. I wasn't sure on what floor he lived. Didn't much care either.

The doors opened, I excused myself from the back and was about to cross the threshold when Mr. Mature said, "Hold the elevator while I walk my girlfriend to her door."

Can you imagine my shock? I don't know when the last time was that I blushed, but I felt the heat rise on my face. I blamed him for my embarrassment. I glanced at the occupants of the elevator and noted a smirk on Eleanor's sourpuss. John, the only black in the elevator, flashed an even row of very white teeth, and his brows rose like feathery angel wings against his dark skin. What is it with men and their eyebrows?

Mr. Mature put his arm out to hold the elevator door and I stepped across to the carpeted hallway. "Wait for me," he said as he turned to the others.

I tried to hide a supreme sense of satisfaction. I couldn't deny it—to myself that is. He certainly wouldn't know the enjoyment I felt at his rather courteous display.

We walked to my door without a word spoken. I turned the key in the lock and his hand pressed on mine. He said, "My dear Mrs. O'Banyon, I promise not to embarrass you at euchre if you will be my partner tonight."

I could hear the elevator thumping against itself, as the doors held open. In addition, I thought of all those metal walkers and canes lined up, patiently waiting for the return of the Otis to the ground floor. My crotchety old self turned a smile on him, couldn't help it, it just happened, just like that. "I'll meet you in the card room at seven."

We stayed after the game was finished and ate cakes and drank decaf tea. Mr. Mature seemed as though he had something on his mind. He'd done well at euchre, but then I wasn't a slouch either. He placed our plates at a table for six, but no one sat with us. The chocolate icing on the cake is my favorite. I'm a bit of a piggy with icing.

Mr. Mature set his cup down. "I'm interested in family history."

"Why is that?" I could feel a bit of icing on my upper lit and wiped it off.

"In a purely academic way I assure you, Mrs. O'Banyon." His whiskers, matching the pure white of his eyebrows, lifted at the ends. "My life's work was establishing archives for search and discovery of our ancestry."

My cake-free mouth dropped a bit. "Are you the one who came up with all those little leaves scattered on the pages of ancestry.com?"

His blue eyes twinkled. "As a matter of fact."

"And that's why you were reading over my shoulder the other day."

"It's a bad habit, I know. Nevertheless, the age of the letter was obvious. I couldn't help myself."

I folded my napkin, settled my hands in my lap, and scrutinized Mr. Mature. He could be the answer to my fuddling about with all those letters hovering over me. Could he possibly assist me with all the confusion at the daunting task ahead?

I leaned forward in my chair and placed my hand atop his. "Mr. Mature, would it be presumptuous of me to ask your advice on a project of mine?"

His eyes twinkled, his mustache widened and his brows flagged high. I took that as an affirmation and patted his warm hand.

THE END

A Deathbed Promise

Karen Dean Benson

On the veranda of my home, *Cantico del Rio*, I rock in my chair, a rug warms my legs. I look to the west as it stretches across the low hills to the Pacific with its sandy beaches tucked between cliffs of black lava. Our adobe affords a panoramic view of Carmel Valley. Beyond the valley toward the ocean are the God-given sunsets of every shade of oranges, pinks and purples that streak the sky like floating gossamer.

My padre had a book in his library of the two years he spent on the Peninsula of Florida before the Franciscan Abbot in Spain ordered him to San Carlos Mission in Carmel, Alta California. Someone water-colored the sunsets over the Gulf of Mexico and it's that picture I am reminded of as I enjoy my evening treasures. Brush strokes of color across the sky calling us to whisper prayers of gratitude.

Hawks on the hunt and the babble of Carmel *Rio* rolling toward the ocean adds luster to my musings on this pristine afternoon. Today, spring is in full bloom with its gift of another blue-eyed sky. A hint of white scatters above the horizon. I push against the floorboards, setting my chair in motion and make the sign of the cross on my old bones grateful to be alive in 1882.

On days like this, I wonder what my life would have been like without that deathbed promise so many years ago? It was another spring in 1826, the year I was twelve and a skinny little horrid *niña* with a razor tongue. I've earned the right to chuckle now, but my padre's favorite neophyte, Islay, used to refer to me as a *cabra montés.* Demanding and willful I admit, but calling me a wild goat made the others chuckle and served to reinforce my stubborn ways.

Through the years, salty dust on my lips brought a pungent remembrance of Carmel Mission, home for my first twelve years. Today it is a crumbling ruin. A tantalizing warmth spreads over me as memory of my childhood floats round about. I've been many places since that day my beloved padre died. I remember when I used to inhale the air giving my nose the responsibility to know if my search had ended.

But, even now, after more than sixty years, my heart remains at Carmel Mission. My tongue still tastes the dust, my nostrils quicken with the scent of salt and sun warmed earth and pine sap. I used to fear I would never know another place that I could call home. A place that would belong to me in not only a spiritual sense, but also a piece of land where I could scoop a handful of the earth and claim it mine.

I was twelve the day *Seňor* Viandante forced me from the newly dug grave where my padre was buried. My heart was broken. I was not forewarned I would be taken from my home when my padre died. When the fierce *hacendado* dragged me from the cemetery and put me astride my pinto, I learned of my fate. My reaction was horrid. I wasn't considering the future without my beloved parent. I wasn't smart enough to think beyond the moment. A searing, knife-like pain stabbed me senseless with the loss of the only person to ever love me and care for me. I wasn't thinking of how weary he had become of late. I only thought of myself.

My mother died giving birth to me. I used to rest my cheek on the warm soil that blanketed her. I did that as a child for many years. I thought I could hear her whisper to me. I envisioned her soft melodious tones of a childish lullaby mingling with the swish of the leaves. I lived but a few steps beyond her grave so I did not feel abandoned.

In retrospect I never should have. Padre Tomas Sandoval, a Franciscan Priest who governed San Carlos Borromeo Mission, delivered me from my dying mama. She had washed ashore in a tender and I was born as the small boat rocked with the gentle slap of the waves. My madre died quietly and at ease in my padre's arms moments later. The Indian women who also attended my unusual birth named me Chenoa. A loose translation means *white dove* in the neophyte's tongue. My certificate of baptism records say Lani Chenoa Sandoval, in the year 1814. *Lani* is the only sound my madre uttered during my birth. My padre wrote it on my certificate as part of my legacy.

Perhaps because I am an old woman now, I babble about the past, like the *Rio*. So let me tell you a little story. There have been three men in my life. Do women boast of more? Or less?

Of the three, the first I've never met. His seed created me. To this day I don't know his name, his origin, nothing. I only know that my mother's pregnancy wasn't another virgin birth ... so blasphemous. Forgive me, Lord.

The second man, Padre Thomas Sandoval, raised me. I will always think of him as my true father. My heart and soul were created from him. My mind was his to mold. My beloved father. My eyes mist, as I tell you this, I loved him so. My heart quickens. I miss him so. He died as my arms clung to him and my lips implored him to live for me. Understand, at that time, I was a very selfish *Nina.* Nonetheless, to this day I crave the presence of him in my life. He had been the center of my being. The sun rose with his hand on my cheek moments before he gave me Holy Communion, and the moon came up with his kiss upon my brow after vespers in our chapel. Life had been simple and lovely where the sea sparkled in the sunlight, its breakers curling lazy fingers around wild and rocky shores. Crimson paintbrush and golden yarrow colored the land.

I had grown up with the *Rumsen* and *Esselen* Indians at Carmel Mission. It had been quite by accident I realized I wasn't one of them. I never questioned the color of my skin, nor the green of my eyes or hair that was sun streaked. Actually, my personal attributes had been quite dirty most of the time. This is not a confession of my health habits. I hadn't known better and it was beneath my padre to broach the subject.

The Indian women, for the most part, recognized me as Padre Sandoval's *property* and would not trespass as a form of etiquette. So, there I was, dirty as a small brave, allowed to ride astride, dress as a male child, still, I was educated in Latin, French and English. Cipher, I refused. Music, I had no time for. Philosophy, I loved. Probably that was the part of me that was so contrary most of the time. He introduced me to

Socrates who taught that every person has full knowledge of the truth in his soul and that a person need only be spurred to reflection for self discovery. That was a challenge my padre presented to me often.

Which brings me to the rest of my tale.

I said there were three men. The first two gave me life. One physical, the other, intellectual and spiritual. I was a young branch, tender and supple. Eager for life; but this third man—ah, yes—this third man, he gave me a future.

Our first meeting was on the day my beloved padre lay dying. We exchanged heated words, this third man and I. At least I spit words of anger. *Seňor* Viandante, was the soul of comportment. Fear welled up within me that day and it spilled out of my mouth in the worst imaginable display. At some point, I offered apologies, but there was a distance of many months between my insult and my apology. Oh, my infuriating pride. I truly acted like a *wild goat*.

That single, horrid day began unremarkable enough with Mass in the chapel, whispered words of devotion to the *Santos* and Padre Serra, the consecration, Holy Communion. My padre spoke more softly than usual. He required assistance walking to the altar. There were eleven or twelve of us in attendance. Two years before, Carmel Mission had been ordered to secularize and had steadily diminished in size. Before the order, several hundred would come in from the fields for Matins. Now only Islay, padre's faithful plum-colored neophyte, the women from the kitchen, their children and me. I sat with the latter. We younger participants in the Holy Sacrifice of the Mass had plans for the time after breakfast.

My skillful riding had been challenged. I was quick to rise to the taunting and itched to prove my accusers wrong. To sit near them was to ensure they not forget the insult, or my eagerness to rectify their misconceptions.

So wrapped in my own injured self, I did not notice Islay carry my padre from the chapel. I swear to you, had I taken notice of him faltering and grabbing at the sacred linen altar cloth to right himself, I would not have run from the chapel as the last words of prayer were uttered. I would not! But I did not see, so self-absorbed was I. It wasn't until later in the night Islay recanted the altar mishap to me.

My next hours were spent astride my pony, given to me especially because he wanted me to have a childhood of some normalcy. I had been an infant birthed of a white woman in this dark skinned and brown-eyed land. He felt I had lost so very much. I could never convince him I would not trade him or my life with him for a mother and father and brother and sister. Perhaps I could not convince him because I was never really sure myself.

However, being a man of great wisdom, he knew unquestionably what he meant to me and, I to him. I have drawn strength and comfort from this knowledge in the years since.

And, as I have said, this was the day I met *Seňor* Viandante, the third man in my life.

After my contest of daring in the hills, I returned to the Mission in search of my padre to seek assurance for my skill. I was told he was in his room, a sparse, whitewashed room with one tiny window for air and light. The tiles, worn by the padding of many feet, were cool to my step. The day's heat had not yet risen full. Upon entering the room I saw Islay and my padre, who was on his cot hands folded across his grey-robed chest. I knew immediately that something was wrong and dropped to my knees at his side.

I'm sure I babbled of seeing to his comfort, and scorned Islay for not informing me. My small frame was garbed in the only pair of breeches and shirt that I owned. The shirt was a faded pinkish shade not unlike pictures in padre's library of flamingos from his native Spain. My sash, which kept my breeches from falling about my ankles, was the color of an orange-ripened sunset. My hair was quite short. It curled of its own free will. And, as I disliked having to comb and fuss with it I insisted on keeping it cropped close to my head.

From a dark corner, a deep English-speaking voice jolted me.

"Allow him to rest, *Niňo*. It has taken much out of him to converse with me this morning. Your histrionics will tire him even more."

I turned to this intruder, angry that he thought me a boy but far more degraded that he had witnessed my vulnerable display. I eyed an immaculately dressed *hacendado* with piercing blue eyes rare in our part of the world. My lips curled around sarcasm. "Then perhaps you should leave him to me, *Seňor*. I will not be as ignorant as you of his welfare."

A flicker of ridicule crinkled the corners of his eyes. He laughed. A rich sound, uncommon at the Mission of late.

"For a mere child, you are waspish, forcing me to conclude you are truly of the fairer gender. Accept my apology, *Niňa*."

I saw those crinkled lines mock me further and my chin rose, the better to glare my defiance.

His words were low and soft, "If it is beneath you to speak civilly in this room, it is right to keep silent, or I will have to ask you to leave."

I remember placing balled fists on my hips rather than his stomach. "It is I who live here and you who will leave at my order." And, as if I needed to further embarrass myself, I commanded, "Islay, take this man from here. I do not like him."

Islay's gaze cast heavenward in a gesture of futility. Little did I know at the time that I was in danger of jeopardizing my padre's grand plan. Before another glance was exchanged, my padre experienced a coughing fit that sent the three of us into motion.

I dropped once more to my knees in prayer quickly promising anything to all the *Santos* in heaven in exchange for his relief. The *seňor* and Islay lifted his frail figure to ease the need for air. At length, he quieted and his watery eyes lifted with much effort, drinking in the scene before him.

The length of his rope rosary drifted from his waist. I grabbed it, fervently caressing the three knots reminding us of Christ's scourging. As I caressed each knot between thumb and finger, I was most intent upon a child's negotiation with God to spare him. Innocent desire filled me with desperation and when his coughing ceased, I opened my eyes to behold the suffering man who was the center of my life.

"Chenoa, child..." His hand lifted a fraction. I moved closer and took it in mine as if it was the host of Christ drifting through the air. I brushed the cold fingers with my lips, tasting him.

"You must be strong when his time comes. He would not want you to be weak," Islay cautioned.

I felt my face pinch with an unfamiliar fear. "His time?"

Islay bent on one knee alongside me and placed a warm hand on my shoulder. "Our beloved padre is gravely ill, Chenoa. Even he knows his time has come. *Señor* Viandante is here at Padre Tomas' request. He made a promise to our padre to take up the care of you."

Like someone in a dream I turned and glared at the tall stranger, then to the dying figure on the small cot. His breathing was deep and labored as though he dug far into his lungs for the precious air required to live yet another moment. His eyes were closed as if in sleep though his hands tightly clasped mine.

I denied the evidence. "No! No! It is not so. You have been ill before and gotten better. I will tend you. Please, my father, tell me you will not die. I beg of you." I pleaded with him until the sobs racked my frame and I could no longer speak clearly.

He was my father!

He was my life!

Moments passed, until the painful truth came to me and I knew my childish outburst would not change the certainty of what was to come. His hand lifted to my cheek spidery with veins across the parchment skin. His God was calling him and yet he comforted me, reached out for me.

"Child of my heart," he whispered. I was not to hear him speak again. Those loving, marbled hands that held mine eased their grasp. I was told I screamed; a high pitched scorching wail that rang throughout the adobe walls and filled the corridors announcing my father's death to all who heard. The stranger and Islay pried me from him and peeled my fingers from his. I was more rigid in pain than my padre was in death.

It was in that very moment that I was thrust from one world to another. From poverty to plenty, from benevolence to indifference, and from loving guardianship to emotional neglect.

Eventually, with maturity gained from years spent in a convent, I accepted my padre's wisdom.

The third man, *Señor* Sebastian Viandante and I have shared all the years since. Our many children grounded me in a life full of love. A few leagues from our ranch is the crumbled edifice of Mission San Carlos Borromeo. Once a year I take a wagon load of children and baskets of food to the Mission grounds and we sit under the old oaks that edge the cemetery and I tell them tales of my first twelve years.

This makes me wonder what my life would have been like without that deathbed promise. Or, perhaps going back further in time, what if the Franciscan Abbot in Spain had not ordered my padre to leave Florida and go to California.

THE END

About the Author

Karen Dean Benson

A member of SWFRW since 2008, Karen divides her time between Michigan and Florida. She grew up in Detroit, Michigan. A graduate of Northwood University. She loves research, history, and tales of the convoluted lives we all lead.

Her novels frequently involve young women navigating the social constraints of the 18th and 19th centuries. Her short story *A Deathbed Promise* presents a character from her novel *Mission Song*, while *The Fishy Place* is based on letters written over a span of 100 years by her grandmother and mother.

Serious about her craft, Karen belongs to a number of writing groups: Romance Writers of America, Gulf Coast Writers, Florida Writers, MSU Creative Writers, Peninsula Writers of Michigan and three different critique groups. What she doesn't much like is housework.

Karen can be reached at:

www.facebook.com/ Karen Dean Benson.
www.karendeanbenson.com (currently under development)

Fred—A Dog Odyssey

Patricia Campbell

My little sister, Mei-Mei, and I were very worried. Our water dishes were empty again and we hadn't been fed since the day before. All my brothers, sisters, and cousins were very hungry and thirsty. We hadn't seen the good lady who took care of us, and played with us, for a long time.

A couple of sunrises ago a small lady with long, dark hair opened the gate and entered our yard. Hurray! We were so excited. We barked, ran and jumped up and down. Someone was finally going to fill our water dishes and feed us.

I jumped and barked in front of this new lady. She kicked me very hard and yelled at us to keep away from her. I yelped with pain. I couldn't breathe for a minute, and just lay on the ground, wondering what I had done to be punished. No human had ever hurt me before. Did I frighten her?

The bad lady cut open a large bag of dry dog food and dumped it on the filthy ground. It didn't smell like our regular food. Nobody had come to clean up our play area for a long time. It was very hot. Flies buzzed everywhere, trying to get in our eyes and noses.

After filling the water troughs with the hose the bad lady yelled at us again before she locked the gate and left.

We were so hungry and thirsty that we began drinking and eating the minute she closed the gate and left. I drank lots of water, but my side hurt so bad I couldn't push myself through the crowd of my relatives to reach the food. When I finally found an opening there wasn't much left. Very few kibbles scattered here and there on the dirt.

Mei-Mei looked sad and bedraggled. Like the rest of us she was dirty. We hadn't had baths or haircuts or been brushed by the good lady and her helpers in such a long time, I didn't think our mothers would have recognized us. I was in much worse condition than my sister because I had a lot of fine wavy hair that must be kept trimmed and brushed. Mei-Mei only had hair on the top of her head, pointed ears, tail, and feet. We were Chinese Crested, both from the same litter, but we looked different. Mei-Mei was very beautiful, and she assured me I was the handsomest of all our other siblings and cousins, even with my long wavy coat and flopping ears. I, and the others who resembled me, were called Powderpuff. The girls don't mind that name, but some of us boys find it embarrassing.

My official name was Chopsticks, but the kind lady who loved us called me Fred. I liked that much better. It was bad enough being a Powderpuff without also having a silly name like Chopsticks.

Mei-Mei and I found a little piece of shade in the corner of the play yard. Mei-Mei and the others like her needed shade so they didn't get sunburned. She worried about me. It was so hot. Each time I panted to cool off I got a sharp pain in my side. Mei-Mei knew I hadn't had much to eat.

Soon the sun went down at the edge of the big water. This is the time of day the good lady usually brought a chair to our kennel and sat with us.

No one came to our kennel, and the house where the kind lady lived remained dark. I fell into troubled sleep and wondered what the new day would bring.

Very early the next morning, the sun barely up, two big trucks pulled up next to the fence of our play yard. We were awake instantly, wondering what was about to happen. Several men got out of the trucks and stood around talking, pointing, and nodding their heads. A very large man opened the gate.

None of us ran to greet him. We were much more cautious with these strangers than we had been with the mean woman who was here the day before. I was curious, though.

The big man knelt down and spoke in a gentle voice, coaxing us to approach him. I slowly inched forward, wagging my tail to let him know I was friendly. The other men stayed outside our yard.

"There's a good boy," he said, and patted me on my head.

It felt so good to have that kind hand touching me. Soon all the others crowded around wanting the gentle touch we'd all missed.

"Okay," the man said. "Bring in the cages." He stood and gestured for the others to enter the kennel. "Let's get these poor pups rounded up and into the trucks. Doctor Sanchez will have her hands full when we get them over to the clinic."

This was very good news. We all knew and loved Dr. Sanchez. A visit to her cool clinic would be a welcome relief from the hot, stinky kennel. All one hundred and forty of us were soon settled down, two to a cage, and on our way in the two trucks.

Mei-Mei and I snuggled in our shared carrier for the short trip. When we approached the clinic the other truck turned into Dr. Sanchez's parking lot, but ours kept right on going. We thought our driver must be lost. We traveled for quite a while, and then slowed and turned into large yard with a small house surrounded by a fence.

The nice driver and his helper came to the back of the truck, lifted down our cages, and carried them to the gate of the yard. Mei-Mei and I worried and wondered why we had not been taken with the other truck to see Dr. Sanchez.

"Okay, open up the gate and put them inside the fence," the driver said.

We soon found ourselves with our cousins on a large green lawn. There were big water tubs for drinking and large clean pans filled to the brim with fresh, sweet smelling kibble. We forgot our worries and ate and drank to our hearts' content. Mei-Mei followed me to a large shade tree where we rested on the cool grass. My side was beginning to feel better, but when I licked it I could feel a large lump.

"We're finished here for today," the truck driver said to his helpers. "This bunch will go to Dr. Sanchez day after tomorrow."

"Too bad about the old dog lady," one of the helpers said.

"She'll be back on her feet soon," the driver answered. "But she's too old to be running that kennel alone. They've shut her down."

It sounded like we would be seeing our siblings and cousins again in just a few days. Mei-Mei and I snuggled together and fell into a sound sleep. Our tummies were full and I had pleasant dreams of the kind lady who always took care of us.

The next morning the far side of the big lawn erupted with fountains and sprays of water. Many of us ran there to play. I couldn't run, but I wanted to get under that water. When I finally did, it felt so good pouring down on my head and back, soaking all my hair.

Mei-Mei yipped with excitement, dashing in and out of the fine spray, chasing our cousins. A man and a small boy came to the fence and watched us. They laughed and pointed at our antics. The sun grew warmer, and my fine wavy hair dried. It wasn't the same as a nice grooming, but I felt a lot cleaner.

The man and boy entered the yard when the water went off. They walked around with small shovels and plastic bags to pick up our messes. From our piece of grass in the shade, Mei-Mei and I watched the man show the boy the best way to do the job. Soon we dozed.

Later our food and water got replenished. We soon forgot what it was like to be hungry and thirsty.

The big truck and the men with cages came to take us to see Dr. Sanchez. When one of the men lifted me, I yelped with pain. He set me down and looked for the source of my discomfort. Soon, he called one of the others over.

These men were gentle when they touched my ribs. They put me in a separate cage by myself. Mei-Mei's eyes grew sad. She whined when they put me on the truck alone. We had never been separated. I was relieved to see them load all the other cages and put them in the back of the truck with me. At least I wasn't being sent to a different place than my sister.

When we arrived at the clinic the men pulled the other cages out of the truck. I watched anxiously from my dark corner. They closed the door and the truck pulled away.

They forgot me!

I barked and barked. They didn't hear me over the roar of the big engine. The truck rumbled along, my lonely cage bouncing in the big empty, dark space. I was afraid I'd never see my sister again.

After a while I gave up barking and tried to sleep, but my ribs hurt and I was very thirsty. We drove and drove. Then I heard the truck slow, and finally stop. When the big door rolled up, I barked as loud as I could and blinked at bright light streaming inside.

"What the heck? There's still a dog in here." The driver shook his head and stood staring at me with hands on his hips. "What now?"

The three men, their eyes wide with surprise, climbed inside and looked at my cage. "We can't go back, it's too far," one of them said. "We'd better give him a drink, or we'll have a dead dog on our hands."

The driver knelt down. He looked at my tag. "His name is Chopsticks. He's the sick one. We'll drop him off at the animal shelter. They'll probably put him down." He patted my head. "Sorry, boy." He stood. "Give him some water. We'll get back on the road after we eat."

I was shaking from head to toe, too nervous to drink the water they gave me. Where were they taking me? What would happen to me?

The men got down from the truck and pulled the door closed. I was in the dark again. I was afraid and hungry.

Soon the truck engine roared to life, and rumbled back onto the road. I tried to stop shaking because it hurt my ribs, but I was so afraid and lonely that I couldn't.

They stopped again and the door opened. Blue and orange filled the sky. Nearly sunset. I stared out the back of the truck at the water. It looked like the familiar view of the big water in the Gulf of Mexico, from our home with the good lady. Maybe I wasn't so far away after all. Hope bloomed in my belly. Maybe I'd see my sister and cousins soon.

The big truck driver stood away from the back of the truck. He talked to a strange lady for a while. I couldn't hear what they were saying, but there was a lot of gesturing as they approached.

"We took him to the animal shelter, but it was closed. The poor little guy is sick. I hoped you'd have a look at him, maybe take him off our hands and deliver him to the shelter tomorrow."

"You know darn well I won't take any dog to that place. The nearest no-kill shelter in southwest Florida is fifty miles from here. Bring me the cage and I'll have a look at him." She didn't sound very happy about it.

I stood when the man set the cage at the door of the truck and opened the wire door. I was afraid to trust this lady. She seemed kind of angry, and I didn't want to be hurt again, so I backed up.

The lady spoke. "That's okay, boy." She didn't reach for me. "He's a filthy mess, but he doesn't look sick to me. Come, boy. Good boy. Come."

I crept forward, but was prepared to back up. I wagged my tail to signal that I wouldn't bite. My heart banged against my sore ribs.

"What a good boy. That's it. Let me have a look at you." The lady reached in her pocket and held a handful of kibble toward me. It smelled good. I wanted to take it, but I was afraid.

"You men back off," she said, and then dropped some of the kibble where I could reach it. "I know you want to get on the road, but I need to gain his confidence, so move away, please." The driver and his helpers disappeared around the side of the truck, out of sight.

I cautiously ate the kibble as the lady watched me. She held her hands to her sides. Finally, I stepped out of the carrier and obeyed her signal to sit. She spoke softly and held out another handful of food. "What a smart boy you are. Come."

Her touch was feathery soft on my chin. I trusted she wouldn't hurt me, and I let her run her hands over my back and sides. When she found the sore spot, I winced, but remained still.

"What happened here?" she asked, but of course all I could do was stare at her soft blue eyes. "Somebody must have hurt you. Let me look at your eyes, baby." She stroked me softly and checked my eyes then she very carefully looked at my teeth. "You're not sick, are you?"

I wagged my tail. She lifted me out and carried me to the edge of the sand. Glad to be off that noisy vehicle, I sniffed around and found a good spot. What a relief!

She slipped a leash over my head and led me toward a fenced area with a large pond in the center. Surprised to see odd, tall, pink birds standing in the water, I huffed.

"It's okay, boy. You've never seen flamingoes? They're my pets, Wilber and Orville. They won't hurt you." She slipped off the leash, closed the gate and left me to stare at the strange birds.

The men strolled to meet the lady outside the gate. The driver told her, "We left their pedigree papers with the vet, Cora. Too bad he's sick. He's a purebred, probably worth a bundle."

"That dog is not sick." She flapped her hand. "He's been hurt. Looks to me like somebody kicked him. I'll keep him a few days and see how he does, but you know I can't afford vets. You took advantage of my soft heart by bringing him here, Tom." She scowled at the big man and shook her head.

Tom put his hand on her shoulder. "Sorry, I didn't know what else to do with him. We have to be in Atlanta by morning. Next time I'm down this way I'll bring you a couple bags of dog food."

"Forget the dog food. Twenty dollars will do." She held out her hand. "Cough it up."

Tom chuckled and shook his head. He reached in his back pocket and pulled out a square lump of brown leather. He handed her a piece of colored paper. "You're a hard woman, Cora."

She took the paper. It didn't look tasty like a dog treat. "I'm not hard, Tom, I'm tough. I need to be, or people would drop every abandoned animal in the county on my doorstep. You get along now, and don't show your face around here for a while."

The truck soon pulled away. Cora leaned on the fence and smiled. I stumbled over a small tortoise on my way to her. The good lady who used to take care of us had several of these same creatures. I never did figure out what good they were.

"Let's get you some food and water. Does that sound good, boy?"

It certainly did.

Cora dropped a pile of blankets under a huge strangler fig, and patted them. "You can sleep here, boy. Tomorrow I'll give you a bath and maybe we can see what you should look like."

That sounded good too.

The smell of salt water hung in the warm humid air the next morning. Everything was damp, me, my blankets, and the grass. I raised my head and took a good look at my surroundings. The pink birds had their heads tucked under a wing. Nothing moved. Not a breath of air riffled a leaf or a blade of grass. I was a long way from home.

Sadness filled me when I thought of Mei-Mei and my cousins. I dropped my chin on my paws. Somehow I knew I'd never see them again. What would become of me?

The familiar sound of a rooster shattered the morning silence.

My ears perked up when a screen door slammed.

"Okay, okay. I'm coming." Cora went into a small shed and picked up a bucket. My eyes followed her when she crossed the property and opened a wire fence. The sound of chickens clucking built louder and louder when she scattered feed on the ground. Then she dumped the contents of the bucket in a wooden trough. The good lady had chickens too. The sound of them comforted me.

I stayed with Cora for a long time. She complimented me on my beauty after my bath and a good brushing. She also took the scissors to my hair and cut a good deal of it off. That felt so good in the muggy weather.

Bright colored lights began to appear on Cora's house, and I watched her string great lengths of them in the trees and shrubs. I felt so much better and even enjoyed barking and harassing the flamingoes. Cora admonished me when I upset them. They flapped their wings with great excitement while they squawked and croaked. It was great fun.

One day a woman and a girl came to visit Cora. They stood at the fence and talked to me. The girl said, "I think we just found Larry's Christmas present. Let's ask Cora if this little ragamuffin is available for adoption."

That was puzzling. I knew I was a pup, a dog, and a Chinese Crested, but had never heard the term ragamuffin. Had they confused Powderpuff with ragamuffin? They were friendly, so I saw no reason to make a fuss over it.

Later that day a strange car parked in front of Cora's house. A man with large eyeglasses stepped out and knocked on Cora's front door. Cora was in the chicken yard so I barked to let her know the man was there.

"Larry, hello! I'm out here," she called. "Have a look at Chopsticks and tell me what you think."

Oh dear, the name on my tag. I'd almost forgotten it. The man strolled to the fence and beckoned me. "Here, Chopsticks, here boy."

He had a friendly face and voice, so I trotted to the fence and stood on my hind legs, enthusiastically wagging my tail. There was something compelling about this man. He smelled wonderful and kind.

"What a silly name for such a handsome guy." He handed me a small dog biscuit. I politely took it in my mouth then spit it out. I don't like dog biscuits.

"Ah, particular are we?" The man laughed and scratched my chin. He called to Cora, "May I take him out for a stroll on the beach?"

"Sure, Larry, go ahead. He's shy of the surf, but enjoys running now that his side has healed. Take him. There's a leash on the hook by the gate."

I hurried to the gate. When the man called Larry knelt to put the leash over my head, I extended my front legs around his neck. When he tried to pull me away I held on for all I was worth. He laughed.

Larry stuffed the leash in his pocket and carried me to the beach. I wouldn't let go when he attempted to set me down, so he just walked for a bit. He sat on the sand and petted my back and head. "What's the matter, boy? Are you afraid I'll leave you?"

Yes, I was afraid. I wanted very much to stay with this good man.

"That's okay, boy. Let's just take a walk." He pulled me away and set me on the sand. I stared into his eyes with my most sincere, pleading expression and wagged my tail.

He stood. "Let's go." He walked toward the water. I followed close on his heels.

We strolled for quite some time at the chasing water's edge. I walked next to his left leg as I'd been trained to do by the good lady at home. When he stopped, I stopped and sat, gazed into his eyes, and waited for his next move.

"How would you like to come home with me?" He sat on the sand again and I crawled onto his lap. "We do need to do something about that name of yours though. Let's decide on a better one. What do you say?"

I grinned and wagged. Larry went through a long list of names. I sat quietly as he continued, and hoped he'd finally hit on the right one. "Boy? Buster? Whitey? Louie? Barkey? Fluffy? Fido? I'm running out of names here."

I fixed my gaze on Larry's eyes, encouraging him not to give up.

He stared, and a light of inspiration sparked in his eyes. “Hmm. Let’s see. How about Fred?”

I sprang up and covered his face with kisses then hopped off his lap and chased my tail in a happy circle.

Larry laughed and stood. He brushed the sand off his pants. “Okay, Fred it is, let’s go see if Cora will allow me to take you home.”

I bounded ahead of him in a state of joy. Cora watched from the gate, where the grass edged the sand. I raced past her to the pond where I proceeded to bedevil Wilbur and Orville. They’d be very glad if I went home with Larry.

Finally I dropped from exhaustion and lay on my belly, frog-style, and watched the sun as it sank closer to the water. Larry dropped the leash around my head and led me to his car.

“Be a good boy, Fred. I have someone I’d like you to meet. The little lady has been down in the dumps ever since I adopted her last month.” He peeked in the car and lifted me to look in the open window. “There she is. I call her Sister.”

Mei-Mei stared back at me for a split second, sniffed, then jumped to her feet and barked. I leapt from Larry’s arms, through the open window. Little Sister and I were so excited to be reunited that we tumbled off the seat onto the floor, and hopped back up again. I licked her face and she batted me with her front paws.

“What’s all the racket?” Cora called.

Larry laughed. “Look at these two. You’d think they knew each other.”

THE END

About the Author

Patricia Campbell

I wrote my first novel at the age of six. It was titled "The Mouse," and it was only a couple of pages long—including illustrations! My mother saved that *first edition* and every now and then I take it out and laugh over it.

When my beloved husband suddenly died while we were vacationing in Switzerland, writing became my personal grief counselor. As a mother of two adult sons, and the owner of a busy retail travel agency, with plans to add a coffee bar, my two best stress relievers were walking and writing.

At first the writing allowed me to pour out all my sadness. Then, the more I wrote, the more I realized I would go on, I would be happy, and I had a lot of living to do.

I wrote the first few chapters of a story and gave them to an author friend to read. She said it was a good start, but "then what?" I didn't have a clue how to plot a story, develop memorable characters or format a manuscript. I needed to take writing classes.

I've had two contemporary romance novels published now, but my first two finished manuscripts still reside on a CD or thumb drive somewhere around here, and I certainly hope they're never found. I can't bear to erase them because they're mine, they're loved, and like a crazy relative one hides in the attic, they reside in a quiet, safe place.

As I worked to learn the craft, I developed a whole new circle of friends and fellow writers. I joined a writing group in Los Angeles, and then later here in Florida. I know and love writers of every genre, some published, some working toward publication, and some who've timidly dipped their toes in the vast, cold writing ocean.

Visit my Website: www.pattycampbell.com
Email me: patricia@pattycampbell.com
My Blog: http://pattycampbellauthor.blogspot.com
Facebook: Patty-Campbell-Author
Amazon: https://amazon.com/author/pattycampbell
Goodreads: https://www.goodreads.com/author6560120.Patty_Campbell

The Fundamental Things Apply

Allan Dyen-Shapiro

The info-feed to my Google specs cut out the instant the Everglades puddle jumper touched down at Fort Myers' RSW International Airport. The regional authorities blocked most electronic communication, ostensibly to promote tourism. "Get away from the prying eyes of the business world," the glossy poster lining the jetway proclaimed. And some travelers did come to vacation. More came to exchange secrets.

Secrets are my business, and my business found me strolling toward the security checkpoint, gazing at the sun rising behind glass. My employer this week, the Shariah Law Enforcer for the Islamic Caliphate of North Africa, disliked secrets because they allowed conspiracy. Sure, some in Mali doubted that Allah transported Mohammed's child through time to rule in our present, August 2024, but if they kept their beliefs to themselves, they were no threat.

Others were. And so the Caliph, the supreme ruler sent by God, fancied American mini-drone technology. He wanted it all to himself. My assignment was to acquire the know-how from industry leader American Homeland Corporation and then kill the engineers who kept the technology secret for the corporate minions of Satan.

The Caliph paid me well, in advance. He bought my expertise, but he overspent. Money wasn't my motivation.

* * * *

The double door under the Ground Transportation sign slid open. The wet heat reminded me of Delhi, as did the porters groveling at my feet for the chance to earn my pocket change. Dozens of them, only one of me. The other travelers swatted them away as they did the swarming mosquitoes, apparently the customary way to treat the poor in Florida, as in Delhi. The Internet blackout meant no augmented reality, but with a blink, the specs converted to mirror shades that concealed my expression.

A man with a receding hairline and prominent razor stubble, dressed in a taxi driver's starched denim work shirt and pressed slacks, beckoned to me. "Come this way, my friend," he said in a Russian accent. When I ignored him, he unzipped a belt pouch to offer a moment's glance at a .22 magnum mini-revolver. "March."

Four steps toward the rear of the cab and several dozen racing heartbeats later, panic subsided as my eye caught the pink flamingo on his taxi's license plate. The sign.

Knowing my host wouldn't kill me before the Caliph paid for his services, I surrendered my baggage, keeping only my water bottle. As he stowed my suitcase in the trunk, I clambered through the front passenger door.

The instant my back met the cushion, the belts snapped closed, pinning me to the seat. My mother had warned me gypsy cabs in America were dangerous.

"Alex." The man extended his hand toward mine.

Although I grew up with *Namaste* and later learned American greeting customs, the restraints made either bowing with pressed palms or shaking hands difficult. I rotated my wrist to extend an appendage, gripped, and felt a needle stick. As he retracted his arm, he revealed his blood cell DNA identification device.

"Ali Acharya, welcome to Florida." He smiled. "I will, of course, extend you the same courtesy." With a turn of his wrist, he offered his left palm.

Restrained, I fumbled and managed to slide my identifier from a pocket. I poked. The extracted drop of blood revealed his identity as Alexander Belyakov, chief technology officer for American Homeland

Corporation. The model I had was enhanced with functions Belyakov's lacked—its supplementary window displayed the letter B.

"We go," he said.

As Belyakov pulled out into traffic, worming his way through cars leaving the airport, I typed the letter C on my ID contraption keypad, hoping changing lanes had distracted my adversary. He didn't seem to notice, nor did he react when I jabbed myself, this time with the dispensing needle, before closing the gadget and sliding it back into my pocket.

I checked my watch. I had twelve hours.

* * * *

The ride passed in silence. A few kilometers from the airport, we picked up I-75. The green light as we passed through the enclosed on-ramp meant neither X-ray nor mass spectrometry found anything in our car that constituted a risk to corporations subscribing to the highway security service.

Belyakov took the fourth exit. Palm Beach Boulevard.

"This morning, I carry nothing, but later, I give you software. Just the software."

Which explained how we negotiated highway security—no hardware to detect. He was smooth. I'd need the software. I couldn't kill him. Yet.

We passed burned-out trailers and makeshift shanties. At an intersection, a bus displaying the name of an all-inclusive resort loaded uniformed workers. Helmeted police officers trained their rifles on the orderly line.

Security contractors. They'd worn the same uniform in Delhi in the years just before I left, the bad years. Prior to that, we'd managed to feed people. I trained and then worked as an agricultural engineer, helping to wrest control of the food supply from the corporations, to win a victory for the poor of the world. But then the ag conglomerates sent the viruses that destroyed our crops, and famine killed my wife and son.

I lived. Alone and angry, but with skills I could peddle. I'd told the Shariah Law Enforcer I was a freelancer, happy to take contract work in the fight against oppression. He'd thought he comprehended.

Belyakov, all business, didn't waste time attempting to understand me. "The hardware you pick up at first stop from idiot who knows nothing. He will recognize you. I tell him to watch for nerdy Indian with fashion sense typical of engineer."

After a moment spent pondering the meaning of this description, I resolved to adjust my shirt pocket's contents, once Belyakov freed my arms, to conceal the graphing calculator. A pity—the blue color matched my Google specs and coordinated with my brown, short-sleeve dress shirt in a way my mother had found dashing. Engineering's gain was Bollywood's loss, she'd said.

"At second stop, you meet Jenna Laszlo. She works on University of Michigan team who developed mini-drone technology back in 2013. You learn how to assemble from her. Then you come back to me."

A hard right turn brought us past a sign proclaiming the area to be Manatee Park. A tourist site, from the looks of it, but I'd left my Fodor's guide in Miami, as my corporate hosts generally didn't allow time for sightseeing. Even when they didn't plan to kill me.

The car screeched to a halt. Belyakov reached in his pocket, extracted a set of car keys and handed them to me. "You see white Toyota at other end of parking lot? Yours for today." The belts unlocked and snaked back into their receptacles.

Belyakov passed me a black box with a red button. "Shortwave radio, we own band at two thousand kilohertz." Presumably American Homeland also owned the bureaucrat in charge of suppressing the broadcast spectrum for the less connected. "Press six times, pause, six more. Your Shariah Law Enforcer picked code. Same signal after you leave Ms. Laszlo, same on beach at sundown, after I give you software."

Then funds would transfer between bank accounts, and I would become expendable. Neither retirement benefits nor life insurance was standard in my line of work.

"Now, go. My idiot, he wait for you. Be careful. He think our rivals watch him."

I had eleven hours, twenty minutes.

* * * *

After stowing my gear in the Toyota, I crossed the parking lot and strolled past the interpretive center, a shack with vending machines peddling trinkets inside and benches facing a video presentation on manatees outside. A five-year-old Japanese girl was shooting video of her brother making his gift shop purchase, a plush, lavender toy manatee, with the words "Welcome to Fort Myers" branded on the side. Their parents glanced at the video while consulting an English translation app on their cell phones.

With my specs out of commission, I grabbed an interpretive map from a plastic dispenser nailed to a wooden post. The trails all led to a power plant discharge canal that emptied into the Orange River. Manatees, the brochure explained preferred warm water during winter months. Moreover, the industrial effluent killed noxious weeds and harmful algae, allowing marine mammals to flourish.

A curving, two hundred-meter path led to the first observation area, where an overgrown boy scout swept unblemished heads of Romaine lettuce from a pickup flatbed into the water. The sea creatures circled the splashes. The leaves were the only greenery in the chemically sterilized waterway, and the manatees seemed to enjoy them. The purple bruises in the shape of a billy club on the gentleman's face suggested the employees also enjoyed what salad they could steal.

As I navigated the path fronting the canal, placards situated every few meters explained the trail's flora and fauna. The exotic vegetation attracted butterflies released daily from a regional laboratory thanked in the brochure. The lepidopterons cavorted among the foreign weeds between insecticide fumigations.

I glanced again at the brochure. The park had won an award for environmental stewardship. From the petroleum industry.

Three blond-haired children hung over a wooden railing at the next observation area. Their pointing fingers tracked manatees as each surfaced to gulp oxygen and again submerged. Their nanny, a gentleman in a brown suit with a plaid bowtie, stood a few paces back, arms crossed. His Glock-22 pistol poked out of his blazer.

The butterfly trail emptied into the main observation area, behind a circular fence built to accommodate a crowd of several hundred onlookers. This early in the morning, the park was near-empty: only two women in matching business suits out for their morning constitutional passed by, and neither glanced at the mammals.

So, why was the snack bar open for business? Aha. Beside the menu on the front of the slate-gray trailer, the sign said, Pink Flamingo Snacks and Sodas. I crept forward to steal a glance at the attendant before he saw me.

Too late. His eyes fixed on mine. An expressionless stare, but the constant movement of his fingers against the napkin dispenser betrayed his nervousness.

The man Belyakov employed to attend this culinary establishment bore the unkempt gray hair and sun-ravaged skin typical of those who slept in a tent on the public beach, the type who had sunk his savings into a dream home only to lose it in the last real estate crash. Or the one before.

I waved, showing both hands empty, crossed my arms and kept them in his view as I approached. "Good morning, sir."

"Here's lookin' at you, kid."

Apparently Belyakov's idiot had acquired his education in the American fashion, via television. The edited version of Casablanca shifted Rick's farewell to the beginning of the movie and spliced Ilsa out of the scene. It made time for an extra commercial break. The guy thought the line meant "Hello".

"Would you like a breakfast sandwich?"

Uttapam with fresh tomatoes, onions and chilies would have been my preference, but I acquiesced to a white bread roll with egg-and-sausage patty. With an oversized spatula, he snatched my McBreakfast from the display case and inserted it into an aluminum foil wrapper, dropping it twice in the process. He then exchanged his wares for my currency.

"You're open early," I said.

"Breakfast until eleven, lunch until four. But our desserts are lousy. You should go to The Bubble Room." He slid me the restaurant's take-out menu, which included a skeletal map with directions to Captiva Island. In pen, he'd underlined the words *orange crunch*. "Best cake in the world."

A map to my next destination procured, all I needed was the electronics. "May I have utensils?"

"Forks are at the side window." He gestured toward a shelf that topped an open space. A metal carrying case sat just inside the opening.

Before I could thank the man, he whipped a handgun from beneath his apron. I ducked, fell hard to the ground and rolled left. He fired three shots into a passing manatee.

"Spy camera, on the animal's back. They found us. Grab the suitcase and run."

I didn't look back. Belyakov judged character well.

I trusted American Homeland Corporation's rivals to attend to kill him if Belyakov didn't do it first. In Southwest Florida, violators of the Marine Mammal Protection Act rarely went unpunished.

I had eleven hours.

* * * *

When I was certain no one followed, I pulled off Palm Beach Boulevard into a weed-choked lot and opened the case. It was packed with electronic equipment—standard stuff, nothing you couldn't purchase at a hardware store. I extracted a sampling of tools and components and stashed them in the glove compartment before closing the kit. In that jumble of metal, the items wouldn't be missed.

I pulled back out onto Palm Beach Boulevard. A kilometer or so down the road, I followed a sign for "Beach Expressway." Just west of the highway, the Toyota lurched upward and hovered. With barely a second for a what-in-the-world, the car shot down the road.

An automated female voice explained, "The route we'll follow runs above Palm Beach Boulevard through the downtown area where it merges into MacArthur Boulevard, which ends at the Summerlin Avenue lead-up to the Sanibel Causeway. The image you're seeing is of an actual royal palm tree, one of those that lined MacArthur prior to the disturbances. The Fort Myers Chamber of Commerce is pleased to announce this part of the surface level route has been reopened to the public. Be sure to ask your resort concierge about visiting the restored Edison and Ford Estates. We hope you enjoy your stay on the beautiful beaches of Sanibel and Captiva."

I didn't. It took me an hour to get to my destination, an hour I couldn't afford. As I approached Captiva's only four-way stop, I glimpsed the sign for The Bubble Room. I crossed the intersection, turned into the lot and parked.

I had ten hours.

* * * *

The takeout menu promised displays of 1930s and 1940s kitsch—Hollywood and the like. To an eager customer anticipating vintage movie posters—Bogart and Bergman in black and white—the restaurant served up disappointment.

"They aren't open for lunch until eleven."

I turned to see a mid-thirtyish woman with plastic frame glasses and off-brand, faded jeans, with a graphing calculator—same model as my own!—hooked through a belt loop. Alex's engineer.

"Too bad. I was looking forward to a piece of their orange crunch cake."

She acknowledged my half of the protocol by unfastening the top three buttons of her blouse. Treated to this view, I was the only heterosexual man in Florida whose eyes would have focused on her pink flamingo necklace.

Well, they did at first. My eyes soon strayed. I envisioned my fingertips tracing her hyperboloid form, over and over, rotating a differential of theta at a time. I imagined her lips parting with my touch, her tongue tracing my digit. Shunting aside my hand, she'd smile, invite me close, and…"

"You like what you see?"

I forced a sheepish grin. "The hardware is in the car."

"Grab it. We can walk from here. My name's Jenna." She offered a clumsy handshake before re-buttoning her shirt.

Carrying the case, I followed her down a road that led past a cluster of island stores and into a gated resort area. Or what used to be a resort area. It was still gated. And guarded, heavily. After crossing a parking lot, we ambled over a wooden boardwalk and emerged facing an overflowing garbage dumpster.

She pointed to a building with most of its windows blackened or busted. "Fifth floor. Elevator's out of service. Sorry."

I made a mental note to submit a less-than-five-star accommodation rating to Fodor's.

We took the stairs. At the top, she extracted a key from her pocket. The moment she opened the door to her suite, a stench of rotten fruit assaulted me.

"Food for the beetles. You get used to it after a while."

"Beetles?" And I'd thought women with a thing for cats were odd.

"Yeah, for the mini-drones." She paused and stared at me. "You don't have any idea what we're doing here, do you?"

I didn't. "My employer would prefer you don't know what I do or don't know."

Her smile said she didn't care. Or perhaps she fancied an Indian gentleman? I could hope.

She drew the curtains, dimmed the lights in the suite's living room and flipped the on-switch to a hologram projector. A chamber with numerous restraints appeared, complete with metal spears of some sort. A torture device! I tensed and sprang back to avoid a trap. Her attractive exterior concealed the claws of a sadistic monster.

Or not. "You're looking at the insect modification chambers, magnified one hundred times. It kinda looks like something from a vintage Japanese Godzilla film, doesn't it?"

Relieved, I nodded.

"The metal implements are magnetized. I use nickel wire to tie most of the pieces to hooks on the beetles' surface."

"And the hooks…"

"Insect surgery. Hold your horses, I'll demonstrate."

And she did. I marveled as the hologram projection of her fingers maneuvered a green June beetle, which Jenna said had the flattest dorsal structures she'd found, into the restraint. One harness for each leg, pulled tight, rendered the insect motionless.

Spellbound by the holography, I jumped when a high-pitched whine, not unlike the sound made by an electric drill pierced the air. "What was that?"

"An electric drill. Fitted with a really tiny drill bit." Like a skilled mechanic working on a car, she drove the power tool in smooth motions, fashioning a hole on each side of the head and several along the back. "The electrodes screw into the head. I connect them to a miniaturized wireless receiver and transmitter."

"Those go in the other holes?"

"No, they're teensy. I just glue them on."

As she demonstrated, my eyes flitted between the holoimage and the soft brown hair brushing her shoulders, shoulders that pressed against the thin fabric of her blouse, a blouse that clung to her curves, curves that made me…

"Voilà, the guidance system."

The what? Oh yes, the 2013 paper—she'd been a technician—for that publication, they'd used electrodes to jolt the bug's brain so it favored either the left or right wing. Wireless communication had been the next logical step.

"The transmitter also sends GPS coordinates," she said.

"Not much use in a wireless-free zone."

"Bingo. It's why we assemble here. It's the last place you'd expect to find our manufacturing."

And they were letting the Caliph's man in on the secret? Something was wrong. I shuddered involuntarily.

As if reading my mind, she added, "We're short on cash."

Maybe.

My engineer brain shifted to the tech specs. "How do you power the thing?"

"Piezoelectric generator wired to the head, attached via rods to each wing base. That's a microwatt of juice just from the beetle's flight behavior. The rest comes from an ultrathin solar cell I glue on. It's really cool. Watch." She added these pieces.

What magic was this? "Why aren't you looking into the microscope eyepiece?" Was I watching a recording?

She dispelled my doubts. "Don't need it. It just takes practice. Easy peasy. I'll have you up to speed, assembling them in the backseat of a car by mid-afternoon."

Assembly in the car wasn't a bad idea. Still, my mind considered other possibilities for a backseat and the two of us.

"So far, everything I've shown you is what we published in Michigan with the DARPA funding. The next part is how I've earned my keep at American Homeland."

She opened a small envelope and spilled the contents on the table while I watched the hologram. The devices resembled miniature hypodermic needles.

"You can fill these with the poison of your choice. I hook them onto the bug's surface and wire them up to the same receiver used for guidance. The trick is I've made them super-lightweight." Her hands finished the latest manipulation and she stood up. "Behold, an assassination drone."

I beheld, marveling at her skill. It looked hard.

Indeed, despite her tutelage, the procedure proved tricky. I mangled many of the delicate tools in Belyakov's hardware kit, which no longer seemed overstocked. But with her patient hands guiding my own, movements that brushed her body close to mine numerous times, by late afternoon I'd mastered it. I complimented her teaching skills.

"In another lifetime, I'd have gone on for my Ph.D. and been tenured somewhere by this age."

"Why didn't you? You'd have been terrific."

She hesitated, not appearing accustomed to compliments.

"Would you unbutton your shirt again?"

Her toward-the-ceiling eye roll lasted only seconds. The buttons yielded to her nimble fingers and she shrugged off the blouse. It fell to the floor.

"Now please open the pink flamingo locket and show me what's inside."

Her shoulders slumped, her lips contorted into a scowl. I wasn't every woman's idea of a catch; loneliness must have fogged her reasoning. Of course, my mind was crystal clear. I was on duty. Just because she was brilliant and lovely and shirtless…

She flicked open a lever and exposed a photo of two little girls. "My kids. To support them, I drifted from job to job, after their Dad's subversive activities got both of us fired from U. of M. When he went to prison, we came here. They stay with their grandmother outside the trailer-shanty zone, near Alva. My salary pays the mortgage on her farm, the crops they produce feed the town. No one starves."

She was married. Darn. "Your husband's still in jail?"

"They killed him." She picked up her blouse and put it back on without showing emotion.

How she suppressed her feelings, I couldn't fathom. Her words charred me like burning oil. Accepting dharma I understood, but I didn't buy her nonchalance. "So you honor his memory by working for a bioweaponry outfit?"

"Kids have to eat."

Chicken droppings. "Michigan had lots of other research groups. You didn't have to dedicate your life to making mini-drones."

She launched into an explanation of potential benefits for agriculture and environmental restoration.

"With Defense Department funding?"

Her eyes cast downward and she exhaled. "I was naive. Then angry, but I've matured and now I love my job working for the best employer an engineer could desire." She motioned toward a light fixture with too many wires protruding.

So she lived her minutes under watchful eyes. The corporate tool ethos was merely a veneer.

Had she guessed my secret? Understood where my loyalty laid? She shot me a knowing glance that said she did.

But wouldn't tell. She bounded forward and wrapped her arms around me, her lips meeting mine. As surprise subsided, I relaxed, and she probed the recesses of my mouth with her tongue. I reached out and caressed her cheek, then ran my hands through her hair. It was soft. I hadn't kissed a woman since my wife's death—my work precluded shared intimacy—but in Jenna's arms, the universe melted away. With Jenna, my intellectual equal, my fellow survivor of the hell our planet had become, I allowed myself a daydream of tomorrow as a fractal outgrowth of this moment.

Her tongue traveled around to my ear, and between nibbles of the lobe, she whispered, "Beware of Alex. He intends to kill you. Now push away and act like you're rejecting me."

With much reluctance, I complied.

The look of hatred she shot slashed me like a rusty switchblade, even though I knew she was acting for the camera. Teeth bared like an animal stalking prey, she ripped open a drawer and withdrew a plastic bag. She scrawled something on a piece of paper, shoved it in, and sealed the bag, which she subsequently threw at me. "Go away!"

I scrambled toward the door and let myself out, then paused to examine the bag's contents. Sunglasses? I turned them over and saw the logo: Lover's Key State Park, my next destination. The bag also included another tourist map, with driving directions. And her note. "The problems of two little people don't amount to a hill of beans in this crazy world."

We'd always have Captiva. At the risk of displeasing the Caliph, I let her live. I sent the shortwave signal to the Shariah Law Enforcer.

I had two hours.

* * * *

Getting off the island was smooth sailing—same road in as out, and the surface road leading to the bridge to Fort Myers Beach wasn't any worse than Palm Beach Boulevard. The same security contractor patrolled the residential areas, the same buses sent those lucky enough to be employed on to their jobs serving the well-heeled and the well-connected.

The bridge was another story. The economic model my outdated Indian textbook had called "American entrepreneurialism" held sway.

Four young men dressed identically in blue converged on my vehicle. "Get out of the car or we'll blow your face off," the apparent gang leader said.

Confronted with four AK-47 machine guns, I did what I was told.

"Hey, foreign boy. I guess nobody told you to buy a bridge toll sticker, did they?"

Apparently my employer had been remiss, expecting our new business partner to make arrangements. "Sorry. How much?"

"They aren't sold here. But you can buy a pedestrian pass."

"And the cost is…"

"Your car. Get your crap out of it."

I shifted the electronics from the glove compartment to my valise, sealed it, and backed away from the automobile.

"And your water bottle. We like the cars clean."

It was careless of me. I thanked him for the reminder.

One of the toughs took my keys and drove away. Another waved me over to the lane partitioned for foot traffic. A third offered tourist advice: "You can catch the trolley on the other side of the bridge. Our guy will keep you safe all the way down the island. If he likes you. Last stop is Lover's Key—one of our taxis will take you to the airport from there. They take cash. You got some, boy?"

I assured the gentleman I did.

"Good. You wouldn't like what my buddies do to those who don't."

For this advice, I expressed my thanks, then I bid him good day. I hoofed it up to the top of the bridge, gazed out, and to my surprise, found great beauty. On the bay side, small fishing craft dotted the water; quaint restaurants and marinas lined the near banks with wild stands of mangrove trees in the distance. On the beach side, luxury hotels and tourist shops in pastel colors predominated. The area bustled with bikini-clad beauties and old men in brightly colored shirts and baseball caps. Fort Myers Beach catered to tourists, oblivious to the cauldron of despair and suffering that simmered beneath the surface of every luxury vacation spot.

As the information bureau had advised, a clean, yellow trolley pulled up to a shelter at the foot of the bridge. I hustled, and the driver waited for me.

"Twenty dollars."

I retrieved a money clip from my pocket and peeled off two crisp green bills, double the fare. The Fodor's guide had suggested tipping men with guns.

He nodded, accepted the money, and motioned for me to take a seat. To the windowless back of the bus I headed, leaving benches meant for enjoying the scenery to the tourists. The slow ride that stopped every few blocks allowed me time to organize the contents of my suitcase.

Ever the engineer, I inventoried the pilfered electronics, finding all components and tools necessary to put the skills I'd learned into practice, and organized them atop my change of clothes. I next opened the waterproof interior compartment and inserted the bottle I'd been carrying. As an afterthought, I swapped my Google specs for the sunglasses Jenna had given me—they cut glare from sun sinking over water better than the specs did—then I sealed up my bag.

At the end of the line, the trolley pulled into Lover's Key and stopped at the main parking area. Although I was the only human passenger by this point, a hungry swarm of mosquitoes entered through the window. Two bit me before I could exit the trolley.

The sun peeked out over the mangroves that framed a path leading to the beach. Almost dusk. Near the path, at the edge of the parking lot, leaning on a palm tree fronted by a tacky lawn ornament—a pink flamingo, of course—stood Alex Belyakov.

The trolley rang its bell. So much for the element of surprise.

I had thirty minutes.

* * * *

I approached Belyakov. “So, Alex, this is a major tourist attraction. Why are we the only ones at the beach?”

“Red tide outbreak.”

“Engineered?”

Belyakov smiled. “The bloom will dissipate by tomorrow.”

I explained the situation with the car, and he apologized, blaming local hoodlums for stealing the sticker from the Toyota. He didn’t seem perturbed about the vehicle. But a hovering mosquito elicited multiple angry slaps to his exposed neck. “They drive me crazy, and they’re most active at sunset. We go to beach, much breeze, blows them away. Walk.”

And a strong breeze would muffle the sound of a gunshot. And the sand dunes would conceal my dead body. The Fodor’s section on Fort Myers Beach sunsets had overstated their romantic appeal.

I walked in terrified silence across a fishing bridge that traversed a mangrove swamp, past a display on local seashells, and onto the beach. A gun to my back, my precious minutes ticking away, I feared my end drew near. Was my fate to die alone on this beach? To surrender the world to men like Belyakov? To never see Jenna again?

“Turn around,” Belyakov said. He proffered a manila envelope containing four typed pages.

“Ancient technology—the hard copy. Software for guidance system is printed out in Courier font. Screeners at airport would never notice. Pity you won’t make your plane.”

The code seemed genuine. “I’ll get the shortwave out of my carry-on.” I unfastened the clasp, swung it open and retrieved the transmitter.

If he noticed that I also nudged the zipper to the waterproof compartment, he didn't react.

"You remember signal?"

"Yes."

"Forget it, I lied. New signal is first line of computer program in Morse Code."

I set the printout on my valise to free my hands, knelt down on the sand, and sent the message. "I assume the bank transfer from the Caliph just went through."

"I'm certain it did." Belyakov pointed the handgun directly at me. "You don't really think I let you go, do you?"

I flinched when a mosquito bit me. Belyakov laughed, thinking he brought about my discomfort. With the next four bites, I managed to conceal my reaction.

One bit Belyakov, and he slapped the side of his neck. Then he keeled over dead.

The bites would hurt me for several days. You'd think coming from Delhi, I'd be used to them, but these mosquitoes were bred to be large. And to mature quickly from the larval stage—they pupated over the course of the day in my water bottle and emerged as adults during the trolley ride. After feeding inside my suitcase compartment on my blood mixed with B toxin, they morphed into natural killers, even without the injectors Jenna had taught me to use.

I checked my watch. Just in time, five more minutes and my serum levels of antitoxin would have fallen below the point of efficacy. The product I'd dialed that morning on my souped-up ID device, the one specific for my "C" genotype, was designed for only twelve hours of stability. The pharmacokinetics were an important design feature—my body would metabolize the rest down to undetectable levels before I crossed security to board the puddle jumper going back to Miami.

A victory for the poor of the world. With the latest in mini-drone technology, the Caliph would prevail and set them free from their capitalist oppressors.

As the sun sank below the horizon, I dragged the body to the parking lot, popped the trunk of Belyakov's car and shuffled him into it. It would be a day or two before an airport parking attendant would find him. A week if I tipped well.

When I reached Miami, I began work for my new employer, BioDefense USA, American Homeland Corporation's main rival. I had a few days to practice attaching electronic components to mosquitoes before flying to Mali. There was no need to reset the ID device, the Caliph also carried the B gene, and the dispensing needle screwed directly into Jenna's injectors. The next mission required this improved technology; the mosquito's proboscis wouldn't retain toxin long enough. A saltwater mosquito naturally flies a few hundred kilometers in its lifetime—a guided flight of that length would reach the Caliph's palace. I also checked the Internet to be sure the Timbuktu Hilton had free Wi-Fi.

It will be another victory for the poor of the world. BioDefense USA will set them free from their theocrat oppressor.

And I'll Skype Jenna this weekend. Her mom's place in Alva has wireless service.

THE END

About the Author

Allan Dyen-Shapiro

Allan Dyen-Shapiro is a Ph.D. biochemist, whose nonlinear career left him with tales to tell of the worlds of biotech, ecology, academia, agriculture, computers and patent law. He's sold a couple science fiction short stories and is working on his first novel. He currently resides, with his wife and two children, in Southwest Florida. In his "Clark Kent" job, he spends his days teaching high school students.

For my Stephanie –
You inspire me in oh-so-many ways. It was an honor to name my "true friend" heroine after you!
Fondly,
M.A.

Sunsets and Second Chances

M. A. Ellis

Stephanie Hunter wrapped her hands around the cold, stiff neck and tugged harder. Maggie, her best friend for the past five years, did the same, but she had a hold of the spindly legs.

"We've almost got him. One more rest," Maggie huffed, releasing her grip completely to shake circulation back into her arms.

Relaxing just enough to flex her fingers, Stephanie looked down at her quasi cat burglar getup of black yoga pants and matching zippered hoodie. The lightweight fabric clung to her sweaty back.

"We should so not be doing this, Magdalene," Stephanie said, using her friend's full name in a last-ditch effort to stop the lunacy of which they were currently a part.

As if to reinforce her point, the dark grey clouds that covered a nearly full moon shifted toward the east, illuminating the front yard of what used to be Maggie's humble abode.

Her words, not mine.

Stephanie had always found the opulent home at the end of Rum Row a modern monstrosity. Harsh angles and ninety percent glass, it was out of place with the neighboring estates, both the ones that mirrored French villas and the ones that stayed true to the old Floridian color palette of sherbet-inspired pastels and stark white trim. As far as she was concerned, the behemoth's only redeeming quality was corner frontage on the Gordon River. A short boat ride and you could be in the Gulf. Fishing until your arms ached, tanning to your specific shade of bronze, and watching swirling hues of orange, pink and indigo transform into the best sunsets on the planet.

"C'mon. One more big pull and I think we've got him," Maggie said.

Her friend's voice was fierce, a tone Steph had heard more often lately, and it didn't fill her with ease.

"Could we not have done this a few weeks ago?" Stephanie grumbled. "You know, when Mother Nature wasn't lending her built-in spotlight to the task?"

She would have preferred not to get involved in Maggie's latest bit of pre-divorce retribution at all. But Stephanie was familiar with the consequences of letting her friend go off half-cocked. The very uncivil divorce antics between Magdalene and Henry Delacroix had become worrisome. The incarceration of one or both, parties seemed a real possibility to Stephanie. She figured lending a little upper body strength to her friend's latest plan was better than trying to raise bail money on her surgical tech's salary. Which is what she feared would happen if she let Maggie to her own retaliatory actions.

"Henry isn't home. There's a cribbage mixer at the club."

"What the hell's a cribbage mix—"

"And he shouldn't have taken the Baccarat snail to consignment," Maggie interrupted. "He was supposed to leave everything as it was. The lawyers made it clear that if he was staying in the house, so were all contents. The bastard knew it was my favorite."

No good could come from reminding Maggie she had made the fatal mistake of leaving the residence when Henry had told her he wanted a divorce. Storming out with dramatic effect, according to the housekeeper, who had told Stephanie the story while being prepped for arthroscopic surgery on her left knee.

It was easy to imagine Maggie shrieking at Henry from the top step of the semi-circular entrance stairs. Yelling for all the neighbors to hear that she'd take a suite of rooms at the Ritz. Which she had. Until Henry called and cancelled her black Am Ex.

Stephanie would talk to the owner of the consignment shop. The woman had been in to the surgery center numerous times with her partner, a six-foot-four former tennis pro with chronic discs issues. Stephanie could ask her to give a call if Henry showed up again, priceless knick-knack in tow, looking to make a quick dollar. Or two hundred, which was probably more the case where the faceted mollusk-in-question was involved. But right now she had to get Maggie's harebrained mission over and get home. Tomorrow was a work day.

"Like I have enough expendable income to buy back my own crystal paperweights," Maggie grumbled.

Stephanie gritted her teeth and pressed her lips into a tight line to stop the flow of unkind remarks from spewing forth. Expendable income and crystal weren't words Stephanie tossed around in everyday conversation. There were times her friend didn't have a freakin' clue.

"Isn't it brilliant?" Maggie asked. "How I disabled the solar lighting. So it wouldn't give us away."

Understatement, Stephanie thought. Shattered remnants of glass and plastic littered the ground. The signed Louisville Slugger that had been Maggie's weapon was propped against the rough bark of a palmetto.

"Can we just get this over with?" Stephanie asked, repositioning her legs for better traction. "Before some crazed socialite on neighborhood watch comes out and caps our asses." All she wanted to do was get the five foot, hundred and ten pound cement flamingo into the back of Maggie's luxury SUV and get the hell out of Dodge.

"The Homeowners Association prohibits firearm usage within the confines of the development," Maggie replied, as if she knew Stephanie's train of thought would eventually lead to that topic. "Anyhow, I watched the landscapers install it. There are three metal stakes and they aren't very deep. And I did my homework. The fact we waited until the flowerbed was watered makes it easier."

"Yippee," was all Stephanie could muster in response. She'd been trying not to think about the fact her good running shoes were in an inch of reclaimed water. As was the case with every development in the area, the timed sprinklers still went on whether there had been a torrential downpour that afternoon or not. And there had been.

She looked at Maggie, only a few feet away. The gleam in her friend's eyes was a tad frightening.

"If it doesn't come free this time, my ass is outta here," Stephanie warned.

"It'll come. It should have already. One last try. That's all I'm asking," Maggie asked.

Stephanie bent at the knees and tightened her grip.

"One…two…threeeeeee." Maggie's voice got higher as a loud, muck-sucking "pop" filled the air and the heavy flamingo became as weightless as its real life counterpart.

For all of two seconds.

The bird's flight unfolded in super slow motion, just like the heart-stopping accident memories people were always quick to share. This entire escapade would, henceforth, be considered nothing short of a train wreck. Maggie lost her grip and toppled sideways toward the blooming Key Largo hibiscus. For a split second Stephanie considered the tragedy of crushing the carefully cultured hybrid. Until the full weight of the statue propelled her backward, the polished beak coming straight at her face.

Reconstruction nose surgery runs five grand, turn and duck!

Stephanie obeyed the voice in her head, the cedar bark mulch growing closer and closer. She closed her eyes and the air whooshed from her lungs as she hit the ground. The water-drenched soil was harder than she imagined.

The hard tip of the flamingo's curved beak grazed her midsection and Stephanie reflexively pushed it away, but not far enough. It bounced against her upper thigh and the proverbial stars people always talked about materialized. They actually looked more like dots as they danced against her closed eyelids. Big and white, like the kind found on vintage halter dresses.

Inhaling with pain, Stephanie blinked her eyes open. The football shaped body of the bird careened sideways onto the thick, well-manicured lawn. Its weight forced droplets of dirty water upward, a speck landing on Stephanie's lower lip as she gasped for air. The soft flesh of her upper leg pulsed in tandem with the throbbing at the base of her skull. She sort of liked the beat, welcoming the way it began to carry her into the darkness.

Her friend's maniacal laughter brought everything into focus again, the polka dot pattern and steady rhythm evaporating.

"We did it, Steph. We *fuckin'* did it."

During their years of friendship, Stephanie had heard Maggie swear less than a handful of times. It had always been at something wildly monumental. Like the time the drummer from Bon Jovi tossed her his sticks at a pre-Super Bowl party in Tampa. A burly guy wearing a Motorhead t-shirt had grabbed the other end but Maggie hadn't let go. She wrestled him for the prize, the litany of profanity spewing from her lips forcing everyone crammed around them to take a step backward, just in case she turned on them.

Or when they were standing in the home theater area of Best Buy, looking at projection TVs and CNN announced that Martha Stewart was on her way to a Federal prison camp in West Virginia. Maggie had dropped the F-Bomb and burst into tears. The customer associate had been horrified. Stephanie always suspected his response had more to do with the fact Maggie was in the midst of her Susie Homemaker phase than the actual profanity. No one expects that sort of language from a June Cleaver lookalike.

"What the *hell*?" Maggie whispered, confusion clear. "Look at this!"

Stephanie rolled to her hands and knees, wincing as pain shot down her leg.

"Hey. Thanks for the 'Are you okay, Steph? Sorry you almost lost an ovary'. You're a true friend."

"You don't even want kids," Maggie said offhandedly, crouching to study the slight depression in the flowerbed.

Now wasn't the optimal time for Stephanie to tell her friend she'd been reconsidering a life less chaotic. Biological clock and all that crap. Maybe kids weren't the crazed hellions and income-sucking menaces she first believed them to be. She wasn't a woman to cast blame, but in this instance, her older siblings and their parenting skills—or lack thereof—might have played a part in her lifelong commitment to keep her womb a "No Loitering" zone.

Maggie picked up a cable. "What the fuck *is* this?"

Uh-oh. Twice in one night. This isn't good. Mission gone bad!

The voice of reason never sounded frantic. What the hell was up with that?

Abort, abort, abort!

High wattage lights flashed on at each corner of the house. The blinding intensity was reminiscent of someone throwing a switch on during a prison break. Stephanie tried to clear her head. The massive amount of brightness flowing over the front yard, the driveway and the surrounding flowerbeds wasn't helping. Not even a little. Palm trees weren't meant to have auxiliary security lighting attached to them. That wasn't the Florida way.

"Run!"

Stephanie turned at the command and watched Maggie scramble to her feet and grab the bat. Stephanie's fingers missed closing around her friend's tiny ankle by a hair. The mastermind of the plot fled across the yard, hopped into her Volvo and fired up the engine.

"Maggie! Get your ass back here," Stephanie cried.

Movement at the front door caught Stephanie's attention as the SUV squealed out of the driveway, the dual exhausts echoing through the night.

She struggled to her feet. Bent at the waist, both hands on her knees, she glanced down at the nearly liberated flamingo, wondering how much of the truth she should tell the man running her way?

It wasn't Henry. Stephanie knew that from the way the dark form jumped from the top step. Henry didn't jump. The expenditure of energy would have resulted in his trademark paisley ascot becoming askew. One could *never* allow that.

Stephanie giggled. The jolt to her noggin must have been more forceful than she thought. She pushed herself upward. She could tell the man she was part of a grassroots organization committed to freeing all yard ornaments—from gnome to Neptune—that were being bound against their will.

"Don't move," a voice ordered from a few yards away. Deep and husky, but with a familiarity that immediately forced Stephanie to her full height. She blinked the haziness at the edges of her vision away. She must have hit her head harder than she thought to be imagining voices from the past.

The man stepped closer, into the arc of light that transformed him from a shadowy silhouette into something recognizable and far more imposing.

"Stay right there." The deep voice ordered. And then, "Stephanie?"

She expected more shock on his part. Definitely expected more astonishment from herself.

His bare chest was wider than she remembered. He crossed his arms, hands tucked beneath biceps that flexed, then jumped. He'd always been fit, but not like this. Not in a sexy, magazine cologne model sort of way. Could a person get an entire upper body implant? She'd have to ask Dr. Gathar next time she was slated as his surgical nurse.

Stephanie gave herself a mental shake, one she hoped he wasn't able to perceive, just to make sure she wasn't imagining his presence. Why was he in Maggie's front yard? The two didn't even know each other. He was a chapter of Stephanie's life that had played out before her move to the Sunshine State. Years before. So why was he here, in all his half-naked glory?

"It's been a long time, Greg." The minute the words left her lips, Stephanie wished she could pull them back. Wished her surroundings weren't so bright. Wished she had missed the way his jaw clenched.

"Eight years, Stephanie. Eight years, four months and..." He glanced down at the heavy diver's watch on his right wrist. "Thirteen days."

Silence filled the night. Even the pesky tree frogs had stopped their high-pitched croaking.

"But who's counting?" Stephanie offered a shaky chuckle. Her heart drummed in her ears, and she doubted her words came out the way she intended. Jovial, not lame. A little humor couldn't hurt when you were caught red-handed trying to pilfer statuary. Caught by a man from your past. A man who obviously hadn't forgotten you the way you hoped he would.

Could it get much worse than that?

He took two steps forward, into the landscaped island, the rough cedar bark apparently no discomfort to his bare feet. He stopped, close enough that she felt the warmth rolling off his body, forcing her to tilt her head backward to see his face. Still gorgeous despite the fact his full lips were pressed into a firm line.

"Who's counting?" His unamused tone forced her gaze to his eyes, mossy green and more clear than she remembered.

"I'll tell you who's counting, Stephanie. The man you left standing at the altar. That's who."

Hell, it could get worse. Much worse.

* * * *

For years, Greg Wingate's peaceful dreams had been interrupted by visions of his former fiancée. Oh, they'd lessened with time, but her bright hazel eyes and mane of silky chestnut brown hair had been invasive. Almost to the point of obsession, according to one of the best counselors in the greater Cincinnati area. Of course, that was months after his circle of friends had offered their own diagnosis. He'd known them since junior high and they never hesitated to call him out on any number of bad ideas or missteps. And on a blustery Saturday night in early November, exactly one year after she'd walked out of the church, as a unified group they had told him Stephanie Hunter had been one of those missteps. He'd railed against them. Together. Alone. It hadn't mattered. Called each and every one of them stupid, self-absorbed fuckheads who didn't know jack shit about relationships.

They had sat quietly and let him rant, then told him he needed to get his shit together and forget Stephanie's sorry ass. Someone had suggested therapy. He'd resisted at first, but eventually gave in.

It had been years since Greg had purged his system of 'what if' negativity.

Then why is the first thought going through your head, when you see that hurtful bitch after all this time, is how your kids would have definitely had green eyes?

There was a time when Greg would have told that irritating inner voice to shut the fuck up. He could feel however he wanted to feel toward the woman standing before him. But in the few seconds it took him to recognize the identity of the front-yard thief, the bone-deep longing he thought he had purged rose to the surface. Front and center. Manifesting itself as a dull ache in the center of his chest.

He really should be pissed at himself for wasting numerous hours and out-of-pocket deductibles for those psychologist co-pays. His friends would toss him out of the bro-hood for what he was considering, but right now, he didn't care. He still wanted Stephanie Hunter.

And here she was. Staring up at him as if the past had never happened. Trying to make a joke to defuse an uncomfortable situation. She'd been the master of diversion, her skill serving its purpose more times than Greg could remember. With him, as well as with people in general. Steph's goofiness had saved him from more than a few altercations. And, quick learner that he was, he hadn't minded walking away while some half-in-the-bag asshole called him a pussy. He had just smiled and kept moving, knowing that when he and Steph got home, they'd be naked before they hit the living room. His girl got off on brains, not brawn. At least that's what she'd always told him.

He wasn't so sure that was the case anymore, not the way she was staring dumbfounded at his bare abs.

She took a step backward and blinked. Maybe she was taking a stroll down memory lane, too.

Greg tunneled his fingers through his hair, stopping before he pushed it behind his ears. Would she remember it was one of his tics? What he did when he was trying to buy time and think of exactly what to say.

Dude. She doesn't remember because she doesn't think of you at all.

"I'd like to tell you this isn't what it seems," Stephanie said, interrupting his thoughts.

Her tone was apologetic, but her posture said something altogether different. Her once reed-thin body had changed. She had hips now. Wide enough that she could stack her fists on top them in an age-old pose of defensiveness. Wide enough that if he was so inclined, he could grab a hold as she straddled him, force her hips into a faster rhythm without fear of hurting her.

Greg cleared his throat and her gaze locked on his.

"I know exactly what this is," he said, stepping to the right, his body nearly touching hers as he stared at the supine flamingo. He was testing himself. Seeing if he could be that close and not pull her into his arms and slant his mouth over hers. Give her time to adjust to the shock before he stroked the bottom of her upper lip with the tip of his tongue. Three featherlike strokes had always ensured she would step closer. Mold her body tighter to his before he kissed her senseless.

The pounding in his heart, the throbbing at the base of his cock told him the experiment could go either way.

Greg mirrored her stance, arms and legs akimbo. "Henry told me to be prepared for retaliatory action, but I honestly thought he was being paranoid."

"So, he hired you?" Stephanie asked.

The soft accusatory tone made the hairs at the base of his neck rise. She was the one who should be on edge. That whole show of confidence was a bluff. Stephanie had tics, too. Greg waited until the thumb of her right hand began tapping against her skin.

"He did," Greg replied just as softly.

"What are you, now?" she whispered, her gaze drifted down his torso and up again. "Bodyguard to the rich and famous?"

Her gaze darted to his arms and Greg barely stopped himself from flexing, just to show her she wasn't the only one whose physical appearance had improved. He'd never forgotten how the mere whisper of the word "fireman" forced Stephanie, the most intelligent woman he'd ever met, to lose complete focus. It had never been a big deal to him because, at the end of the day, Greg had thought she would always be his.

He offered her a guarded smile. "I'm just the house sitter, Stephanie."

Her eyes narrowed. "You've never been *just* anything your entire life, Greg," she said, the tapping against her lower waist increasing in tempo.

An image of her sliding her hands downward over the tight fabric of her black exercise pants had Greg standing up straighter. Suddenly, in his mind, she was totally nude, water sluicing over her porcelain skin as the shower heated up their small bathroom. Fingers splayed against her thigh as her thumb rubbed tiny circles around her hidden nub while he stood there watching.

Greg shook the scene out of his head and focused. On her being here, in the very real present and not on what they had shared in the past.

"You always did have a knack for knowing just what to say to boost my ego, Stephanie." He watched her bristle. Heard the long exhale of the breath she'd been holding.

"So what are you going to do?" She let her arms drop to her sides, and then quickly crossed them over her breasts.

She was nervous. That would work in his favor.

"I'm not going to do anything," he said, stepping around her body to study the angle of where the flamingo had fallen. "It's already been done."

"What the hell does that mean?" From the corner of his eye he watched her follow his steps as he inspected the hole in the ground, the trampled landscaping and the fallen flamingo.

He walked up to the palm tree, stepped close and turned toward Stephanie. He held her gaze as he leaned his back against the trunk, trying to ignore the way the bark dug into his flesh.

"What do you think about sucking my dick?" he asked in his best nonchalant tone. Her eyes widened, mouth parting to form an "O" of silent disbelief.

"Wh—*what*?"

"Too soon?" he asked in mock innocence. He moved away from the tree and lowered himself to the ground, grimacing when the wetness seeped into his lounge pants.

Hands back on her hips, she glared at him. She was going to let loose an oration of epic proportion, he knew that. Dull, flashing hues of blue and red cut through the dimly lit street.

"You called the cops?" she asked in a tone of total disbelief.

"I hit the button on the alarm panel."

"You *what*?" She looked anxiously from the street to him and back again.

"I didn't know it was you. Come here." He reached his palm upward.

She looked at it, then back at him.

"Bullshit. You knew it was Maggie," she accused.

"Henry's crazy ex could have hired an army of goons for all I knew. One or two, I can hold my own, but more than that…"

He let his words trail off for effect. His heart was racing with every second Stephanie delayed. In a no-sirens zone, it was hard the gauge how far away Naples' finest really were. The colored lights grew brighter and despite what might be swirling through her head right now, Greg had no intention of letting her be taken away.

"Stephanie, give me your hand. You've got about five seconds before the cops pull up."

She took another look toward the curb and then her hand was in his, fingers cold and shaky. Greg gave a tug and then let go, catching her as she tumbled downward. In one smooth motion she straddled his hips and gripped his shoulders, her knees squishing into the damp ground.

Her face inches from his, Greg impulsively leaned forward and placed a quick kiss on the tip of her nose, raising his knees until his upper thighs were flush against her bottom. Their bodies had always fit well together.

"Just like old times, sweetheart."

"Not really." He felt her body stiffen and grabbed her waist before she could dismount. Tunneling his hands under the edge of her hoodie, he hooked his thumbs in the waistband of her pants and yanked them downward until her ass was partially exposed.

"How 'bout now?" he questioned, ignoring her gasp as he ran his palms over her bare flesh.

"Gregory—"

"That tone isn't going to work anymore, Steph. I'm a different man. We'll have to talk later about when you started wearing thongs, but right now, I suggest you play along."

He slid her body upward until her warm core teased his shaft.

"Are you *hard*?" Her incredulous words echoed in the night. They were followed by the distinct sound of screeching tires.

"Just a little," he chuckled. "Maybe just the tip."

"Oh my god, this isn't funny."

He caught a glimpse of two bodies heading their way. "Let's hope you're ass is as alluring as it used to be."

"Where were those backhanded compliments six years ago," she muttered.

He didn't have time to consider her words.

"Police! Hands up where we can see them."

"For once, shut the hell up and follow my lead," Greg ordered, wishing he'd have been given a few more minutes with her, breasts to chest.

"I'm not going to kiss you," she replied, her determined voice barely audible, but he felt the tremor that went through her body.

The thudding in Greg's chest quickened and he gave her ass a little squeeze.

"We'll see, Steph. We'll see."

* * * *

Stephanie had imagined if she were in a situation where law enforcement was yelling "freeze" she'd be so petrified she wouldn't be able to think. Which wasn't the case since her mind was racing. Logic fled the moment she obeyed their command to raise her hands. The movement forced her more firmly against Greg's semi-hard erection. A split second of wondering why he hadn't gone limp was replaced by memories of sweaty bodies, tangled sheets and let's-try-this enthusiasm. Their sex life had never been an issue.

"Miss, get up and move aside." The officer's tone was firm, but not at all threatening. It didn't sound as if he'd fling her to the ground and wrap one of those plastic ties around her wrists before dragging her to the squad car. The neighbors across the street would be watching, probably videoing with their smart phones. That was a sobering thought.

She took one last look at Greg, arms above his head and naked chest, and nearly slipped back into the land of remembered orgasms.

"Should have planted one on me when you had the chance," he whispered, then winked.

"I'm getting up now," Stephanie said loudly. She'd seen that a million times on television. The perpetrators letting the police know they were going to comply. There were two officers and they moved closer, into her periphery. She moved one knee, then the other. The loud "ooof" that slipped from Greg's lips when her full weight was on him reminded her she was no longer the lithe, hundred pound princess he'd fallen in love with. Arms still above her head, she struggled to her feet and turned around. Greg was by her side a second later.

Each of the officers had a flashlight and a holstered gun. That dose of reality made Stephanie stand up straighter. No nightsticks, though. She wouldn't have to worry about broken kneecaps. A tiny laugh escaped and she pressed her lips shut. Stephanie knew it was a physical reaction to anxiety. The police would probably take it as insubordination.

"I'm sorry you had to come out, officers. I accidentally hit the call button on the alarm panel," Greg explained. "I'm Gregory Wingate, house sitter for Henry Delacroix. I'm on his permanent guest list with the guard. Mr. Delacroix is in Jacksonville for the week."

Beams of bright purple light moved back and forth between Stephanie and Greg. The cop to her left honed in on her face then moved lower. Her stretchy pants had slid back into place during her dismount so at least she was covered. But she was sure they'd seen her bare butt when they were storming the front yard. And the cop seemed fixated on her shoes. What could that mean?

"Whitmyer," the other cop barked, interrupting Stephanie's thoughts. "Call the gate. Tell them we have this under control. No need for their security. And make sure he's on the guest register."

"On it," came the quick reply.

The officer in charge waited a few seconds then said, "Go ahead and lower your arms."

As soon as the words left his mouth, Stephanie realized how bad her shoulders ached. Her arms felt like lead and she dropped them to her sides. She wanted to reach up and massage the back of her neck but thought better of it.

"Mr. Wingate, I'm Officer Pendry, why don't you tell me what's going on?" The policeman walked in front of them, crouching down to look at the flamingo from every angle.

Stephanie became mesmerized by the way various areas of his bald head glowed, depending on where he was standing. She would love to take a step out of the circle of light and fade into the darkness.

As if he read her mind, the officer stood up and moved closer to her. It would only be a matter of time before he started asking her questions. Would she have to throw Maggie under the bus?

"My companion and I were having a leisurely evening—"

The cop reached toward his gun side and Stephanie froze.

He pulled out a leather-bound notepad and small pen and began taking notes.

"Companion? As in escort?" he asked lightly, as if answering calls that concerned high-end prostitutes was an every evening occurrence in the high society section of town.

"No," she and Greg answered in unison, her tone indignant, his as even as ever. Stephanie looked down at her clothing, wondering which part of it screamed vagina-for-hire.

"She your girlfriend?" the cop asked, his gaze focused on Stephanie.

She knew how to play the who-blinks-first game. Greg would tell him they were together. Explain it all away and the cop would put his pad away, take his flashlight and Officer Whitmyer, who was walking briskly toward them, and get back in the squad car and drive away.

"Sort of," Greg replied.

Sort of?

Stephanie didn't like the tinge of sheepishness in his voice. She didn't have a clue where he was going with this and her stomach knotted. He was the one in control and she had no choice but go along.

Unless you just speak up and tell them you're an accessory to larceny. Then you won't have to worry about it. Or him.

Stephanie jumped when Greg's hand brushed hers. He laced their fingers together, his palm immediately heating her cold fingers. Warmth radiated up her arm, so welcomed and enjoyable she didn't struggle when he pulled her to his side.

"Explain 'sort of'," Pendry demanded.

She felt Greg shrug. "She's my … friend with benefits."

Stephanie snapped her head around. He was staring at the officer but she could see the way his lips formed a satisfied smirk. She tugged, trying to pull her hand from his.

"Officer, I am not his—"

"It's okay, baby," Greg said in a sugary smooth voice. "I'm sure the officers don't care—"

"Don't placate me, you big jerk," Stephanie hissed, yanking so hard her knuckles cracked before her hand was finally free. She stumbled a few steps before turning on him.

"She's got an amazing vocabulary," Greg said, ignoring her.

"Screw you, Gregory."

"That's what you were trying to do when these gentlemen pulled up."

"Ma'am, we're not here to judge," Officer Whitmyer interrupted.

"Oh no, not the *ma'am* card," Stephanie groaned.

The younger cop kept talking. "Public fornication is strictly prohibited, so this better be something else."

"I'd like to hear the rest of Mr. Wingate's story," Pendry said.

"Of course you would," Stephanie muttered.

"Excuse me?" The cop turned his full attention to her and Stephanie shut her mouth, determined not to say another word. It would be difficult, but she could do it.

"She's a little beside herself, officer. We've just recently reconnected after five years," Greg explained.

"Son, you don't sound reconnected to me."

Oh, shit. There it was. That tone indicating that male solidarity was just around the bend. Greg must have sensed it as well because he leaned forward in a conspiratorial manner.

"We're trying to figure it out. It's rough sometimes," Greg said in a commiserate-with-me tone.

Stephanie waited. His pause stretched and the acid in her stomach began to churn.

"She walked out on me on our wedding day," he finally said.

Collective gasps filled the night. Young cop, veteran cop, Stephanie herself.

"But here I am, in Florida, helping out a friend and I find out she's here, too. Maybe it's fate, right?"

Stephanie glanced at Greg's audience. Pendry stood stone faced. Whitmyer was nodding.

Great.

"So I give a call, she calls back, next thing you know we're hooking back up, but she makes it clear, up front, no commitment this time."

"Hmm. That's tough, bro," the younger officer said, shaking his head.

"Whitmyer!" Officer Pendry gave the younger cop a warning look then told Greg to continue.

"I was bitter at first. Listened to her explanation of how our lives were headed in different directions and marriage wasn't going to solve that. She wanted to focus on her real estate career."

A knot of anxiety settled in Stephanie's gut. Greg's gaze met hers for a mere second. The weight of upset grew so heavy it nearly doubled her over. She knew how devastated he had been. But she had believed every word she had told him that day. Actually thought he might understand, workaholic that he was.

Her conviction that she was saving them both from disaster had been the only thing that kept her sane during the backlash her decision had spawned.

"She was right, of course," Greg admitted.

The pain in her gut subsided, just a little.

"Back then, I worked way too many hours and she was a control freak. To top it off, when we did find time, for just us, she was into this whole role playing thing and I wasn't down with it. I'm a man, right? I had that 'why am I not enough to turn you on' attitude."

Not true. So, so, so not true. At least that last part.

"Yeah, I know," Greg continued. "Captain Dumbass, huh?"

This time, it was Pendry who nodded.

"So, fast-forward to where we are now, with me trying to be more adventurous. When Stephanie suggested one of those burglar-captured-by-the-homeowner scenes, I said, what the hell. I mean, what guy doesn't like to see a woman in lycra running up the stairs? I thought she'd just race toward the bedroom and I'd corner her there."

Stephanie was pissed, and hurt, and feeling guilty at how the past had turned out, but a vision of Greg chasing her through the house, stalking her around the huge guest room until she was trapped and had no means of escape, made her mouth go dry.

"We were right near the alarm panel and I had my finger hovering over the call button. I've read up on this fantasy stuff, you know. I did that whole 'don't make me call the cops' thing."

Stephanie wondered how on earth the men were buying *any* of this. But from their rapt attention, they were.

"Anyhow, she takes off through the front door and I accidentally hit the call button before I chased after her. Big mistake. I forgot she's into the gym thing now. I had a helluva time catching her."

"The gym," Whitmyer said loudly, snapping his fingers as he looked at Stephanie. "*That's* where I recognize you from. Those shoes. You're part of the Wednesday night Toning To The Tunes class."

Stephanie plopped onto the ground and cradled her head in her hands. When-oh-when was this night going to end? Her ex-fiancé had laid it all out there. For total strangers. Even though all he was trying to do was save her ass. She doubted there could be any more surprises in store.

Greg, on the other hand, seemed to be impervious to it all. He was on an oration of thespian proportions.

"So she runs around the shrubbery a couple of times and I finally get a hold of her, bring her to the ground with me. Tell her she better do exactly as I say or I'm going to have to spank her. That's when you guys showed up," he finished.

Stephanie looked between her knees at the ground, darkened by the shadow of her body. There was a small beetle slowly making his way up a blade of thick grass. She hated bugs. But she suddenly didn't have the strength to get up.

"So how did the statue end up over there?" Officer Whitten asked in an inquisitive tone.

"I was a strong safety in college. Apparently I'm not as good at long dives as I used to be. Misjudged and took him out on my way to Steph."

"And you were able to what? Roll to your feet and into a waist tackle?" Whitmyer asked.

"I was." The pride in Greg's voice forced Stephanie to lift her head and look at him.

"Seems pretty damn amazing," Pendry said, sliding his flashlight back into its holder on his belt. Whitmyer did the same, then closed the gap between himself and Stephanie and offered a hand, pulling her to her feet.

"Not *that* amazing," Greg replied. He turned toward her, his green eyes daring her to look away. "A man can do anything to get to the woman he still loves."

The heaviness in Stephanie's stomach twisted, then rocketed straight to her heart.

He's playin'. Making it sound good for the police. That's all. Don't buy into it.

He didn't love her anymore. How could he? And Stephanie was sure he would never love her again. Greg was just being protective. Men did that, right?

No, not where heartbreaking exes are involved. He's going to screw you. And not in a good way.

"Let's take a walk," Officer Pendry said. "I'll need to see some ID, get estimations of time, take a few more notes. We'll do that inside then let you two get back to your … evening." He gestured with his arm for her to go first and Stephanie silently obeyed, still not able to look Greg in the eye.

The demand for identification should have been more worrisome, but it wasn't. Her purse was in Maggie's car but Greg had done such a bang-up job of explaining to his new fraternal fan club Stephanie decided to let him keep weaving threads to the tale. He'd come up with something plausible. She had way more important things to be concerned with right now.

Like whether or not there was a glimmer of truth in Greg's last sentence. And how she would handle that if there was.

* * * *

Greg was pretty damned please with himself. He'd given the police his ID and went through the fabricated events of his reunion with Stephanie once more, all the while watching her from the corner of his eye.

She had taken a seat on the fourth step of the grand, center staircase, adopting a Rodin-like pose—chin in palm, elbow on knee—seemingly oblivious to the cold marble beneath her butt.

He wondered if he should be worried about how quiet she had become. How she simply stared out the double, cut glass front doors. That demeanor was new. The Stephanie of old was rarely quiet. She would have never allowed him to take charge, couldn't have sat silent.

"Your turn," Pendry said, looking at Stephanie. "Can I please see some form of ID?"

The officer's manner had changed. Politeness seeped into his interrogation and Greg knew the men weren't going to harass them. He and Steph would get by with a warning and probably a promise not to take their sex games outdoors.

"I left it at home." Stephanie spread her arms wide, but remained seated. "A friend dropped me off."

Greg wondered if either of the officers noticed the subtle change of tone when Steph mentioned her 'friend'. He didn't want to be in Maggie's shoes when Steph finally came face to face with her cohort.

"Name and address, then," Pendry said.

Greg listened as she rattled it off. He wasn't familiar enough with the area yet to know the exact location she gave them. But with any luck, he would soon. Steph would need to get home.

Unless you ask her to spend the night.

Right. Like that was going to happen. But at least he had the advantage of keeping her here so they could talk. She'd want to talk after all this time, wouldn't she?

"That'll do. You're free to go," Pendry said in a dismissive tone.

Greg held his breath, waiting to see how Stephanie would respond.

"Thank you, officer," she said, standing up slowly. She didn't look at any of them as she turned and walked toward the back of the house, sneakers squeaking on the polished floor as she retreated.

"Sarge," Whitmyer whispered, tapping his wrist.

Greg glanced at his own watch. Ten thirty seven. It was getting too close to Fifth Avenue's witching hour. There would be a mass exodus of inebriated patrons from the various upscale bars. Would that be less paperwork than a suspected break in? When it was all said and done, he was fairly certain that Pendry and Whitmyer would write it up as an unexplained disturbance.

"One last question," Pendry said.

Greg became suddenly alert. It was always those 'last questions' that hung the guilty out to dry.

"After she breaks your heart, even after all this time goes by, you still love her?" Pendry asked.

Saying that Steph had broken his heart was the biggest freakin' understatement known to man. He remembered the days and weeks and months that had followed her abandonment, the cyclone of conflicting emotions that had gnawed at his gut. Anger had been the front-runner, but in the end, disappointment in himself had pushed everything else aside. He should have seen the subtle changes. Recognized them as more than pre-wedding jitters.

But after all this time, their connection was still there. He felt it the second he came within three feet of his former fiancée.

The constricting claw of pressure on Greg's chest suddenly released. Heat warmed his body and for the first time in years, Greg felt as if the jagged crevices of hurt and distrust had suddenly fused together.

He fixed his gaze on the officer and replied, "It's the damndest thing, but I do."

The cop studied him and Greg chuckled, rubbing the area over his heart.

"Son, I think that's the first honest thing you've said all night." Pendry gave him a half smile, handed back his ID and turned toward the front door.

"Good luck with *that*," Whitmyer said, gesturing toward the kitchen with a quick nod of his head. "I don't envy you, man. That's for sure. She all but screams 'unattainable' at the gym. Even with those rockin' curves, it's not worth the effort."

The younger cop's unsolicited opinion forced a whorl of jealousy through Greg's body. "Thanks for coming out," Greg said quickly, walking to the door and opening it. "I'll make sure I let Henry know how great your response time was."

"It's our job," they replied in unison, Pendry giving the younger officer a stern look as he followed him through the door.

Greg watched them cross the lawn, get into the squad car and drive away. He stared out into the night, glancing at the disrupted landscaping, then back to the street. Was Maggie waiting out there? Waiting until the cops left to come back and get Steph?

If she is, you better move quick, man.

Greg pushed the heavy door closed and locked it for good measure. He wouldn't be denied his time with Stephanie. Alone. Uninterrupted.

He headed toward the kitchen, pausing when he reached the arched doorway of the formal living room. Steph was standing in front of the massive, built-in china cabinet. She had turned on the display light, the shelves of figurines and crystal forming a beacon of glistening light in the darkened room. From the back, her silhouette wasn't defined, but his fingers itched at the memory of her on top of him in the grass, of how he would have welcomed more time to explore her more-rounded shape.

Greg shook his head and kept moving, stopping at the wet bar just long enough to grab the bottle of very nice wine he had opened for dinner. Henry had said to help himself, and considering he was making next to nothing for his home watch gig, he didn't feel bad.

He poured two glasses and by the time he entered the living room, Stephanie had made her way to the final display panel. He offered her a glass and she took it, her eyes never leaving the array of fine porcelain.

"This room always makes me nervous," he said. Without thinking, he clinked the rims of their glasses. It was something they had always done, whether they were drinking fine wine or tap water.

"The proverbial bull in a china shop," she said, taking a sip of wine.

His mind raced for the right thing to say. They had visited Naples and Rome and Venice what seemed like a lifetime ago. Monuments, museums, even the family-owned factory that produced delicate objects like the ones she continued to stare at.

Was she thinking of that now?

"Are you still drawn to all things Old World?" Greg asked.

"You mention fine Italian imports now and I think cannoli, not Capodimonte," she smoothly deflected.

He chuckled. "Your tastes have changed." She'd been as fixated on high end, designer branded products as everyone else in her group of socialite friends. It had bothered Greg, but not enough to change his affection for her.

"Yeah. Life has a way of doing that. I'm not as self-centered as I used to be. Or as disciplined. Hence my new relationship with the gym four times a week."

"You look great, Steph. Ditching the emaciated look has done wonders for you." Greg swallowed a healthy dose of wine to cover his nervousness.

She turned, looked at him, and Greg nearly choked. Her eyes sparkled, the way they use to just before she said something teasing. Something that would have him pulling her into his arms and kissing the smile off her lips.

"I think there's a compliment in there somewhere," she replied. The corner of her mouth quirked tentatively, as if she might be equally on edge.

"There is." He took a step closer, deciding to press his advantage, if indeed that's what it was. He reached forward and trailed his fingers along her lower ribcage before settling his palm against the side of her waist. Her body flinched, but she didn't back away, which was enough to make him smile.

"What are you doing?" Her eyes widened and he wished they were in a brightly lit room, one where he could see if that pale green of her irises were darkening. The way they did when she was excited. Or aroused.

"Taking advantage of your adrenaline rush?" He smiled, wondering if she could still read his body language, the facial quirks that had become blatant indications of what he wanted.

He stared at the long column of her throat, watched the muscles in her neck contract as she swallowed. How would Steph react if he slid his tongue over her throbbing pulse, nipped at her skin just the way she had liked.

"My adrenaline rush was gone the minute we walked through the front door," she said softly.

Greg slid his hand toward the center of her back and when her hips shifted, he lowered it an inch further. The cleft of her buttocks was easily discernible in the tight knit pants she wore.

"That's too bad," he said. Taking a chance, he stroked the small patch of skin with his pinky finger, waiting to see if that simple little motion would have the same effect all these years later. He felt the slight shift in her stance, knew he had her attention.

Leaning close to her ear, he whispered, "Maybe, just maybe, Stephanie, I can give it a jumpstart."

* * * *

Egotistical jerk. On any other day, that's what Stephanie's mind would have screamed. But here, with his warm breath tickling her ear, she couldn't find the strength to reprimand Greg. She hadn't realized how much she missed the sensation of heat spiraling downward to her core. He hovered, his slow easy breathing setting every nerve in her body on high alert.

How was he so calm when her heart was thudding as if she had just encountered the ultimate fear?

Maybe you have.

All she had to do was turn her head to the side and their lips would meet. Did she truly want to take a step in that direction? Or maybe he was being a tease. Get her to the point of showing him she still responded to his touch, only to have him back away and ask her how it felt to have something you wanted slowly walk away.

Memories swirled through her mind at a numbing rate of speed. Date nights, friends' parties, holiday dinners, vacations. The images taunted her and she took a deep breath, trying to force them back into the corners of her mind, the little recesses where she kept them safely under wraps.

She would not allow the happiest moments of her past to drive her to another poor decision.

Another one? Like leaving him the first time?

She shook her head, trying to clear the images and shake off that pesky inner voice all at once, but the motion made his lips brush slightly against the shell of her ear and a jolt of desire rocked her.

"Oh, what the hell," she said in a jagged whisper, turning toward his chest. She knew how to do self-recrimination. She'd have plenty of time for that. Later. When the scents of his musky cologne and pure bare-chestedness were mingling together to form a heady blend she couldn't resist.

Bare chests don't have a scent!

Stephanie straightened the arm holding the wine glass and slid her other hand over Greg's shoulder and up the side of his neck. It was time to silence that voice inside her head once and for all.

She rose up on her toes, kissed his cheek before she aimed her lips towards his. He pulled his head back, avoiding her caress as he stared down at her with a look of ferocity that made her heart falter.

"You expect me to just give you what you want?" he asked, waiting a few seconds before his lips parted in the tiniest of smiles. "With a line like '*oh what the hell*'?"

Relief washed over her, but she tried to hide it by angling her pelvis flush against his hips.

"I expect you to give me what I want because it's obviously what you want, too," she replied in an assured tone. She wasn't certain what she would have said if she hadn't felt proof of his desire.

"Mmmm. My darling Steph. Things are going to be different this time." He gave her ass a little pat and took a step backward, raising his wine glass. "To change," he toasted, waiting for her.

It was stupid, the wave of aloneness that washed over her as their bodies parted. And what exactly did that toast mean…and did she really care?

Stephanie stared into his eyes and her apprehension faded. She was turned on by that promising gleam and his teasing tone. She raised her own glass, but didn't clink the rim to his.

"To change?" she asked. "Not to old times. Old friends—"

"Old lovers?" he interjected. "Definitely not. I've learned it isn't healthy to live in the past."

Steph's eyes began to burn. She knew full well she was the one who'd helped with that lesson.

He tilted his wrist and the ring of crystal echoed through the room as he forced their glasses together. "This time, things are going to end differently," he said, his gaze never leaving hers as he took a long sip of wine.

"How?" she asked, following suit. The rich wine coated her tongue, warming her throat and belly. "Are you going to bang me like there's no tomorrow, then just walk away?"

"Maybe. But there's going to be a helluva lot more before the 'banging' part. And can I just say, I've missed the way you turn a phrase."

Stephanie laughed despite herself.

Greg took her hand and led her around the couch and out the door, back toward the foyer. Stephanie quickly drained her glass and set it, as he did, on the onyx hall table as she followed him to the grand staircase. Now would be the time to tell him she wasn't sure this was the best idea. Before they started upward to the second level guest suites. But that wasn't what was going through her mind as they made the climb.

"So how is this going to be different?" she asked.

"For starters, you're not going to be the one giving commands."

"I never commanded you," she said as they reached the landing.

He glanced over his shoulder, offering her a dubious look.

"Okay," she admitted. "Maybe once in awhile. Like telling you that you needed to thrust a little harder."

"I was talking big picture, babe. Not just sex."

She caught the toe of her sneaker, missing a step or two.

"That thought enough to make you stumble?" He drew her closer to his side, so she wasn't walking behind him. She knew he meant it to be comforting and it was.

"I'm still not made of porcelain," she said, trying to steer the conversation toward sex, and sex alone. "That's all I'm saying."

"Maybe not," he said as they reached the opened door of his bedroom, pulling up short to motion her inside. "But either way, I'm going to make you shatter."

Stephanie's mouth went dry. She walked into the room, not stopping until she was a few feet away from a huge Victorian dresser. The intricately carved mirror above it allowed her to watch his predatory advance. It never occurred to her to doubt his words. Greg had never been a braggart. And he never promised anything he didn't deliver. She shivered at the thought. That and the look of lust reflecting back at her from his eyes.

"What if Henry comes home early from cribbage?"

"He's not at cribbage. He's in Jacksonville, just like I told the cops."

"Jacksonville? For how long?" Stephanie asked.

"One more night," he said, reaching up to pull a strand of hair that had escaped her pony tail back behind her ear.

"Then what if he comes home early from that? He's made unexpected appearances before." She barely got the words out before the dryness in her mouth migrated to her throat. She stood, voyeur to herself as his large hands gripped her shoulders, squeezing lightly before his fingers trailed over her collarbone, not stopping until they reached the zipper of her hoodie.

"I'll lock the bedroom door," he said, lifting the metal tab with one hand, the weight of the other resting against the fullness of her left breast. With infinite slowness he lowered the zipper, exposing the clasp of her front-closure bra.

"But what if he gets pissed that I'm here?" Stephanie thought it was a plausible question, one that was meant to prolong a seduction. And that's what this was. Her ex-lover fiancé seducing her into his bed.

"I'm allowed to have girls over." His tone was innocent, but the way he unhooked the bottom of the zipper and slowly traced the gaping edges upward were anything but. His touch tickled her ribs but the path over the inner swell of her breasts sent electricity through her nerve endings. Her already-peaked nipples tightened and she bit her lips against a threatening moan.

"Even on school nights," he added, yanking the fabric off her shoulders and down her arms with such erotically startling force that Stephanie blurted the first thing that came to mind.

"I have to work tomorrow."

"Good to know," he said, before tossing her hoodie to the floor. She caught a glimpse of his sexy smile before he lowered his lips to the spot where her shoulder and neck met. She watched him press a long kiss on the sensitive patch of skin. He nipped at her neck and desire forced her hips backward, against his body, against his erection. Thick and hard.

"I need to be home by five," she said in a voice that sounded too breathless to be hers.

His hands snaked around the outer curve of her breasts, fingers brushing the upper edge of her knit bra.

"Why?" he asked, fingers hovering over her nipples.

She held her breath, waiting to see if he would tweak her flesh. He couldn't have forgotten how she loved that. But he simply brushed the turgid peaks, so featherlike and torturous that she nearly demanded he stop.

"Why?" he asked again, more sternly.

The tone was enough to snap Stephanie out of the fog of lust.

"Why do you need to leave me so soon?" he asked.

His fingers stilled, suspending her between pain and pleasure.

"Shower," she groaned, still trying to be sensible, but fullness building low in her belly was making it difficult.

He splayed his fingers over her breasts, releasing the pressure. "You can shower here," he said, meeting her gaze in the reflection of the mirror. She stood, staring at the inviting sight they made. She relaxed her upper body against the warmth of his broad chest, unable to deny, even to herself, how good it felt to be in his embrace.

"Then you'll drive me home?" she asked.

He stepped backward and spun her around to face him in one smooth maneuver. Their gazes locked and if he hadn't had a firm grip on her shoulders, Stephanie would have backed away from the unconcealed heat in his eyes.

"By that point, if history is any indicator, I'll probably do whatever you tell me to do."

Stephanie shook her head lightly. "Something's different about you, Gregory Wingate. Very, very different."

His lips parted into the sexiest smile he'd ever offered her, and just that quickly, her own desire was rekindled. "And you're still the queen of inquisitiveness."

"Maybe," she replied, breaking eye contact.

"You're dying to know how my lovemaking's changed."

"Maybe." She studied the draperies as if they were the most fascinating thing in the room.

"How we could possibly be better than we were before."

She offered him a flippant wave of her hand, as if the thought was insignificant, her heart beating a little faster with each volley of the conversation.

Fingers, long and cool, curled gently around her chin and forced her head around. "Then let's can this conversation and let me go down on you until you're screaming."

The mere confidence of his tone made her body tingle with excitement, electricity jolting straight to her core.

"What if the room has audio sensors," she asked, simply wanting to have the last word. "What if my screams set off another alarm?"

Greg's knowing look told her he was on to her. "Then we'll invite Pendry and Whitmyer back inside and offer them coffee and donuts."

His humor cemented her decision to stay.

"You have donuts?" she asked in mock surprise.

He tipped his chin toward his chest until they were nearly eye-to-eye.

"Baby," he said in a promising whisper. "I've got something a helluva lot sweeter."

* * * *

Greg's warm palm covered her shoulder the exact moment Stephanie jolted awake.

"Hey. Time to get up, lazy bones. It's Mr. Bluebird on your shoulder," he sing-songed. The words had barely left his mouth before the glaring light of the bedside lamp assailed her.

She flung herself onto her back and covered her head with the pillow, hoping he'd think it was the early hour that she wanted to hide from, not the fact that they'd fallen right back into the familiar, teasing camaraderie they'd shared years before.

"Ugh," she sighed heavily, her voice muffled as she replied. "A person can't be considered a lazy bones if they're simply trying to postpone the start of their buttcrack-of-dawn job.

"I can think of better ways to postpone hitting the operating room than smothering yourself." His hand began a leisurely exploration of her upper arm, palm replaced by fingers when he reached her elbow. He dipped into the soft skin at the bend of her arm, drawing tiny circular patterns that immediately had her thinking of how he'd done the same thing last night. But he had used his tongue, not his finger. And he hadn't been anywhere near her elbow. The mere thought of his exquisite foreplay made her body flush and she tossed the pillow to the floor with more force than she intended.

"I told you last night you could shower here," he offered, leaning across her body to stare at where the pillow had landed, a hint of confusion knitting his brow.

Stephanie knew that if she wanted to see him again she had to defuse the tension that had whooshed into the room. Either that or let him think she'd turned into a crazy woman.

"I'd rather do it at home," she said, reaching up to trace the line of his jaw with her finger. He tilted his head to the side and studied her. She smiled in return.

"Don't trust yourself, huh?" he finally asked.

She sat up and pushed him hard enough that he rolled back onto his side of the bed. "You weren't *that* stupendous," she lied, wondering if she should take the sheet with her or walk buck naked into his bathroom.

Given what had transpired hours before, how they hadn't left an inch of each other's bodies unexplored, prudishness seemed silly.

"Liar, liar, panties on fire." He stood up and walked around the bottom of the bed, his own nakedness putting her at ease.

"Well they obviously were last night," she replied, pushing the sheet aside. She focused her gaze on her hoodie, tossed haphazardly against a tall Egyptian urn. She didn't want to meet his eyes. Not yet.

Greg reached out his hand and she took it. Although parts of her body were sore, she didn't really need the help. But she wasn't ready to simply say 'break' and go to her respective corner. She had longed for Greg's touch last night and the way her heart was racing, that wasn't about to change anytime soon.

"When did you become such a gentleman," she asked, allowing him to pull her to her feet. A part of her wanted him to take the move further, to pull her straight into the security of his embrace. She had forgotten the sheer pleasure a woman could derive from a strong man.

"I'm always a gentleman when a woman acts nice. You know, like you did last night. Using 'please' and 'thank you' and 'fasterfasterfasterfaster'.

Stephanie tried to duck around him but he caught her around the waist and pulled her body tight against his chest. She really didn't want to think about him and other women. Not now.

"When did you become such a wimpass that you can't look me in the eye?" he asked softly.

She listened to the steady rhythm of his heart and exhaled slowly. The moment was pivotal, she knew that. She could be flippant and maybe that would be the end of it. They could chalk it up as a one-night stand. Or she could be honest and see what happened next.

"I don't know when I morphed into a wimpass. Maybe somewhere between the 'pleases' and 'thank yous' and 'fasterfasterfasters'." His arms tightened around her and Stephanie couldn't stop her lips from parting with contentment.

"Well then," he said, giving her butt a playful slap. "We'll have to work on more eye-to-eye contact."

"Oh, please." She stepped backward and he let her go.

"Don't use that disgruntled tone with me," he warned. She could hear the humor in his voice, but there was a hint of command to his tone, as well. Which was something new. He'd taken control several times during their lovemaking, made her submit before he gave her what she needed, and her body had sizzled with the eroticism of his demands.

"Can we please not talk about this now?" she asked, grabbing her hoodie then going in search of her bra. If he kept bringing up particular details, she'd be horned up to the max by the time she got home.

"Haven't you heard? Communication is the key," he teased. "But have it your way. We'll talk about it later. As in, later tonight."

"I have plans tonight," she lied. Her toe brushed against her forgotten thong and she stopped and quickly pulled it up her legs.

"Another round of grand larceny with your best bud?"

Stephanie stopped dead in her tracks. "Oh, crap. I totally forgot about Maggie."

"Understandable. Considering the fact she left you high and dry last night."

"No," she said, urgency filling her voice. "I forgot to text or call or let her know where I was. Maggie probably thinks I was arrested."

"Well, when she finally asks, tell her you *were* subjected to an interrogation of sorts." Innuendo dripped from his tone but Stephanie ignored it.

"Being asked if I could handle doggy style doesn't count. For crying out loud, where are my pants?"

"Here." As if by magic, her pants and bra landed over her shoulder. She turned, pleased at his amused smirk but shocked that he was already dressed in his sweat pants and t-shirt.

"That was quick," she said, putting on the rest of her clothes.

"Ah. One of the few things the neighbors didn't hear you scream last night," he said, heading for the door.

Stephanie hurried after him in silence. She knew they could go back and forth forever. The banter was one of the best parts of their past relationship. It was confusing how they could suddenly be in sync again. Passage of time aside, she was perplexed by his willingness to even speak to her, let alone fall back into intimate contact.

Maybe he just wanted to take you to bed, show you what you've been missing, then tell you to get lost.

Stephanie tried not to think of that as they entered the huge, six car garage. Greg hit the garage door opener, then led her past Henry's lineup of high performance automobiles, all of which cost well over six figures.

He stopped when he reached a glossy, midnight black Challenger and motioned her by before he opened the passenger door. Stephanie looked from Greg to the car and back again.

"I make no excuses," he said as she lowered herself onto the grey leather seat. "Midlife crisis car, plain and simple."

There was a time when Greg would never have admitted such an ordinary affliction could affect him. He'd put himself at a level higher than most men. He had often explained, usually when he was still in the office at ten at night, that it was what kept him driven, kept him in front of his peers. Heaven knew she'd changed, apparently he had, too.

Stephanie smiled. "That's not supposed to happen until you're in your forties."

"What can I say? I've always been ahead of the curve."

He swooped into the car, startling Stephanie as he gave her a quick kiss then shut the door. Without thinking she placed her fingers against her lips, wishing his mouth had lingered. Just a little while.

Greg slid behind the wheel, buckled up and offered her a wink before the engine turned over and the car rumbled to life. Hair a little too long to be corporate approved, still a mess from their bedroom romp, he looked more like the ultimate bad boy than a trader displaced from Lehman Brothers.

The fingers Stephanie was still holding against her lips began to shake. She didn't even know that was what Greg still did for a career. They hadn't delved into the present. They'd been too busy revisiting all the right moves they'd known from the past. The ones that guaranteed mutual orgasms and contented sighs that led straight to slumber.

She watched his mouth curve into a satisfied grin. "Don't worry, baby. I'll have you home in no time."

An uncomfortable heaviness settled in the pit of Stephanie's stomach. Suddenly, getting home didn't sound so great.

* * * *

Greg gave up trying to make small talk on the way to Stephanie's apartment. He could tell from the way she was tapping her thigh with her thumb she was zoned out, mentally prioritizing the numerous things she needed to accomplish today. Her fingers rested an inch above her knee and a flashback of how she had slid that same hand up her thigh last night and guided him into her for his initial thrust had Greg gripping the wheel tighter.

It was wild, their need to be together. The urgency to get naked. He loved how the years had changed her body. How it had softened in all the right places. But there were parts of her anatomy, the ones directly related to his success at pleasuring her that had remained the same. Which allowed him to dive in and drive her to the brink of release, over and over, until she begged him to take her.

He liked her new verbal openness, but with the haze of lust gone, he didn't want to think about who might have assisted her with that transformation. He'd had plenty of other women over the years, it would be unrealistic to think Stephanie's past was any different.

But the knot in his chest was proof that thinking about her previous sex life wasn't beneficial. Not if he was going to win her back.

And as of last night, that was his new life plan.

"Take a right at the next stop sign, then I'm the second house on the left."

Greg nodded. "So, you work until when?" He wasn't going to let her out of the car until she agreed to meet him later.

"Greg—"

"Don't," he cut her off. "We *are* going to get together tonight and talk. Not dry hump each other in the shrubbery or end up sweaty and twisted in the fifteen-hundred-count sheets. Just you and me with no distractions. You can't just write this off as coincidence, Stephanie. Not this time."

"I wasn't going to," she said, motioning to where he should turn.

"Really? That would be a first," he replied. She had always jumped at the chance to tell him there was no such thing as Fate. Or Karma.

"Yeah. Well enough shit has happened that I now give consideration to the whole 'it was meant to be' thing," she replied. "I haven't forgotten the million times you tried to push that possibility down my throat."

Greg reached over and picked up her left hand, balled it into a fist. He raised it to his lips and kissed her fingers, not stopping until he felt her relax.

"I'm not going to make the obvious reference to pushing something down your throat," he teased. "What time do you get off?"

"I'm not going to make the obvious reference to getting off," she mimicked in a stuffy tone generally used by on-screen English butlers.

Greg dropped her hand and turned into her driveway. He wouldn't give her the satisfaction of laughing. "So, what time?"

"I'm done by 4:30 if there aren't any stragglers. Let's say six?"

Quick mental calculations would put them too late for where Greg wanted them at that time of the evening. "Let's say five-fifteen. Just come home and throw on some shorts and a top. Nothing fancy," he said, putting the car into park. He reached for his door handle and she stopped him with a hand on his arm.

"I'm good. Save the gallantry for later, okay?" She opened her door and Greg forced himself to remain still. His gaze drifted to her lips, wanting to give her one last kiss before she went.

Then, just as quick as he'd been in the garage, she swooped toward him and gave him a brief kiss. One so light, he should convince himself it held zero promise. But the dazzling smile she offered him dispelled that thought. And before the heavy door slammed shut his mind was spinning with plans for the perfect evening.

* * * *

"Hunter. Line five," the receptionist yelled over the partition. "It's your *sister*. Again."

Stephanie tossed her pen onto the chart. Everyone at the surgery center knew she had two brothers. No sisters. She punched the blinking light on the phone hard enough that her finger ached. "What?" she whisper-yelled.

"Don't snap at me." Maggie's voice was equally pissed.

"I'm working. I told you we'd talk later." Stephanie rubbed the bridge of her nose. She had barely made it out of the shower that morning when Maggie's insistent phone calls began. She'd put her friend on speaker and listened to her rant as Stephanie dried off and dressed and threw on mascara, her standard beauty regime on days she worked the operating room. At Stephanie's request, the receptionist had fielded

Maggie's calls. But the day was winding down for both of them and Stephanie would rather talk to Maggie now than later.

"You also told me you have a date *later*," Maggie said.

"For the love of—just let it go, already. Will you?"

"I need to see you. We need to talk," Maggie demanded.

"You lost your bargaining power the minute you drove away and left me in that freakin' flower bed." During her quick shower that morning, Stephanie had decided she was over Maggie's scheme. But now the woman had brought the entire evening back into the forefront of Stephanie's mind.

"Don't tell me there wasn't a moment during the day when you were reliving spending the night with your ex—in *my* house, no less—that you couldn't have picked up the phone and returned my call."

Stephanie counted to ten, keeping her frustration under control. "This may come as a surprise to you, but I have other things to do during the day than lounge around worrying solely about my insignificant, self-induced catastrophes."

Silence. Complete and utter silence.

"Hunter." Stephanie turned at the sound of her supervisor's voice. The woman stood in the doorway, arms crossed over her breasts. "I'll finish that chart. You head on home. You got hands-free in your car, right?" The woman, who earlier that morning had heard bits and pieces of Stephanie's adventures with local law enforcement, motioned with a nod of her head that Stephanie should leave. No one argued with the woman, a near doppelganger for the famous Nurse Ratchet.

"Maggie. I'll call you back in ten minutes." Stephanie hung up, not waiting for a reply. "Thank you, Helen. I'd appreciate that."

"Listen, honey. With the night you had, you deserve to cut out a half hour early. You know, in case you have to get ready for a date, or something."

Stephanie chuckled. There wasn't much that didn't get around their surgery center. It was a tight-knit group. "I don't know if it's a date. We're just getting together."

"Hmph. I know it's been awhile since you've hit the anatomy books, but I'm thinking that's what you two studied last night."

She hadn't elaborated on what went down after the police had left.

But she had slipped up when she mentioned Greg had driven her home and included 'this morning'. Her coworkers had some of the best detective skills around.

"You think that's a mistake?" Stephanie questioned. She respected the older woman's opinion.

"Please," Helen said with a dismissive wave of her hand. "Who am I to judge? I'm just a nurse."

Stephanie snorted. Helen had circumnavigated the globe as relief effort support for the Red Cross. She'd encountered hostile tribes, earthquake aftershocks and numerous bombings.

"I got cold feet. The day of the wedding. I left him at the altar."

"But did you, in actuality, leave him at the altar? I heard it was after the guests had arrived but before he and his groomsmen made their appearance."

Stephanie stared at her, not really surprised that she knew that much. "That's true."

"And the guests still got to party it up on filet and lobster. Dancing along to the DJ."

"That's only because my parents have never met a party they didn't like. They figured everything was in place for a great night so they partied on, while secretly wanting to kill me."

"Hey, they still speak to you now, so that's a plus. And your guests? They had to be pleased they could just return their gifts. Better than you and your man being together for six months then splitting. Nothing pisses me off more than when I shell out for the Wedgewood place setting and things go tits up before the couple even gets to pull out that top layer of frozen wedding cake on anniversary number one."

Leave it to Helen. She always offered a different perspective.

"I'm just a little leery that he's so forgiving," Stephanie said. "I don't think I'd be that way."

"He's probably realized you're the best thing going, girlie." Helen grabbed the back of the chair and spun it so Stephanie's body was facing the door. "Don't over think things, okay? Now get going."

Stephanie stood up, resisting the urge to give the woman a quick hug. Helen wasn't a hugger. She clocked out and was in her car before the ten-minute time frame she'd given Maggie elapsed. Maybe she should make her friend wait a little longer. But really, what would that prove? She hit Quickdial and buckled her seatbelt while the phone rang.

"Hello, Stephanie."

The contrite tone Stephanie had hoped for was absent. She didn't want to argue with Maggie. She just wanted to let the woman say what she needed to, then move on. Stephanie wanted to take a few days before she decided if their friendship would survive.

"Maggie. I'm on my way home, so you have about twenty minutes."

"Wow, when did you become such a bitch?"

Stephanie positioned her car in the middle of the three-lane highway. The best place to be when you were driving and carrying on a conversation.

"Is that what you really want to discuss?"

"No," Maggie replied. "I want to know what compelled you to turn traitor."

"It wasn't turning traitor. You left me. I honestly don't want to think about what would have happened if it wasn't Greg who came running out of the house."

"And that's another thing," Maggie said loudly. "What the hell is your ex-fiancée doing work for Henry?"

"I don't know," Stephanie replied honestly.

"What do you even know about him? I mean, him *now*? You tell me how much you've changed. What about him? I thought he was some sort of techie genius stock trader when you two were together. Shouldn't he be inventing Google or something, not playing house sitter?"

"News flash, Miss Current Event-Challenged, someone's already created Google."

"You know what I mean," Maggie said hotly.

"I'm sure I'll find out tonight when we play Twenty Questions."

"Yeah, right. Since you guys already played Spin The Bottle last night." Maggie offered up a defeatist sigh.

"No bottle," Stephanie said. "But there was wine involved. One of Henry's vintage Bordeaux, in fact. That should make you happy."

Again, the silence.

"Well … maybe a little," Maggie said softly.

"Listen. Give me a few days to figure out if you've been a raving maniac all this time and I haven't noticed or if I'm going to forgive you for leaving me stranded," Stephanie said.

"I dropped by your place today. Went around back to the lanai and tossed your purse and phone as far as I could in the doggie door."

Stephanie smiled at the olive branch. "Thank you, Maggie."

"Hey. Those pavers are super hard. You need a bigger rug out there." Design advice from the queen.

"Well, you're just not used to being on your knees," Stephanie teased. She didn't hate her friend.

"Not without being handed a rectangular box from Tiffany's first," Maggie replied. Stephanie could tell she was smiling.

"I'll let you know how things go," Stephanie promised.

"Just be careful, okay." True concern echoed through the speaker. "He might just be playing you. Trying to hurt you for hurting him."

Stephanie's intuition told her that wasn't the case. "I'm off tomorrow. I'll be in touch."

"Text me where you're going," Maggie said. "And when you get home."

"Even if I end up back at your ex's?"

"Especially if you end up there. He's got a 1982 Château Margaux stashed in a secret hiding place in the wine cellar. Text and I'll direct you to it."

"It's always about revenge with you, isn't it?"

Maggie avoided the question. "As long as it isn't all about revenge on your ex's part."

* * * *

Stephanie heard Greg's car coming and her palms began to sweat. She hadn't noticed this morning how loud the exhaust pipes were. She'd have to wait and see if one of the condo commandos turned her in for violating the noise restriction clause. But she knew that wasn't what was causing her discomfort.

She glanced at the small backpack sitting on the couch. Seconds were ticking by to her big decision. Should she carry it out to his car and nonchalantly toss it in the backseat? She had a change of clothes, a few toiletry items, and her swimsuit packed, just in case he invited her to stay overnight. Having the following day off work meant they wouldn't have to wake up early and search for her scattered lingerie.

If he gave her the option, she'd sleep with him again. Tonight and any other night. After ending her conversation with Maggie and driving the short distance home, Stephanie's mind had zipped through scenario on top of scenario where she and Greg were concerned.

Some included him being a selfish prick solely set on revenge. Others had them wrapped in each other's arms every chance possible. One had her doing an early morning walk of shame. Another played out with them spending Saturdays hitting the thrift stores and Sundays watching football.

The advancing rumble of the car turned to a softer, steady idle and she walked toward her front door, snagging the backpack and tossing it over one shoulder. She opened the door before he got a chance to knock, not caring if she seemed anxious.

"Wow," Greg said. His gaze took in the sunglasses perched on the top of her head to the lime green flip flops on her feet, and everything in between. "You look great. Don't forget a jacket."

"A jacket?" That was something she hadn't packed. "It's eighty-four degrees."

He slid the backpack off her shoulder and carried it to the car. She quickly unlocked the front door, snatched up her sweater, locked up and then followed him to the trunk of the car.

"Nice," Stephanie said, seeing everything they needed for a beach visit. "I haven't seen the water in over a month."

He laughed. "Good thing I didn't want this to be a surprise."

"Hey. How many beaches are in southwest Florida? You haven't told me where we're going."

He slammed the trunk then opened her door. "Get in, Steph. Quit asking questions."

She didn't move. "There are tons of questions I'm sure we both want to ask."

"We'll have plenty of time." He motioned her in and then they were off, down her street and westward. When he hung a right onto Highway 41, Stephanie offered a guess.

"Wiggins Pass?"

He smiled. “Nah. I’m looking for something really memorable. How was work?”

“Work was work. My manager let me go early. Due to the fact Maggie kept calling the office every half hour.”

“Did you talk to her?”

“I did,” Stephanie said. “I told her I’d touch base tomorrow. You know, after you and I got together again. She warned me to beware, you know, in case you were simply plotting your revenge.”

There, she’d thrown it out there in casual conversation. It wasn’t like he’d admit it, but she watched his response closely. His jaw clenched then he splayed his fingers wide, relaxing his grip on the steering wheel for just a moment before holding on again.

“Is that what *you* think?” he asked.

Stephanie shook her head, probably answering too quickly. “I don’t. Am I being stupid, Greg?”

“You’ve never been stupid. Well, except for that one time on November eighth.” He offered her a half smile.

“Would it do any good to say I’m sorry again?” She clasped her hands to keep them from shaking.

“Babe, there’s no need. I’ve recovered from it. Really.”

They turned west onto Beach Road and Stephanie tilted her head, studying him. “Are we going to Fort Myers Beach?” she asked.

He shut her up by zigging in and out of traffic, faster than she would have gone, and turned onto Barefoot Beach Drive. He slowed down and pulled up to the guard house. “Hey, Dan. Just headin’ out to the beach.”

The guard bent down and looked inside the car, offered Stephanie an easy smile and said, “Sounds good, Mr. Wingate. Have a good one.”

Greg nodded to the guard then reached over and gave Stephanie’s knee a little tap. “Almost there.”

“Barefoot Beach?” she asked. “One of the sweetest stretches of white sand and you and the guard are tight?”

“It’s another home watch gig. What can I say, I’m a blessed man.”

“So you watch Maggie’s place and this one?” Stephanie asked. They pulled into a three-storied house, the wooden siding painted a deep shade of aqua.

“This one I check from time to time. No sleeping over, so don’t get your hopes up," he teased. "Water's shut off, humidistat is on. I just stop by to look things over once every few weeks. I was at Henry's for a different reason. One you can guess."

They opened their car doors and she met him at the trunk. "Henry wanted to make sure Maggie stayed out. Is that what you do now? Check on people's homes?" Stephanie knew it was a big business in areas where many residents were seasonal.

"Only for a select few. My boss's son owns this place."

Stephanie took the blanket he handed her. "Now we're getting somewhere," she said. "Who's your boss?"

He lifted a small rolling cooler from the trunk and slammed the lid. She followed as he rolled it over the crushed oyster shell driveway. He led her to a small, wooden walkway close to the side of the house, nearly hidden by the eight-foot high, silver buttonwood fence row.

"I work for Harold Strong. Dean of the Literature Department at the University of Cincinnati."

"Dean … you work for a university? What happened to the trading?"

They stepped onto the powdery sand and watched the blinding ball of brilliant sunlight that was creeping lower in the sky. It was gorgeous but Stephanie didn't have time to tell him that. He was continuing to explain.

"That went right down the crapper, as you can imagine. My psychologist suggested, when I first started seeing her, that I take a few night classes to get me out of the office early but still let me feel like I was being productive. It was a way to break my habit of working like a madman."

"How long did you see a psychologist?" Stephanie had thought about it, but never had the nerve to actually go see one. She had been afraid of what the person would tell her.

"Not past tense, Steph. I still call or go in when I feel like I need it. There's no shame in that," he said, as if he could read her mind. "Where looks good to you?"

She pointed to a spot forty yards or so down the beach. She really didn't care where they sat. She wanted to hear more about Greg.

"Sooooo, you're a professor?" Stephanie asked.

"No. Adjunct. Online intro to writing classes."

"You're a writer?" She couldn't keep the shock from her voice as she picked up a blanket.

He stopped and pulled the blanket out of her hands. "Freelance. Which hardly pays the bills, so I teach. And housesit."

Stephanie mulled that over. The man who had planned to have his own firm had done a complete one eighty. He was laid back. Not overly worried where the next dollar was coming from, apparently.

And what do you think of that?

She let the seconds tick by. Did she care?

Not really.

She plopped onto her knees on the blanket and opened the lid of the cooler, smiling up into his face. There was tension there. He was trying to hide it, but she knew him well. "I'll bet your acid reflux has diminished to nothing," she said.

He laughed, real and genuine, and joined her on the blanket. "I made your favorite," he said.

"Chateaubriand?" she asked, arching a brow, knowing that wasn't what was in the cooler.

He frowned. "No. Wisconsin Cheddar and Goldfish crackers. I threw in some Triscuits just in case you've grown up a little. Oh, and white wine."

She thought he was teasing but wasn't sure. When he didn't immediately reveal their beachfront buffet, she took a chance. "I never liked Wisconsin Cheddar. That must have been one of your other girlfriends."

"Yah. Must have been," he joked. "Good thing I brought some Bitto."

"Oh, Greg." Stephanie leaned forward, shocked that he'd remembered her favorite cheese. They'd happened upon it while on vacation in Lombardy. Where had he found it? While she wasn't in the habit of dropping fifty dollars for a pound of cheese these days, she might have been tempted if she knew there was an outlet nearby.

"I was kidding about the Goldfish, too."

She reached over and wrapped her arms around his neck, kissing him as if he'd been gone for years. And he had, of course. Last night, she hadn't thought about that fact overly much. But here, with him showing her he still held their memories in his heart and mind, she wasn't about to hold back.

"How can you be like this?" Stephanie asked.

"Like what?" He reached down and grabbed the bottle of wine and she slid her arms back to her sides.

"Like I didn't break your heart and turn your world upside down. Like you still like me."

He uncorked the wine and filled two plastic tumbles halfway. "I do still like you, crazy girl."

Stephanie felt moisture pooling in her eyes. She didn't want to cry. Not in front of him. She'd look like a complete dope. She needed to focus on the questions she wanted to ask and not the softness of his tone.

"So you didn't hunt me down, here in Florida?"

"Wow. Tell a girl there's still a spot in your heart for her and you're suddenly a stalker," he teased.

She tried not to focus on the heart-holding-her-dear part and stay on track with her questioning. "It's just some willy nilly thing that you're watching Maggie's place?"

"You're just going to keep at it, huh?" He sat down and crossed his legs, the sun brightening the side of his body facing the Gulf. Toned and bronze in the ebbing rays of light.

Stephanie would *not* reach out and touch him. She wouldn't.

"Henry Delacroix is my psychologist's brother. When she mentioned he was down here, traveled a lot, and had a house he needed to guard from his crazy soon-to-be ex wife, I said I'd help. Then, my dean told me about his son's place and it seemed like Florida was definitely calling my name. Now it's my turn to ask you a question."

She didn't completely lower herself to the blanket, just stayed there, kneeling before him.

"Are you happy I'm here, Steph? Happy I gave in to fate?"

She gazed into his mossy green eyes. The teasing glint was gone. He was staring at her, all seriousness.

"I'm happy you're here. I'll try not to over think how all these years have passed us by, but we end up falling back into each other's arms. Remembering everything that makes us perfect together. How that could happen after everything I put us through."

He nodded his head in understanding. "I know you too well and I know there's a 'but' coming."

She swallowed hard. "Every part of my being tells me we can have what we did. That the way we've grown as individuals can only make the relationship better. But I have to believe there could be a day when Florida won't hold the attraction it does now. That someday you'll leave. And who would I be, to try and stop you?"

Stephanie threw her biggest fear out there. That life would repeat itself all these years later, with her being the one left terribly hurt.

"Why would I leave? I can freelance from here. I can online teach from here. Why would I ever consider bailing? This is where I can have it all."

"You consider having to deal with Maggie 'having it all'?" The little laugh she offered him reflected her nervousness.

Greg shifted his hips on the blanket and rose up on his knees, scooting forward until they touched. His warmth reached her, not just her outer skin, but a part of her soul.

"Let me rephrase," he said, entwining their hands. "Why would I leave when two of the best things on the planet are right here?"

"What two best things are those?" she asked, her voice barely a whisper over the thud of her pulse racing in her ears.

"Sunsets, for one." He stopped short of clinking their cups and looked out at the swirling hues of a vibrant sunset.

Stephanie held her breath, waiting for him to elaborate. But he was going to make her ask.

"So what's the second reason?" she asked, raising the cup to her lips but not drinking. She let it hide her features, waiting for his response.

"Other than sunsets? he asked. He turned his gaze on her, his eyes bright. His smile widened as he brought the rims of their cups together and his lips closer.

"Second chances, Stephanie. Second chances."

THE END

About the Author

M. A. Ellis

M.A. Ellis is a firm believer that everyone should pursue their dreams…no matter how long it takes to achieve them. She stepped out of her neat little writing boundaries in 2007 to devise tales of hot encounters and steamy romances that always have a happy ending. It's a vocation she truly loves.

Originally from the land of perogies and black & gold sports memorabilia, she now resides in southwest Florida where she's never at a loss for inspiration. The sunsets are always amazing, the fishing is stellar and weekly beach volleyball is undeniably a 'research' mission.

In non-writing moments, she's either trolling the local consignment shops, watching HGTV, or honing her master baking skills. She loves mermaids, pin-ups, kickass heels, vintage June Cleaver dresses, and the realms of cheesecake and chocolate…which happens to be her favorite alliteration in the entire world.

http://www.maellisromance.com/
https://www.facebook.com/author.m.a.ellis
https://twitter.com/AuthorMAEllis
http://www.amazon.com/-/e/B0036YAF70

First Class All the Way

Sonja Gunter

The chill of an April morning in Illinois greeted Ava Rice as the front door of her house closed behind her. She put in her ear buds and adjusted the volume on her iPod Nano. After zipping her jogging jacket to her neck, Ava stretched, and sprinted down the street for a mile run.

No, time for the normal four-mile sprint today. Tomorrow, I can make it up by running extra on the beach.

An airport limo would be arriving in a few hours, and she still had to finish packing for her big Five-Oh birthday Florida getaway. Her three best friends Gina, Lori, and Karen had helped plan the vacation: days of lying in the sun, nights of dancing, and long beach walks.

Girl time! Boy do I need it.

At the corner of Pingree and Grandview, she waited for a white delivery truck to turn into the subdivision before crossing the road. Her phone vibrated. Running in place to keep her muscles loose, Ava answered.

"Hi, Karen. What's up? I'm doing my run."

"I have bad news. I'm not going to be able to go today."

Ava came to a complete stop and pulled away her ear-buds.

This can't be happening. Gina canceled two weeks ago. Lori last week. Now Karen.

"No, you have to go! I can't go by myself. I don't want to celebrate my fiftieth alone." Ava gulped into the phone.

Everything's going wrong. Crap! All I wanted was to celebrate with friends. What am I going to do? Stay home alone on my birthday? No way.

"Sorry, Ava. Luke called. Sara's having labor pains and they're on their way to the hospital. As much as I'd love to share your special day, I can't miss my grandbaby's birth."

"I'm canceling my flight, too."

"No! Go and have fun," Karen said.

"I'll stay home. We can go have dinner someplace tomorrow night for my birthday. No big deal."

Ava squatted and raked her hand through her shoulder-length hair. Her best friends had abandoned her. They all had families. She didn't. Why? Because of her two-timing, too-busy-to-start-a-family ex-husband. Her good mood vanished.

Don't cry. The past is the past.

Two years ago, Don came home and asked for a divorce after thirty years. Surprised and prepared to fight him, he told her in his attorney voice his girlfriend was pregnant. The divorce was quick. He'd given her almost everything, the house, the money, and the cars-in exchange for her share of *Rice & Nygaard Associates.*

"Ava? Ava? Did I lose you?"

She stood. The realization she was going to Florida alone sank in, and she brushed a tear away.

"I'm here. I understand. Go be with your family. Promise to at least call me on my birthday."

"You know I…we will! You're our best friend. We'll have a party for you when you return. Oh … Luke is calling. Bye."

"Okay, talk to you soon."

Several cars drove by and Ava stared past them, not really seeing anything. Too frazzled to continue her run, Ava turned and retreated home in disbelief. She walked slowly trying to picture what she'd do by herself.

Alone in Florida. This is a real pisser. Some fun in the sun! I'll have to make the best of it. I'm easy going. I like to talk to people.

Ava brooded over the situation and didn't notice at first the array of pink flamingos decorating her front yard. She stopped and looked around. What the heck?

Damn Gina, Lori and Karen.

In the middle of the fifty pink birds was a sign that said, *Guess Who is Turning Fifty*. She snapped a picture with her phone. Her friends were right, time to move on, experience new things and start fresh. It wouldn't be so bad. Fifty is only a number. She smiled and walked inside.

* * * *

O'Hare International Airport buzzed with activity. Ava sat at her gate, A-24, excited and melancholy. To pass the time, she group texted Gina, Lori, and Karen.

Paybacks are hell. Your turn is coming.

What? It wasn't me, Gina replied.

Then Lori's text.

Pink flamingos? Don't know anything.

Sure. The perfect angel.

A smiling face with LOL came in from Karen.

No Starbucks dates, Ava sent to the three.

Ugh. K it was Gina's idea.

Their texting exchange lasted a few minutes and with no one to talk to Ava people-watched. Most were in a hurry and the ones sitting around her were dressed for warm weather. The screen showed the wait list had grown; the flight was over-booked. She smiled, wondering who was going to get Karen's seat.

A man approached the desk dressed in a Hawaiian themed shirt and dark jeans. He caught her attention right away because he wore loafers with no socks. This combo always seemed funny and odd to her. He appeared to be fiftyish or in his late forties, still had a full head of medium brown hair sprinkled with some grey. No pot belly, which meant he probably exercised. A plus in her book.

Definitely a looker. Lori would call him eye candy for women.

Her lips curved upward as she focused on the man's face. He seemed familiar. Ava's brows knitted together as she tried to remember. The man turned her way, and she caught a glimpse of the bluest eyes she'd ever seen. They reminded her of the morning sky.

Immersed in her appraisal of him, Ava realized too late she'd been staring and he smiled at her. Embarrassed, she stood, grabbed her purse, her Vera Bradley carry-on suitcase, and hurried to the bathroom.

Stupid! He's probably married and his wife witnessed me eyeballing her husband.

Scolding herself, Ava used the restroom and freshened her make-up.

Even if I'm turning fifty it doesn't mean I have to look like I am.

Satisfied, she returned to the gate as they called for First-Class boarding. She walked over the red carpet with excitement and mentally thanked Karen for talking her into splurging. She settled into 2A, a window seat.

"Hello."

Ava turned, ready to greet the other passenger, but her lips parted in surprise and no words came. Standing next to the empty seat was *Blue Eyes*.

The man put a laptop bag in the overhead compartment and took the aisle seat next to her. She couldn't stop staring; he was incredibly handsome up-close.

"First time?"

"Um … flying no, but First-Class, yes. It's a present to myself," she said, recovering.

"Really!"

"Yes, a birthday gift."

"I see. Personally I like the leg room. I'm Christian, by the way."

"That's nice. I'm Ava."

"Well, birthday girl, would you care for something to drink? It's on me."

Ava laughed. Even being a newbie to First-Class she knew the drinks were free.

"I usually don't let men I don't know buy me drinks, but in this case yes. I'd like a Baileys on the rocks," she said with a smile.

They waited for the drinks and Ava removed her iPhone from her purse. She sent Lori, Gina, and Karen another group message.

OMG. Gorgeous man sitting next to me.

Really! Gina texted.

LOL. Yes.

Mile high club, Lori texted.

Whatever.

A man took my seat? Brown eyes? Karen texted.

Oh yeah. Blue. TTUL when I land.

The flight attendant brought their drinks and dishes of warm nuts.

"So, Ava, you sprung for First-Class, this must be a special birthday."

"It is. I'm turning fifty tomorrow."

"Well, I'm past that and still alive. So there is hope for you too."

She laughed and glanced at his hands. No ring but in today's world that didn't mean anything.

"I'm sorry, what's your name?"

"Christian."

"Oh my, I feel stupid. I thought you were telling me you were a Christian. Like in religion."

"Now that is a first for me," Christian chuckled. "Would you like another drink?"

"No, I think one is plenty. I've embarrassed myself enough for one day."

"Come now, it was an honest mistake."

"You're kind. Are you traveling alone?" Ava asked.

"I am. I have a meeting in Florida. I'm staying at the Hyatt Regency Resort and Spa. And you? Meeting friends to celebrate?"

Ava shook her head. "No. My friends were supposed to join me, but their family lives got in the way. I'm booked at the Hyatt, too."

The flight attendant called for attention and announced the safety protocol. Before putting her iPhone away Ava quickly sent one last text to her friends.

No ring. Eye candy staying at Hyatt.

Take a walk on the wild side. You only live once, Lori text.

She clicked off her phone and gave Christian a smile.

Walk on the wild side? Right. Can I? I haven't let any man get close to me since the divorce. It isn't nice sleeping in a king bed alone. I've been going through way too many batteries lately.

"Do you travel a lot?"

"I do. Not because I have to but because I want to."

"I've always wanted to travel. Go to exotic places. I just never got around to it. But I'm going to start. Part of my new outlook on life, turning fifty and all."

"By yourself?" Christian asked.

"Not sure. I'd go with my friends but that's not turning out as planned."

"No husband?"

Ava lifted her left hand and waved.

"Nope. Divorced."

"Fifty and free. I see how it is."

"Yup. Would you mind … like to have … I mean if you're not busy with work. Would you care to have dinner with me?" Ava asked.

Christian's lips turned upward and laugh lines appeared at the corners of his eyes. Ava studied Christian's profile and liked what she saw.

"Tomorrow night?"

"Yes."

"I'd love to. It happens to be my free night," Christian said.

"Are you sure? I'm not imposing?"

"No, it would be my pleasure. Should I be worried? You said you're divorced but is there a man in your life who might get jealous?"

"Heavens no! The only baggage I have is my ex, who decided after thirty years to start a family without me."

"Ouch. His loss."

"Thanks. Their daughter is three," she said and shifted position.

"If you don't mind, what did your husband do for a living?"

"I don't. He was and still is a lawyer, for Rice and Nygaard Associates. Their offices are in downtown Chicago."

"Really?"

"Yea, why?" Ava asked.

"Is your last name Rice?"

"Yes."

"Your ex-husband is Don Rice?"

"Yes, do you know him?"

"I do. What a small world. I used him for several years. I thought you looked familiar," replied Christian.

"I do?"

"I believe you were at one of our dinner appointments. I think it was nearly six years ago at Ruth's Chris's Steak house."

"Umm, I thought you looked familiar too," Ava said excitedly.

She remembered that night. Unexpectedly Don had called, telling her to meet him for dinner. Thinking it was to be the two of them, she was surprised when Don introduced her to one of his clients. The man she recalled had been very energetic, considerate, and good-looking. She hadn't paid much attention to the conversation and when the dinner had ended Don said he was returning to his office. He'd used the engagement as a smoke screen to meet with the *girlfriend.*

Felicitously like before, Christian talked with his hands. However, each time he accidently touched her, a ripple of excitement coursed through her. Her body's reaction surprised her. She hadn't experienced sexual feelings for someone in a very long time.

"You never know who you might run into," Christian said and placed his hand on top of hers.

She looked at him. She saw admiration and interest in his gaze. Her pulse quickened.

"Right, you never know. What have you been doing?"

"A little of this and a little of that," Christian said.

"Come now."

"Okay, I was married too. Her name was Jane. She was a good friend. I'd known her since grade school. The day she learned she had stage two cancer, I asked her to marry me. She was all alone, and I didn't want her to go through the cancer treatments by herself. I took her all over the world before the cancer consumed her."

"Oh Christian, I'm so sorry. Here I've been feeling sorry for myself. Mulling over my life and …"

"Don't be sad for me. I accepted it. The time Jane and I had was very special." Christian sighed and drummed his fingers on the tray. "Enough of sadness. I'll try to get away from work as much as possible. Besides dinner, anything else you'd like to do on your big day?"

Ava sat stunned, unable to resist his flattery. Was this guy for real? He was not only handsome but compassionate. An unusual combination in a male. Before she could answer, the flight attendant announced the airplane's descent.

Christian waited in the aisle with an air of masculinity, a garment bag and a briefcase slung over his shoulder.

"Do you have a bag in the overhead?"

"I do, the patterned one," she said and pointed to her bag.

He pulled the bag down, and Ava threw it over her shoulder and disembarked. In the gate area, she moved to the side allowing the other passengers to walk by.

"I guess this is it. See ya around the hotel," Ava nervously murmured, moistening her lips.

"I rented a car, did you?"

"Oh, crap. Karen did. The reservation is under her name. I'll have to see if I …"

"No worries. We're going to the same hotel, you can bum a ride with me," Christian suggested.

"I really shouldn't. I can get my own car, but what the heck," she replied with anticipation, not wanting their encounter to end.

In the few hours she'd known Christian, a new sense of life had awoken in her. She now knew she wanted companionship. Her days and nights had been too lonely.

Could Christian fill the loneliness and the void in my life?

For some unexpected reason, she found his ruggedness devilishly attractive. His natural good looks and athletic physique were such a contrast from the men she'd usually found handsome. Ava then realized she'd been looking for men like her ex-husband who wore suits.

Can I turn this week into a romantic getaway? He seems interested in me. My week might be sun, fun and sex.

"Do you have any checked baggage?"

"Nope, this is it," Ava gestured to what she was carrying.

"All right, a woman who travels light. I love it. Here's to our adventure."

Christian laid his hand on the small of her back. His touch sent warm shivers down her spine and a sudden rush of desire caused her to shy away.

What is happening to me? He's intoxicating my senses. I can't think.

No, I am thinking. But it's about having sex with a man I just met.

Being awkward and unsure of herself was something she hadn't experienced in a very long time. She was in uncharted waters with feelings that had lain dormant for years. Her dates lately hadn't gone past the first dinner.

But I'm not looking for a man who'd give me a night of hot sex! Right. Yes, I am. I've lived long enough without it.

As they walked through the SouthWest Florida International Airport, occasionally Christian's hand brushed hers. When they reached the escalator, he fixed his hand on her back again. It was a comfortable feeling. At the Hertz desk, Christian rented a yellow convertible Mustang.

"Sorry, I couldn't resist."

Ava chuckled and climbed into the passenger's seat. With windows open, the warm humid Florida air filled the car as they drove to the Hyatt.

"I promise we'll go for a ride with the top down. Do you have a free day?"

"Oh, let me check my calendar … oh right, I'm on vacation. All ten of my days are open. And so are my nights."

Now why did I say that? Oh my, I'm flirting.

Christian threw his head backwards with a peal of infectious laughter. Ava's hazel eyes gleamed with interest at his deep throaty laugh. The sound was music to her ears. She couldn't help herself and joined him.

"I like you, Ava. You're wonderful."

Wide-eyed she turned to find him watching her. Her mind reeled in confusion and she couldn't offer a reply. *Could you really have a sexual connection with someone you just met and know if they'd be good in bed?* Lori swore she could tell on the first date.

Engrossed in the blueness of his eyes, a sudden awkward silence filled the car. Neither speaking. Suddenly her door opened.

"Welcome to the Hyatt Regency Resort and Spa," a young man said.

"Oh …," she squeaked.

The mood was broken. She'd been saved. It appeared Christian wasn't expecting a reply. He lifted the bags and waited for her to join him. Together they walked to the reception desk.

"Good afternoon. Welcome to the Hyatt," the girl said.

"Ava Rice."

"Yes, I have you down for a ten day stay and a king bed."

"Excuse me, please upgrade Ms. Rice to an Island Suite and bill it to me, Christian Newman."

"No, Christian. You can't, it wouldn't …"

"Sure I can. It's your birthday present from me."

Ava looked at the receptionist, not sure what to say.

"I do have an Island Suite available. Should I upgrade your room, Ms. Rice?"

The proper thing to say would be no, but this was her adventure.

"Yes, but … Christian, let me pay for it."

"No, it's a present. Please allow me."

The way he said it, so gentleman-like, all she could do was nod her head.

"Okay, Ms. Rice, one room key or two?"

"Ummm …"

"She'll only need one. I'm not technically with her."

"Here is the key and your room number."

The woman pointed at a number on the key card envelope.

"Thank you, Christian."

"If you wait a few minutes I can walk you to your room."

"You mean, my suite," she laughed.

"Right, your suite."

"Okay."

Ava stepped to the side giving him some privacy. What was the correct protocol when a man you barely knew paid for your room? Did it mean he wanted something in return? Or was he simply being nice.

What would her friends say to all this? Ava withdrew her phone and saw it was still turned off. She pushed the button, bringing it to life. Message alerts dinged. Lori. Karen. Lori again. Gina. She touched the screen message app to reply.

"I've been upgraded to an Island Suite."

"Did you enjoy First Class?" Karen asked.

"More info on the hunk," Lori requested.

"You go girl," Gina replied.

Laughing she typed. "You should be here."

"All right, I'm checked in," Christian said.

Ava jumped a little and tucked her phone in her purse.

"That was quick. The elevators are over here." Ava pointed to the left.

He still carried all the bags as they entered. She pushed number fifteen but the elevator didn't move.

"You have to slide your key card to access the suite levels. Press the floor number again and then slide your key into the panel."

"Oh boy, do I feel like a blonde. Oh, I am," Ava joked.

Christian's deep laugh made her insides do flips. She did what he said and like magic the doors closed.

"Which floor is your room on?"

"Fifteen."

"Oh, you have a suite too?"

"Yes."

The doors opened and they exited. She could feel his presence behind her and stopped abruptly at room 1525.

"This … this is my room."

She slid her key into the door and the green light flashed. She held open the door for Christian.

"No, you go in first."

Ava stepped into the suite and gasped. It was more beautiful than she could've ever imagined. Gorgeous cream and teal colors mixed with a Floridian flare. Bamboo-like furniture and two sets of double sliding glass doors. The view took her breath away.

"Oh, my goodness! This is awesome. Come look at this spectacular view. All the palm trees!"

"It's beautiful, just like you."

Ava slowly turned and found Christian standing next to her. He was gazing and smiling. She returned the smile, and he leaned in closer to her.

Oh my, he's going to kiss me!

And he did, but to her disappointment, only on her cheek. She inhaled and was rewarded with a musky aftershave scent.

"My room is down the hall, 1531."

"Oh, right. Would you like my phone number? I know the man is supposed to ask for it first but I think in this case … since we have a date … I didn't mean a date-date … since we will be having dinner together, I thought you might like my number. You know, in case something comes up or …"

She exhaled and could've hidden in the bathroom from embarrassment. They didn't have a date. Simply sharing dinner together.

"Yes, I'd love to exchange numbers. And I have no problem calling our dinner a date."

Smiling, not trusting herself to say anything, she added his number to her phone contacts. He did the same, but an awkward silence followed.

"If you need me, call. I don't have much planned for today," Christian said.

"I don't either. Maybe I'll see you at the bar or the restaurant later."

"Now that could be arranged. Maybe I'll be having dinner say … around five-thirty. Should I get a table for two?"

She smiled. This was too easy.

"Five-thirty it is."

He walked to the door, turned, and smiled before leaving. Once the door shut she sank onto the couch.

Maybe turning fifty isn't going to be so bad after all.

* * * *

Whistling, Christian strolled to his suite. Today turned into one hell of a good day. He stepped into his room and wondered if he should've kissed Ava on the lips instead of only on the cheek.

Damn! I'm playing it safe. I should've given her a kiss to remember. Tonight after dinner when I take her to the beach, I will.

The image of them on the beach, the sunset in the background and Ava in his arms, played in his mind. He wanted tonight to be a romantic pre-birthday gift.

Christian put his luggage next to the couch, sat down, and removed his iPad to log onto the internet. His lips curved upward in an easy smile. Six emails from Ava's friends. He'd nicknamed them *The Three*

Musketeers.

Last year he'd joined Ourtime.com dating service hoping to find someone to share his retirement and interests. He'd gone on a few dinner dates with some of the women but none held his admiration.

Then, before the holidays, he'd scored big time. An invite to meet someone came through, but when he read the email, he thought it was a joke of some sort. The invitee asked him to go on a date without the person knowing. At first he hadn't wanted to go along; the set-up seemed a little devious.

But when he received a picture of the birthday girl, he was stunned. The woman the invitee wanted him to go on a blind date with was Ava Rice, his ex-lawyer's ex-wife. He hadn't been able to turn down the chance to be a birthday gift to the woman he hadn't been able to forget all these years.

Christian folded his hands behind his head and slouched down, relaxing. After he'd consented to be part of the plan he was bombarded with emails from not one, but three ladies saying they were Ava's friends.

The fact that he'd known Ava's ex-husband, Don, for several years, and the man had been his attorney until recently hadn't deterred him from wanting to date her. The three ladies hadn't known he'd been looking for a way to be introduced to Ava.

For years when he'd visit Don, their meetings would start with Don talking about Ava and showing off her picture. Then one morning Ava dropped off a cup of coffee and muffin for her husband. She'd glanced his way and smiled.

He'd instantaneously been attracted to her. It was wrong, but she'd been so captivating. Christian scheduled his bi-monthly meetings for mornings to be able to catch a glimpse of her. He'd fallen in love with her smile and laughter.

Sometime after Jane's death, he no longer saw Ava bring Don his coffee. He noticed her picture was missing too. When he asked Don's secretary what was going on, she told him Don and Ava were getting a divorce.

Excited, Christian surfed the dating websites for Ava but never found her. Until six months ago.

Dingggg donggggg. Dingggg donggggg.

Christian focused on the incoming email.

"Mr. Newman, thank you again. As to your inquiry, Ava likes shrimp, chocolate martinis and enjoys dry red wines. If you have any other questions email. Lori."

Interesting choice of drinks. Martinis.

Dingggg donggggg. Dingggg donggggg.

This email was from Ava's other friend, Karen.

"Mr. Newman, one of Ava's birthday wishes is to walk on the beach at night. Plus be kissed in the moonlight."

Christian laughed.

I don't think Ava would tell anyone she wanted to be kissed. Her pals are trying to make things happen.

He chuckled and typed.

"Karen, thank you for the info. A moonlight beach walk is now on the agenda."

He knew how to charm a lady and didn't need the help of *The Three Musketeers.* When he'd checked in at the airport gate, he'd spotted Ava right away. She'd given him the once-over, and he thought she might've recognized him.

She'd only seen him in business suits and glasses. The glasses he'd dumped last year by treating himself to Lasik surgery. The best thing ever. No glasses. No contact lenses. He'd changed some but not much in the four years since he'd seen her.

Ava too had changed. Her short brown hair was now blonde and long. She appeared to have lost weight but looked healthy.

Crap! I'm falling hard and fast.

She was the woman he imagined her to be. He now had to convince Ava he was the man she needed. No, wanted. First he had to plan what he was going to say to her.

* * * *

Dressed in a cotton, blue floral sundress, Ava left her room to explore the hotel before dinner. In the hallway she glanced towards Christian's room, hesitated, but changed direction to the elevators.

I shouldn't push my luck.

Happiness engulfed her in spite of her friends' abandonment. She was alive for the first time in years. All thanks to Christian. Her stomach turned in mayhem with the anticipation of the upcoming evening.

The mixture of fresh and salt air greeted Ava. The afternoon warmth of the sun made her skin tingle. It boosted her courage a notch. She walked to the pool.

Gorgeous!

Several huge lounge chairs with green cushions surrounded the pool area. Most were vacant so late in the day. A pathway to the right caught her attention. The sign posted said it led to the beach. Considering a walk before dinner, she decided to save it for her morning run. After a stroll around the pool, she headed to the main restaurant since Christian hadn't said which of the three to meet him at for dinner.

"Hi, I didn't make a reservation and I'm not …"

"Ava, you're early. A nice surprise," Christian murmured.

To her delight he kissed her cheek and the pressure of his hand on her waist sent shivers down her spine. A spicy aroma and freshness greeted her.

"Christian …" Her breath caught in her throat.

Mmmmm, he looks and smells great.

He'd changed. Gone were the Floridian clothes. He now wore grey slacks and a white dress shirt. The sleeves were rolled up to his elbows, and the buttons opened at the neck, revealing a spray of chest hair.

"Table for two. Newman. I called earlier."

"Yes, follow me," the hostess said.

"After you, Ava," Christian said and smiled.

"Thank you."

They followed the hostess to a table by a window, overlooking the lagoon. An uncomfortable silence fell as they sat facing each other. Christian cleared his throat.

"Ava, before we continue, I have a confession."

Oh hell, here it comes. I knew he was too good be true.

"A confession?" Ava asked.

She folded her hands on the table. A surge of mixed feelings swept through her as she waited for Christian and his explosive announcement.

"Yes. I wasn't going to say anything …"

"Good evening, welcome to the Tarpon Bay. Can I get you anything to drink?"

The waiter cut off Christian's announcement. Ava kept her eyes on Christian, weighing her options.

Should I leave or stay? Is he worth my time? And here I am falling all over him like a sex crazed woman! Damn, now I'm jumping to conclusions. He only said a confession. What do I have to lose?

"A Chocolate Martini," Ava said to the waiter.

"Grey Goose on the rocks, with stuffed olives," ordered Christian.

"Maybe we should wait and not ruin our night," she said with a little sarcasm.

"That's so sweet. But I have to tell you …," Christian paused and took hold of her hands. "I'm your birthday gift from your friends."

"What?" Snatching her hands away from his, she added, "My present! A man … you. Like I need to pay someone to go on a date with me. They are going to die for this embarrassment."

"Don't be mad at them. It fell into my plans."

"Your plans?"

"Remember I said we'd met, went to dinner, you and your ex-husband."

"So? You've been stalking me?"

"No. He was my lawyer. I used to see you bring him coffee."

"I'm sorry. This isn't making any sense. You're pulling my leg, right?"

Ava sat straighter in her chair and observed Christian closely as the waiter set their drinks on the table. Her hand encircled the glass, raised it, and she took an enormous gulp.

This can't be happening. They'd never do something like set me up on a long distance date. Would they? But they were acting strange before I left.

"I answered their request on Ourtime.com."

"Let me get this straight. Lori, Karen, and Gina paid you to be my birthday present?" Ava looked around, leaned in and whispered, "Are you a gigolo?"

"Heavens no! But thanks for the compliment."

She saw an amused sparkle in Christian's eyes. His laughter was heartfelt but confusing. Ava's memory of the time he mentioned was faded. It had been the low part of her marriage. She'd still been in love with Don at that point. His clients were all blurs.

"I'm sorry, this is all very strange," Ava retorted.

"I'm sure it is. When I learned you and Don were divorcing I tried to find a way to meet you."

"Me?"

"Yes, Ava, you. I wanted to get to know the woman who, out of love, would deliver coffee and a morning treat to the man she loved. I registered on Ourtime.com in hopes of finding you. That's where your friends found my profile. They asked if I'd be interested in a blind date. I wasn't going to accept but then they forwarded your profile. And there you were. The woman I couldn't erase from my mind."

Ava lowered her head in embarrassment. Why would he lie? Somehow her friends arranged for a man to be her escort for her fiftieth birthday.

How pathetic. First fifty pink flamingos in my yard and now a planned date. Like I need help to find a man. Wait till I get home. I'll find a way to even the score.

"Well, Christian, I'm sorry you've come all this way for nothing. I don't need my friends to find a date for me. You can forget tomorrow's dinner too! It was nice to meet you," she said and stood.

"Please. Please sit down, Ava. I've been brainstorming on a way to get in contact with you," Christian pleaded.

"What do you do for a living that you met with my ex so often?"

"That's a fair question, but I reserve the right to tell you later."

"You're full of secrets. How many more do you have?"

He sounded genuine. She sat down and took another sip of her martini.

"Again, it's not what it seems. Give me a chance, Ava. You won't be disappointed."

"My friends are in deep shit! I'm going to call them right now," she reached into her purse.

"Are you ready to order or do you need a few more minutes?" The waiter asked.

"Ava?"

"Fine. I'll take the salmon with a Caesar Salad."

"I'll take the same."

The waiter's eyebrows shot upward at her tone. He recovered, nodded and left.

"Can we start over?" Christian asked.

She hesitated. Gina, Lori, and Karen were in so much trouble. Her anger subsided, knowing her friends did know her likes and dislikes. Christian did have possibilities. He was handsome, well built, great sense of humor, and the prettiest eyes. And the big plus, he'd made her feel things she hadn't in years.

"Hi, I'm Ava. I've been divorced for two years. Haven't dated since I met my ex in high school. I'm turning fifty tomorrow."

Christian laughed and she did too.

"It's nice to meet you, Ava. I'm Christian. You don't know me but I've heard a lot regarding you. I'm fifty-five. A widower. I'm retired."

"Wow. Do you really have a meeting here?"

"Yes, you."

"I'm flattered."

"By the way, you look very lovely tonight."

The praise threw her guard off. Don hadn't said those words to her since high school. They were simple words but meant so much more. Shifting in her chair, not sure how to respond, she decided to be straightforward.

"I think you're very handsome. I do have to say I like the dressy look better than the casual."

His eyes opened wider and she thought she saw a little pink flush on his cheeks.

"You know flattery will get you whatever you want on my end."

"I see how you are. And you're NOT a gigolo?"

"I don't charge if I like the woman."

She laughed and relaxed. Their salads arrived, halting any additional comments. Instead they talked and talked, simply enjoying each other's company.

The mood became light and teasing. Every chance Christian got he seemed to touch her hand and a slow warmth started to course through her body. Never quite becoming a fire.

"Would you like the check? I think you still have time to catch the sunset on the beach," the waiter suggested.

"Yes, please. Ava, would you like to walk on the beach with me?"

"I'd love to."

They walked side by side down the pathway she'd eyed earlier. Ava wasn't surprised but delighted when Christian's hand reached and took hers. They strolled to the beach as a couple. Hand in hand.

The water swooshed and roared when it met the sandy beach. The sound was a comfort to her ears. Her first step into the sand caused Ava to stop.

"Time to take off my sandals. The sand is getting in-between my toes."

Regretfully, she let go of his hand. As she bent down a wind gust came and her dress billowed upward.

"Oh, no!"

Ava dropped her shoes and anxiously pulled at her dress.

"That was a nice sight. You have a great body for someone who is turning fifty."

Her head snapped upward, her dress forgotten, and Ava stared at Christian. Their eyes locked, his hand touched her shoulder and then her cheek. His other arm slipped around her waist, pulling her to him. She rested her hands on Christian's chest.

"Ava …"

He leaned in and captured her partly opened lips. His lips moved over hers in sweet tenderness, making her quiver.

Too soon they left hers. She breathed in lightly. Her emotions whirled fervently to lustfulness.

Who is this man? Menopause be damned!

"Should we watch the sun set before we go to my room?"

"Now that is an offer I'd like to accept," Christian said.

He kept one arm around her waist, and they turned to the west. Ava laid her head on his chest. Three monochromatic hues; red, orange and yellow touched the blue water.

"Do you hear it?"

"Hear what?"

"The sizzle. The cool water touching the hot sun."

Laughing, she stood on her tippy toes and kissed his cheek.

Mmmmm, heaven.

"I don't think I heard the sizzle, but I do feel a burning."

"Um, I might be able to do something concerning your fire. But I'd like to take my time trying to extinguish it. Sometimes you have to let it burn itself out."

"You can take all the time you want, Christian."

"In that case, your suite or mine?"

"I've never invited a man into my hotel room before. So let's make it a first."

They watched the water and the sky become one before turning away. She was so blissfully happy to share this special moment with someone who might be able to complete her lonely life.

Once again, hand in hand, they walked. When they reached the elevator he used his card to access the fifteenth floor. Alone, he emptied the space between them and framed her face with his hands. He claimed her lips with his. Their tongues met and his traced her lips ending the kiss.

Binggggg.

The doors opened and they pulled apart.

"Wow! I'm thankful no one witnessed our kiss. It was not G-Rated. You're a great kisser."

"Remember I've had more experience than you, being a gigolo and all."

The mood lightened. Their passion held at bay. When they came to her room she opened the door.

"Just so you know, I haven't done this in a very long time."

"Ava, we don't have too, we can sit and talk, or watch a movie."

She reached over and touched his cheek.

"You're so sweet! I'll be right back, have to pee."

"Okay, I'll use the other bathroom."

Good heavens, now what. Should I tell him to leave? No! I want him to make love to me.

Ava shut the bedroom door and leaned against it. She hadn't brought any sexy pajamas with her. Crap! She'd have to improvise.

* * * *

In the bathroom, Christian braced his hands on the sink. Ava was everything he'd hoped she'd be in person. Funny, sweet, and gorgeous. She appeared nervous, and he too was having second thoughts.

Before dinner he'd stuffed a Viagra into his pocket. Now he held the blue pill in his palm and stared at it.

He'd been diagnosed with ED, erectile dysfunction, around the time he'd married Jane. They'd never had sex because she'd been so sick, and he hadn't been with anyone after her death.

Should I take it? Better to be safe than sorry.

Quickly he placed the pill on his tongue, turned on the faucet, and scooped water into his mouth. According to the directions, it could take up to a half hour for the pill to act.

I'll to have move more slowly.

Christian shrugged his shoulders and breathed deep. The sands of time had been depleted. The woman who'd captured his attention was waiting. He walked into the sitting room to find the bedroom door still closed. He opened the mini bar, took out two small bottles of wine, and emptied them into the hotel glasses. The sound of the bedroom door clicked, and he turned to greet Ava with the filled glasses.

"I found some wine. I can't guarantee it will be good but … Ava …"

She stood in the doorway, not in the sleeveless dress she'd been wearing but in a pair of sleeping shorts and a tank with her nipples pushing through the fabric.

"I'm sure it will be fine."

"No, you're fine, Ava. You take my breath away."

She smiled, turned and walked into the bedroom. "Are you coming before I lose my nerve?"

"Oh, yeah."

He followed and handed her a glass. She sipped hers. He almost drained his. Christian set his glass down, took two steps and reached her. Placed one hand on her waist and with the other removed the glass from her hand. He set her half-filled glass next to his, leaned in, pulled her closer and kissed her partly opened lips.

Ava surrendered to him. His hand slipped under her tank and welcomed the softness of her skin. Her arms wrapped around him. Leaving her lips he kissed and nibbled her earlobe.

"Ohhh," she moaned.

In a gentle but possessive gesture he eased her to the bed. She sat on the edge and looked up at him, her blue eyes bright with desire. He lifted her tank over her head, then traced the outline of her breast with his finger and cupped the mound. Her fingers tugged and unbuttoned his shirt. He stopped, discarded his shirt, shoes, and slacks, leaving on only his boxers. She moved to the middle of the bed and lay on her side watching him.

I hope the pill works. I'm so nervous. I hope she doesn't notice.

"Ava, I haven't done this in a very long time either. I took a Viagra … it's the first time," Christian said and moved to the bed.

"So you thought we'd be having sex tonight?"

"Yes … no, I just took it a few minutes ago."

"Really?"

Christian sat on the edge of the bed and felt Ava's hands gliding over his back, and then pulling him towards her. He slid further onto the bed and turned.

"I was hoping we would, and I wanted to make sure I satisfied you."

"You're so sweet, Christian. You could've taken me on the beach."

"Now that could be arranged too."

They laughed. Without hesitation, he moved his hand up her abdomen and caressed her breasts. Her head fell backwards and he gently kissed one of her swollen nipples. Letting the pent-up desire take its course, he placed his hand on her thigh and ran it up and under her pajama shorts, finding her wet. He tugged the shorts over her hips, down her legs, and tossed them across the room. His boxers joined hers on the floor a moment later.

Her legs lay opened. Christian's eyes met hers. She smiled letting him know it was okay. He shifted and lay on her, skin touching skin. Her hands again roamed over his broad back and down to cup his butt cheeks. She pinched him and giggled.

"Nice ass," she whispered.

"Thanks."

Christian kissed Ava's opened lips. He was ready and she was ready. In one natural motion, he slipped inside her. Ava arced her hips and matched Christian's tempo as they became one. His dormant desire gained strength and burst only after he'd seen her climax.

* * * *

Ava awoke abruptly when a hand touched her. She lay still, as the last few hours played through her mind. Christian had made love her to three times. He'd been fantastic.

The room was quiet, their breathing normal. Ava glanced at the clock. 1:05 am. They'd slept for almost two hours in each other's arms.

It's my birthday! I'm now half a century old. I don't feel any different.

She hadn't turned into an old hag with long grey hair and no teeth. All the expectations and waiting for what? Nothing.

Christian snored and Ava smiled. She'd actually invited a man she'd just met into her room. Enticed him by wearing a stupid pair of short pajamas. They hadn't been very sexy, but they were the only pj's she'd brought.

For a moment she imagined what would've happened if she'd come out totally naked. Probably the same thing. She smiled and made a mental note to call her devious friends. They'd be shocked by her impulsiveness. It had been one thing for them to arrange a date for her, but she'd gone the extra steps of taking her date to the extreme.

After they'd made love the first time Christian had been so sweet. They talked, drank more wine, and to her surprise made love again. The second time had been better than the first. She'd actually made love to him and rode him like a wild filly. Blushing in the dark she reached over and placed her hand on his. He was real and he'd stayed.

Now what?

Do I want a man in my life again? Someone to be there for me and to share this new phase of my life?

At that moment, Christian's eyes opened, and he gave her a sleepy smile. Her heart leaped. Her decision was made. She wanted this man.

He raised up on one arm and the sheet fell, covering only his lower half.

"It's not morning yet, is it?"

"No."

"Sorry I fell asleep," he groaned and touched her shoulder.

His hand slid lower, making her skin tingle. He tugged the sheet down exposing her breasts.

"We fell asleep."

"Maybe I should leave," he said jokingly and covered her breast, making her nipple taut.

She tried to keep her breathing slow and easy.

"No."

Ava shifted and moved closer to him. He pulled the offending sheet away from her body and pulled her even closer.

"Happy Birthday, Ava."

"It is my birthday. Now that I'm an old woman maybe I shouldn't be making love to a stranger."

"You're funny. I'm not a stranger."

He kissed her lips. Their tongues battled for a moment before he let her win.

"Oh, I'm so glad my friends set me up with you. You're the best birthday gift I've ever received."

He laughed, kissed her again, and took his time to get to know her mouth and neck.

"Ava, I think I'm in love you."

Mood breaker! He loves me?

"You love me?"

"Yes, I've been enamored with you since I first saw you in Don's office."

"Christian, I wasn't born yesterday! Love?"

"Oh yes, love. I'm not going to let you get away. I think we'll be great for each other. You and me. You want to see the world; we can go together."

She laughed.

"I don't have enough money to travel the world. Coming here for my birthday was a huge expense."

His grin made her pulse race and she met him half way, pressing her lips against his. The kiss was tender and short.

"No worries. I have plenty of money. I won the Florida lottery several years ago. That's the reason I made appointments with your ex so often. You know, investments, taxes and lawsuits. Do you want to see my winning ticket?"

"You carry it with you?"

"I sure do. It's a copy of the original. A reminder of how your luck can change in an instant."

He stood naked and reached for his slacks. He returned to the bed holding a laminated piece of paper. He looked like a little kid, excited about telling a secret.

"This is very awkward. We just met. We've had sex. And now you tell me you're rich and love me."

"Yes, to everything."

"This is too much to handle," Ava said.

She took the lottery ticket and read the numbers aloud: 10-23-37-44-49-16. They lay over the image of a pink flamingo with the official Florida lottery seal. As she studied the ticket, she remembered Don mentioning one of his clients was very wealthy.

"Just how much did you win?"

"I took the lump sum, so after taxes, three hundred and sixteen million."

"Oh my, only three hundred and sixteen million."

Fingering the card as if it would disappear, she raised her eyes to study Christian. She was too old to fall in love. Love was for the young and foolish. But here she was: heart racing, stomach lurching, all from a simple word. Love.

"Ava? Are you okay?" he asked and touched her cheek.

She blinked several times. Christian was real. It was her birthday. And she'd found someone who wanted to share life with her until she was old and wrinkled.

"I don't know what to say. You've surprised me. I thought I was too old to fall in love again."

She leaned over, kissed him, and smothered his reply. He pulled her close and covered her body with his. The hardness of his arousal pressed against her.

Thank heaven for Viagra!

"Christian ..."

He silenced her with his lips as his hand caressed her thigh. Ava opened her legs as Christian slid into her warmth.

"Will you marry me, Ava?"

"Christian! We don't even know each other."

"I know all I need to know. If you won't marry me today, tomorrow will do."

"Tomorrow?"

"Yes, we could fly to Las Vegas. Get married and fly to wherever you want for a honeymoon."

"Slow down. I think we need to take this slowly. Date for a while, before we tie the knot," Ava said.

"See, that's another reason I love you. Okay, I'll court you for a year. That will give you enough time to plan our wedding. How does next April sound?"

He brushed the hair from her face.

What is wrong with me? He wants to marry me. "Oh my, you're terrible. Yes, let's date for a year, but I'm not going to guarantee I'll be able to wait."

"Good, I knew you'd see it my way," he said in a tone laced with huskiness.

She glanced up and found his blue eyes sparkling with tears. The love she saw and felt from him softened her heart to the point of no return.

"Yes. Yes."

Their lips met, sealing their agreement as the age-old rhythm of passion took over. She yielded heart and soul to her newfound love. Moans of pleasure filled the room, followed by heavy breathing. Neither heard the pings of their phones.

THE END

About the Author

Sonja Gunter

Born and raised in the cold and beautiful Minnesota, she escaped to Illinois for seventeen years to raise two boys, and now calls Florida home. She and her husband, who's always her hero, have a new family to worry about; Cookie, an Assui-Po dog, Oreo, a black and white cat who thinks he is a dog, and Chip, a Ragdoll cat, that their sons compare to Eeyore.

She loves to travel, read, shop, and bowl. You can catch her writing her next novel at the lanes.

Sonja encourages you to check out her web site, www.sonjagunter.com , Facebook- Sonja Gunter—author page. Or email her at guntersonja@aol.com.

Don't be surprised if she lets her Norwegian heritage come through in her stories. You betcha!

Sheldon,
Thank you for
your friendship.
4 July 14

This story is dedicated with love to B. Joyce Henderson. Co-founder of The Southwest Florida Romance Writers. My friend, mentor, and the lady in the portrait.

The Portrait Conspiracy

M. L. Joy

I wake to the sound of the spring-loaded door of my room clicking shut. I'm groggy from my nap, but since the rooms here at Sunset Cove Elderly Home are almost too small to turn around in, it's not hard for me to figure out the only picture I have of my wife of fifty years is missing. It's an eight-by-ten Hollywood style headshot. A glossy black and white, taken back when Joyce was in her twenties. She'd never been a model, but she could have. The picture always reminded me of Lauren Bacall. For most of us, memories are all we have left. Stealing a man's photos here in the Home is a big deal, and I had no doubt it was that bastard Mitchell, again.

My damn hearing isn't what it used to be, but still, Mitchell must have parked his walker outside to keep from waking me. That contraption of his is a yard sale reject. It creaks and clanks through the hallway, as if he was carrying stolen silverware from the dining hall.

I slide off the starched sheets and into my slippers in one fluid motion. I might be old, but I can take advantage of gravity when I need to. I grab my wheeled walker and roll toward the door. If I hurry, I can catch him and wrestle the picture from him before he gets away.

I pry open the door. It feels like the damn thing has gotten heavier overnight, and step into the hallway. Mitchell has already made it down the hall, just outside his room. My enthusiasm immediately sinks into my belly. I drop my butt to the padded seat of my rolling walker. When the hell did he get a motorized chair?

He looks back at me and squirms out of the driver's seat, his toothless smile triumphant. He holds up Joyce's picture like a trophy and disappears into his room.

He may think he's beaten me this time, but I'll get that son-of-a-bitch.

* * * *

Mealtime at the Home can be an adventure. Sure, sometimes the food is a little suspect: the pureed vegetables practically ooze off the tray, the meat only comes in gray, and the mashed potatoes pose a choking hazard. I would give my left kidney for a shaker of salt.

But the adventure? I'm talking about the chaos created when you gather this many geriatrics in one place and serve them food—on trays. Not that our keepers make us carry the trays. Oh, no. The staff delivers them to our tables and picks them up, but even so…a bunch of them end up on the floor anyway.

Usually, it's because one of my friends here forgets they don't have to clear their own dishes and they drop their tray on their way to the kitchen. Other times, you get a cranky resident that's just sick and tired of life in here. The food, the staff, or the fact their kids never visit, so the tray gets shoved off the table on purpose. Both situations can result in other residents tossing trays in solidarity. Believe me, this does not go over well with the administration. If you get caught, it earns you an office visit with Sergeant Moron. This isn't actually a military facility and she's not really an officer, but she barks like my old CO.

I sit at a far table, pushing a pickled beet around my tray and studying Mitchell's back, waiting for just the right moment. I'm pretty sure he's lost track of me. The ladies I sent to sit with him, Dot and Clair from the cribbage club, are doing a bang-up job at distracting him. He's too busy explaining the features of his newfangled mode of transportation to notice what I have and where I'm going. That's good.

When the first tray falls the staff goes into their normal routine, cleaning up the spill and reassuring residents that everything is fine. Cheers from the other residents, like when a bartender drops a glass, are loud enough to mask the sound of me and my walker sneaking up on Mitchell. Once I'm behind him, I dump my mashed peas and orange-colored butterscotch pudding behind the wheels of his motorized chair. That should slow him down a little.

I give the ladies a wink of thanks and shuffle toward the exit. The dishes I leave on top of the trash bin and then punch the handicap button to open the dining hall doors. As they swing outward, I jam my empty milk carton behind the button to obstruct whoever might use it once I'm gone. Like Mitchell.

The hallway is clear. The only sounds are the TVs in the rooms of residents not able to make the trek to the dining hall, the hum of my walker wheels on the tile floor, and the shuffle of my slippered feet. I pass the nurses' command station.

A nurse wearing a V-neck scrub shirt covered in pink flamingos stands. "Where are you going Mr. Zborowski?"

Hunched as my posture is, I had hoped she might not see me. "My room. Where the hell else would I go?" I say.

Satisfied, she plops back down onto her chair and turns toward her computer.

My room isn't my destination and by the time I make it to Mitchell's door, the commotion back at the dining room door has spilled out into the hall. It's hard to hear if Mitchell's motorized chair is whirring my way over the voices of the agitated residents. Hopefully, Dot and Clair are still tugging at his ears. I need every second I can get to pull off this mission.

I turn the latch and push open his door. One step inside and something hits me on the top of my head. I lean heavily on my walker, fearful more blows will follow. When it seems nothing else is coming down, I hesitantly touch my bald scalp. I expect to see blood on these gnarled, trembling fingers, but find none. I'll be fine.

The door tries to swish shut, but a bulbous plastic lamp keeps it from closing entirely. Mitchell must have rigged it above his door as a booby-trap. I'm not sure how in the hell he got it up there, but I'm glad he didn't have strength enough to use anything heavier. I would have been knocked-out cold or worse. The paranoid old fool could have killed me. And how did he get in and out without hurting himself?

Through the partially open door I overhear people talking in the hall. There is no sound of Mitchell's chair and I'm concerned I won't be able to hear it from inside his room. A quick look around and I don't see Joyce's picture. I trudge over to his dresser and open the drawers. Nothing but plain white boxers and ratty undershirts. I move to the tightly made bed, hoping I won't have to lift the mattress. Chances are good I'll probably pull a muscle in my gut and that would slow down my escape. Thankfully, I toss the pillows and spot the silver frame. It's face down. I flip it over and Joyce looks up at me as if it's fifty years ago. I miss her.

I wedge the picture in the waistband of my pants, navigate my walker around the bed to the door, and ease into the hallway. Mitchell is just clearing the nursing station. Dot and Clair are walking on each side of him, still chatting and trying to keep up with that damnedable scooter. I don't think he sees me, but they're too close to my room for me to go that way. I turn and head in the opposite direction. I can double back through the garden unnoticed.

I make it three steps before Mitchell yells my name.

"Zborowski."

I pretend not to hear him and push myself to pick up the pace. The top of the picture frame cuts into my ribs. The entrance to the garden is farther than I remember. Mitchell yells my name again. The drone of his chair is clear now and closing in.

I risk a glance over my shoulder. Mitchell is leaning forward in his chair, his face strained with determination. At the speed he is gaining, there is no way I can make it to the garden before he catches up with me.

I stop and turn to face him. I will not be run over like a dog.

A grin spreads across Mitchell's face. He has no plans of slowing down.

I notice the fire extinguisher on the wall and roll over to it. I might be able to redirect the motorized chair before it crushes me under its wheels. Or, if I'm lucky, I could hit Mitchell with it. At least that would be a little payback.

I remove the red canister from its glass-fronted cabinet. It's heavy and almost takes off one of my toes as it clunks to the floor. I turn my rolling walker around and plant my butt onto the bench seat. I try to lift the fire extinguisher, but I lose my grip and the safety pin comes off in my hand.

Mitchell is close enough I can actually read the manufacturers name on his motorized chair.

I smile as I realize there is another way to use the fire extinguisher. I aim the cone and pull the lever.

Mitchell's charge is lost in a cloud of white powder.

I am shot backward by the blast. The wheels of my rolling walker wobble at the unexpected increase in velocity. I cannot force my fingers to let go of the lever, even as I speed backward, teetering on two wheels. The extinguisher drags along until it expends itself. My walker catches the edge of a floor tile and shoots out from under me. I land hard on my back and slide several feet. It's hard to breathe. I roll on my side and struggle to my hands and knees.

The hall is filled with a choking, white fog and there's no sound from Mitchell or his motorized chair. My hand moves to my waistband, but I don't feel Joyce's picture there. The fall must have knocked it free. The white powder covering the floor makes it hard to distinguish anything. How could I lose the photo now? I reach out and search the area around me, crawling on my hand and knees. I see the familiar rectangle by the garden door.

I recover my walker and use it to help me get to my feet. The dust has cleared enough that I can make out Mitchell against the far wall, slumped in his chair. I hobble to the garden door. My neck and back ache, which reminds me that I have pills I should have taken after dinner. I wince against the pain as I bend to pick up Joyce's picture. The glass across her forehead is cracked. I can fix that.

It takes nearly everything I have to open the door to the garden. I take several steps outside. The air is clear. I inhale a few deep, cleansing breaths. It feels good.

It's then that I hear the whirr of Mitchell's approach. He is heading full throttle toward the open door and me, his face twitching sporadically, as if his chair were giving him electric shock treatments.

I don't bother to move. I'm too tired. I tighten my grip on Joyce's photo.

In a blink, his chair veers hard left, straight into the door frame.

The collision is not as loud as I expect. There is just a thrum of the large safety glass windows vibrating. Mitchell is launched from his chair like a circus clown from a cannon. His arms are outstretched and he is screaming like a banshee. Too dumbfounded to move, the full force of his body strikes me. The momentum carries us both to the ground. Plumes of white powder erupt from us as we hit the concrete and roll. Joyce's picture is knocked from my grasp and skitters across the walkway, coming to rest under an Everglades Palm.

Mitchell's bony fingers wrap around my throat and squeeze. I press my thumbs into his rheumy green eyes.

"Stop it!" someone orders, the tone sharp and demanding.

We both freeze and look up. Sergeant Moron stands over us, hands on her narrow hips, cheeks flush and eyes narrowed.

"You two—in my office—now." She points in the direction of her domain as if we don't know where it is.

* * * *

Sergeant Moron's office is located behind the nurses' station. It's smaller than my room. The shelf that covers one wall is filled with books on management, elderly care and Chicken Soup anthologies. Centered on the opposite wall is a poster of a cat hanging from a bar as if it might be doing chin-ups. On her desk are stacks of bulging folders, small picture frames, and a name plate: Margery E. Murano. She has more personal items in her office than I do in my room. Behind the desk is the only window, one that looks out onto the garden. The sky is orange with the setting sun.

Sergeant Moron has left us in her office to "reflect on our actions". My reflection on these events is that I underestimated how crazy Mitchell is. That won't happen again. But I suspect this time-out is more so the Sergeant can collect herself before she blows a heart valve.

Mitchell and I sit in padded chairs on the guest side of her desk. We are still mostly covered in white dust.

"Nasty thief," Mitchell whispered.

"Dumbass," I replied.

Sergeant Moron strides through the open door with a uniformed police officer. I cringe as she tosses the portrait of my Joyce onto her desk.

"Mr. Mitchell. Mr. Zborowski. This is Officer Garcia. He is here to talk to you about how inappropriate and dangerous your actions were today. Isn't that right, Officer?"

Officer Garcia has a stern look about him. He is a big man and makes the room feel claustrophobic. One hand rests on his holster. He's poised to say something. I wait. Then his cheeks puff out, he puts a hand over his mouth, and laughter bursts from behind it.

"I can't do this," he says, quickly exiting the room.

Mitchell looks at me for an explanation. I have nothing for him but a shrug.

"Thanks a lot, John," Sergeant Moron yells after the officer and sits down at her desk with a huff. "What am I going to do with you two?" She runs both of her hands through her dark hair. "What were you thinking?"

"My wife," Mitchell mumbled, folding his arms across his chest.

"Liar," I say, folding my own arms, but adding a leg cross. "Joyce and I were married for fifty years."

"Not Joyce, Mitchell says. "Pauline. I watched her die of cancer twenty years ago."

"Impossible," I say, brushing dust off the arm of my shirt in his direction.

Mitchell drives his elbow into my shoulder.

It doesn't hurt, but I shove him anyway.

"Enough!" Murano's voice is shrill.

She holds up the picture with both hands like a Bible and shakes it. "I don't know how either of you got hold of this, but this woman has never been married to either of you."

She looks at me. "This isn't your Joyce."

I want to tell her she's wrong, but this is not to the time to poke the bear.

She turns to Mitchell. “This is not your Pauline.”

His hands shake as he grips the arm of his chair.

“This is my grandmother,” she says. “*My* grandmother.”

Grandmother?

Mitchell pushed himself up from his chair. A tear streaks down the white powder on his face. He waves a hand at her as he heads to the door, as if dismissing what she has said.

She shifts her stare to me, waiting for my reaction and I realize one thing. I’m going to have to be nicer to Margery, now I’ve learned she’s family.

THE END

About the Author

M. L. Joy

M.L. Joy, a New Englander now living in Florida, has discovered that the land of sunshine, alligators and snowbirds can be an unusual place, one rife with great characters and unique stories. When he's not writing and researching the bizarre, he's a professor and a drummer.

facebook.com/michael.l.joy

Romantic Notions

Doris Lemcke

With only two days until Valentine's Day and her shipment of handmade jewel boxes MIA, Amy Lindstrom couldn't appreciate Southwest Florida's warm, winter sun. She should have been thrilled that the worst winter on record in the Northeast was sending record numbers of snowbirds to Naples' Gulf Coast beaches, just blocks from her upscale gift shop. But without the exotic treasures she promoted every year for the Global Women Artisan's group, *Romantic Notions* was just another Naples tourist trap cashing in on the Hallmark Holiday.

Amy believed in paying for success up front and returned all of the profits back to the organization so critical to the survival of thousands of home artists around the world. After only three years, the event had drawn the attention of New York's trendy magazines and made regular customers of some of Florida's richest visitors—on both coasts. This year, Valentine's Day was on Sunday. It was Friday afternoon and instead of forty cases of handmade heart-shaped jewelry boxes, she had a back room full of pink, plastic flamingos.

The tinkle of the bell on the front door did little to dispel her gloom as she entered the little emporium filled with everything necessary to create a lasting, romantic-yet-tasteful mood for Cupid's disciples. Sudden tears misted her eyes. *What am I supposed to do with pink flamingos on Valentine's Day?*

"Sandy, has Josh been in yet?" she called as the door closed behind her.

Sandy's blonde head popped up from behind a crystal vase filled with white, dark and milk chocolate roses. "Josh?" she repeated with a sly smile. "You mean that tall, blond hunk in blue shorts who faithfully visits you every day with boxes of romantic gifts?" Not intimidated by Amy's narrowed green eyes and annoyed frown, she added, "It's only three o'clock. Be patient. Prince Charming will be along."

"Oh, stop," Amy responded to her only employee's teasing. She stashed her purse under the counter and tied her chin-length black hair back with a red ribbon. "BPS promised to find my hearts and pick up the birds today. But it's getting late."

"Have some faith, Snow White. Remember the BPS motto is 'we deliver'."

"Not helping," Amy muttered from the office that doubled as a stock room.

After carefully placing the vase in a shaded corner, Sandy crossed the store to put a hand on her boss' shoulder. "I'm sorry, honey, but I'm an optimist. I believe things always work out. And sometimes it's at the last minute. Don't give up hope."

"I really hope you're right."

"I am. You'll see. Oh, is it okay if I leave a little early? I gotta pick up Jen at school and finish her costume for the Valentine Party tomorrow." She winked. "The Queen of Hearts, of course."

"No problem. If I don't get those boxes today, you may as well go to the beach tomorrow with everyone else. No pun intended, but my business will be for the birds."

"Oh ye of little faith," was followed by the angelic chime of the bell signaling Sandy's departure.

With Sandy gone, Amy glared into the painted black eyes of a three-foot tall plastic flamingo yard ornament weighted with fifteen pounds of sand. "Optimist or not, no amount of faith can turn *you* into a jewel-studded jewelry box," she muttered, nose to beak and propped the bird against the doorframe between the stock room and cash register. Heaving a sigh, she left it to peer out the multi-paned window that gave *Romantic*

Notions its old-world ambience.

The store had a great street-front location in a cluster of rehabbed warehouses on Naples Bay. As usual, afternoon traffic on US41 was heavy both to and from the beaches, and she hoped to see the familiar blue van that stopped every day between three o'clock and three-thirty. *No luck.* She hadn't exaggerated about her business being ruined if BPS didn't find her shipment. Her prepaid orders from repeat customers had doubled this year—and she'd used the money to save ten percent on her own prepaid order with the supplier. Her bank account couldn't cover those refunds *and* rent if she didn't get them in time. She was half way through the "snowbird" season and even eating macaroni and cheese every day wouldn't make up the difference.

Where is Josh? In six weeks, eight at the most, the tourists and winter residents would start flying north. Her business dropped more than sixty percent by June and the whole mall shut down in July and August. She needed Valentine's Day like the big box stores needed Black Friday. Without the centerpiece for this year's "Heart's Treasures" event that drew crowds from the posh resorts, she may as well lock up and go home to a glass of wine and a romance novel.

Pretty depressing for a healthy, single, just-over-thirty year-old, she thought, admitting that Sandy's comment about the BPS driver had hit a little too close to home. Josh had taken over her route nearly a year ago. *Romantic Notions* was at the end of it and she'd begun to look forward to their chats at the end of his day when she took over from Sandy for the evening shift.

She'd moved to Naples from Ann Arbor, Michigan three years ago, after her fiancé texted her that he wasn't ready to "settle down with just one girl". Furious, hurt and humiliated, she quit her Human Resources job and moved south to her grandmother's empty condo on the Gulf. After a few months of self-pity, margaritas and sun-bathing—and her neighbor Sandy's insistence that Happy-Ever-After could happen if you believed enough, she poured her savings into *Romantic Notions*. She was surprised that helping couples express their love through heartfelt gifts helped heal her own shattered heart.

She looked up at the grandfather's clock by the entrance. *Three-fifteen.* Maybe Sandy was wrong about Prince Charming. *Damn her for planting that seed in my head.* Maybe Josh didn't have anything to deliver, maybe he was sick, or maybe BPS put him on another route. If the last was true, she missed him already, and not only because his face had replaced the image of more than one romance novel hero in her favorite books.

For nearly a year, Josh had offered friendship without any strings. She was sure the hour or two they shared every day (between customers) had more quality than many couples shared in long-term relationships. They talked comfortably about books, movies, weather, local gossip and even a little politics. The two things they *didn't* talk about were the past and the future—his or hers. To her, the past was still too painful to share and the future too vague to predict. Sandy had told her that Josh's wife of only a year had left him for an Italian real estate agent on Marco Island, at the same time Erik had dumped her for a pole dancer back in Michigan. She didn't ask Josh about it and he didn't tell. It worked for them. Theirs was a friendship between strangers. No strings, no demands, no expectations.

At least that's what she thought when she knew she'd see him every day. Now, faced with the possibility of someone else taking Josh's place, someone who just delivered boxes, she realized that she wasn't just going to miss the conversations. She was going to miss *him.* His wide, honest smile, his deep voice calling, "HayAmy" in one word while twisting his loaded dolly to fit through the door. And she'd miss the way his muscles rippled when he swiped a white towel over the sheen of perspiration on his cheeks after making three trips to his truck in ninety-degree heat and humidity.

And there was the touch of his calloused hand when he handed her the electronic clipboard, those strong arms, and well-defined calves from both his job and his passion for kayaking the local waterways. Feeling suddenly warm, Amy took a deep breath to quell the painful feelings she remembered so well from so long ago. Feelings of loving someone and thinking she was loved in return. The memory of how that turned out brought her temperature down.

"It's just the season," she muttered and took another look at the busy Florida highway crowded with the usual lineup of Beamers, Volvos, Benzes, Corvettes and Italian imports; but no BPS truck.

Three-thirty! She turned too quickly from the bright afternoon sunlight to the cozy ambience of the shop and bumped against a shelf, nearly upsetting a Victorian Kissing Cupid. Legend held that in exchange for a three-second kiss, the Cupid would grant a young maiden's' wish for true romance.

Sandy, Amy thought. Since there was only one on the shelf, Sandy had probably picked it up from a cute novelty salesman peddling to the erotica stores in East Naples. Still, holding the gaudy cherub with puckered lips and shining blue eyes, she couldn't resist wishing, "Send the Prince with my lost hearts soon." Taking a deep breath, she closed her eyes, pressed her lips against the warm red porcelain ones, counting one thousand-one, one thousand-two At one thousand-three, she opened her eyes. Cupid's smile just looked smug and a passing shadow made one eye look like it winked.

"Fake," she accused and put him back on the shelf. She was almost to the counter when the door chimed and a familiar voice called, "Sorry I'm late. I found your hearts."

"Josh!" She told herself it was releif, and not his voice, that made her heart jump and a sudden flush warm her cheeks. The sun behind him highlighted his tall, strong body as he backed in the door with a loaded dolly. Then she saw the familiar Global Woman logo stamped on the side of each box. *The heart boxes.*

He made three trips to the truck and with the office/stockroom already filled, carefully stowed the forty boxes in ten stacks behind the counter. Amy was so happy to have her hearts back she couldn't stop smiling and stifled a giggle when he handed her his digital clipboard to sign. It was a ritual she did five times a week, but this time, every part of her body seemed aware of his heat. Her bare shoulder tingled at the touch of arm brushing across it. Her fingers warmed as they passed over his to take the plastic wand. A deep breath didn't help. Even at the end of his day, he smelled good. Like sunshine and salt breezes. She could hardly write her name.

As if he'd noticed her agitation, he covered her hand a moment before taking the wand back from her. "Are you okay? These must have been really important to you. I mean, I know this is your living all, but do you really believe in …all… this?"

She looked up at him, her breath catching in her throat. His hair was mussed, glowing like a halo with the sun behind him, his smile both amused and concerned. Her face heated again. *Did he see me kiss that stupid cupid?* "Believe? In…what?"

Josh waved at the frills decorating the shop, and nodded toward the boxes. "In all this romantic…stuff. Is this shipment so important for you to be so…shaky?"

Embarrassed that her emotions were so transparent (and gratefully misunderstood), Amy's defenses went up. More often than she cared to count, she'd endured jokes and jeers about her business, even at Chamber of Commerce meetings. At best, people described it as silly. At worst, they compared it to a soft-porn store. Some of Naples elite business scions even voted against approving her shop for the mall. And all of them thought she'd fail by the end of her first season. But she'd survived three seasons. Now, with her precious jewel boxes finally here, she'd make it through four. "What do you mean?"

Josh's smile faded and the sun dipped behind a cloud. But his voice was as gentle as ever. "I mean, do you really think people need all of this to...to be...close? I mean, do women really still need candy, jewelry, and little cupids on cards to feel special? Will it really make someone fall in love—or a relationship last?"

Something in his chocolate-colored eyes told her he wasn't trying to get out of buying his girlfriend flowers. *Maybe he's just clueless.* She smiled. "Is this the 'what do women really want' question?"

Her knees nearly buckled at his deep chuckle when he answered, "No. Not really. Maybe. Well, I guess so. You see, there's a woman I'd like to ask out, but it's been quite a while since I've dated. And no offense, but this stuff all seems kind of phony to me. I just figured, you being in the business and all, you could tell me. So I don't screw it up."

The stupid smile Amy had been wearing ever since Josh rang the bell disappeared and the heart that had skipped a beat when she touched him, suddenly felt heavy in her chest. Apparently she'd missed the Love Boat again. While she was sitting around chatting with him, someone else had healed his wounded heart.

In the space of a few breaths, she beat herself up for hoping that someday she'd see affection instead of friendship for her in Josh's eyes.

Stupid! In a place where Jersey Girls, movie stars and models paraded the beaches nearly nude, she was no beauty. She was too short, with pale skin that refused to tan and a body better suited for the "well-rounded" fifties than the string bikini millennium. It wasn't his fault. He'd never misled her. He'd just never mentioned he had a girlfriend.

"Amy, are you okay?" he asked again, his hand warm on her shoulder. "I'm sorry. I didn't mean to offend you—or put you on the spot. Never mind. It was a stupid question."

Her pity party over, she smiled. Standing there in his blue uniform with "JOSH" embroidered on a patch sewn above the pocket, he looked so…sincere. And more than a little confused, *He may be taken, but I can still be his friend.*

Just to torture herself, she touched his bare forearm. The muscle tensed but he didn't pull away. "Don't worry. I'm not offended. And there was nothing stupid about the question. It's the core of the 'men are from Mars and women are from Venus' dilemma. But it's also really very simple."

She waved at the overcrowded little shop and leaned closer to him. "You see, all women…and men, if you'd admit it, like to feel special." Speaking for herself, she explained, "Some people can't express their feelings well in words or public displays of affection, so little gifts, or a quiet setting with the right lights and music make it easier for them to show how they feel."

Josh suddenly cleared his throat and stepped back, swiveling the empty dolly around and letting out a deep breath. "Okay. I see. Well, it looks like you've got your work cut out for you and I've got extra stops. Season traffic is a pain."

Amy stepped back too, surprised at his sudden change from curious boyfriend-wanna-be, to all-business. *Blew it again, Bossypants.* It's what Erik called her whenever she disagreed with him. *Well the man asked the question!* She wouldn't apologize for answering it.

"Yes. Well, thanks for the delivery." He was nearly to the door when she remembered the flamingos and shouted. "Wait. Aren't you going to take the birds?"

"Birds?"

She pointed at the stock room. "Yes, pink flamingos, fifty of them.

BPS said they'd pick them up."

Steadying the dolly with one foot, he smiled patiently and scrolled through his electronic manifest. "Sorry, pink no flamingo pick up. Maybe the Naples Zoo can help you out."

"What?" Panic made her voice squeak. She didn't have room for both the birds and the boxes. Her store would look like a freaking flea market on Valentine's Day.

He shook his head and touched her arm. "Sorry, I'm not good at jokes. I heard you got a wrong shipment but didn't know what it was. Still, I can't take them back without an order." He glanced at clock now chiming four o'clock. "The office shuts down at three-thirty on Fridays. If you can wait until Monday, I'll check into it."

What choice did she have? Feeling stupid for not getting his joke, and awkward for keeping him, she looked at the pink bird lounging against the door jamb. *Maybe I can hide the shipping boxes for the jewel cases under tablecloths and set up the champagne and chocolate fountains on top.* At least she'd save a few bucks on the caterer. *And maybe one or two of these monsters posed together to shape a heart would add some whimsy to the night.* She suddenly regretted that Sandy hadn't bought more kissing Cupids.

"Amy?" brought her back from her disaster recovery plan.

"What? Oh, okay. Thanks. I…I'll figure something out."

He sounded disappointed when he echoed her, "Well, okay then. I guess we're both pretty busy. We can catch up later."

So the phase-out of the friend is beginning. She tried to smile. "Sure. Later."

Amy used the slow time between the early-bird dinner specials and sunset in Naples to begin unpacking. With no room in the office, she settled on the floor behind the counter to put together the tiered, display shelves to showcase the unique, jeweled and shell-covered boxes. Her back was to the door jumped when the bell signaled someone's entrance and she jumped.

"Damn," she whispered when needles stabbed her left leg and she nearly fell over trying to stand. There was no feeling at all in the same foot and she rose slowly, rubbing it back to life. When she finally looked up, a teen-aged boy dressed in gray gym shorts and a lightweight hoody, was standing behind a flower arch, peeking out the front window.

The sun was low in the sky now and shadows darkened his face. Instinctively, she stiffened, all the while hoping he was just a teenager coming in to buy his girl a trinket. When a police car drove by, lights flashing but no siren, the boy crouched deeper into the shadows.

A hard lump formed in Amy's throat and for the first time in three years, she reached under the counter for her grandfather's police night stick. Holding the stick behind her with her right hand, her left rested on the counter. She tried to sound cheery, "Can...can I help you?"

The boy jumped and turned slowly to face her. When his gaze met hers, Amy forgot about the fire ants still running up and down her awakening leg. Her heart slowed and her mind seemed to watch her from…somewhere else. "Don't be afraid," the little voice in her head told her. "If you are, he'll know."

He stepped toward her to pause under the largest of six strategically-placed chandeliers. Her blood began to thaw when she saw that he was just what she thought: young, fifteen or sixteen. Just a boy. The sigh of relief turned into a sharp intake of breath when he pushed back the hood. His eyes were dark, angry and wild, like the pit bull in her neighbor's yard that lived its short, miserable life at the end of a six-foot chain. But more than the boy's eyes, his voice chilled her to the bone.

"Maybe, lady," he growled and came toward her, one measured step at a time. "What you got to offer?"

She slid along the counter, closer to the stock room door, where she'd left her cell phone on the desk. Her voice held a calm she didn't feel. "Well, why don't you tell me what you want?"

His laugh made her flesh crawl. "What d'you think I want, bitch? Your money—first. Then, maybe a little romance."

The boy's eyes were even more frightening up close, dilated and watery, the whites bloodshot. There was a rash around his nose and mouth and a sickeningly sweet smell mixed with his rancid body odor. *Inhalents!* The latest drug of choice for America's teens. There was no reasoning with someone under the influence of inhalents.

That's when she stopped being afraid and became angry. She brandished the night stick like a tiny baseball bat. "No! Don't come any closer. I have a silent alarm," she lied. "I tripped it when you came in.

The police will be here in minutes."

He cocked his head and took another step. "Funny, I don't hear nothin' like sirens."

Knowing he was so high he felt invincible, she stood her ground as he advanced in short, staggering steps, stopping when he was so close she saw the acne scars on his sallow cheeks.

His rancid breath was hot against her cheek. "And I wouldn't be wavin' that little thing aroun' 'less you know how to use it." He moved so fast, she barely saw his hand when he snatched the impotent stick out of her hand. Then he stepped back, howling in laughter and waving it like a sword until a killing blow to the granite counter shattered a hand-blown glass heart.

Amy had turned to run toward the stock room when he broke the heart, but he caught her by the back of her camisole top and pulled her close to his own sweat-soaked hoody.

"Where is it?"

She twisted away, bumping into the doorframe when he smashed a heart made of mother-of-pearl this time. She bit her lip, tasting the blood her heart pumped at high-speed forcing her mind to slow down and assess her situation. The boy blocked her path to the front of the store, and a wall of boxes filled with flamingos stood between her and the cell phone ringing with a call she couldn't answer, Then she felt the hard beak of the abandoned flamingo press against her back.

"Okay, okay," she bargained, waving one hand toward the mess on her counter while the other one wrapped around the curved plastic neck. "I'll give you everything I have. Just don't break anything else."

He raised the night stick again, this time over her head.

"No, no don't," she screamed, nodding to her left. "It's in there. In…the…desk. Nearly $5,000."

Under the hanging Tiffany lamp above the counter, his eyes glittered like the shards of colored glass shimmering on the granite surface and on the floor. "Where in the desk?"

Suddenly, she wasn't afraid anymore. Her ex-fiancé had proved that drugs and greed made you stupid. This boy confirmed it. She stepped a little to the right, as if making room for him, and forced her voice to quiver. "The center drawer. It..It's not locked. Just take it and go. I won't call the police. I promise."

He cocked his head, smiling at his victory over an unarmed woman half his size. "Don't move. I ain't done with you yet."

As soon as he broke eye contact, she tightened her grip on the flamingo's graceful throat, dipped her shoulder to take her championship girls' softball stance, and swung with all her might. There was no aiming the "S" shaped bat, but the heavy pink body caught the boy on the shoulder. The blow sent the night stick flying back into the store and knocked him off balance enough so Amy had him trapped in the stock room.

They faced off, the night stick out of reach by the Kissing Cupid and her brave flamingo bleeding sand at her feet. But the boy showed no fear. He smiled wide this time, His well-capped teeth told her he was no street thug and had no fear of punishment. Then he pulled a knife from his designer hi-top sneakers. "Looks like you struck out, honey. Now get on your knees."

A sudden flash of red light tinted the entire store pink and a siren screamed from the street once, then went silent. Panic wiped the sneer from the boy's face and a hint of sanity cleared his eyes. Still, he waved the knife. "Okay, I won't hurt you…this time. Where's the back door?"

Amy didn't speak but he was cunning enough to follow her glance past him at the old delivery door partially blocked by boxes. It opened onto an alley that ran behind the mall and ended at the bridge connecting Tin City to West Naples. The front bell rang just as the back door slammed behind the exiting intruder.

"Amy? Are you still here?" Josh's voice instead of policeman's, pulled Amy's gaze from the flapping back door and he turned. Her vintage camisole was ripped at one shoulder, her hair mussed and her entire body shaking, the mutilated yard ornament dangling from her arm.

"Oh, God," he shouted and ran to her. He pulled her to his chest just as she started to tremble, and held her, whispering against her cheek, "It's all right. I'm here. What happened?"

"I fell," was all she could whisper between uncontrollable shudders that opened the way for a torrent of sobs and tears.

He held her until her breathing slowed and the trembling subsided, and then led her to a wicker rocking chair. With one arm still holding her up, he threw off a half dozen antique needlepoint pillows embroidered with homey Victorian sayings, onto the floor. Placing her like a doll in a toy rocker, he knelt on one knee in front of her. “Hey, I’m sorry. I didn’t mean to scare you. I’m a volunteer fireman. I bumped the siren and light switch when I got out of my truck. What happened? Are you okay?” he asked for the third time that day.

“Yes,” she answered for the third time. “I…fell.”

But this time he shook his head. He looked around at the mess of broken glass and beads, bits of pink plastic and the trail of sand on the floor ending at a nearly decapitated flamingo. “That was quite a fall.”

At the question in her eyes, he explained, “I...got off late, but thought I’d come down and give you a hand putting out your...heart stuff. I thought maybe we could have dinner...or something...after.” He gestured to the army of regular cupids on the Victorian display behind the Kissing Cupid, armed and ready to fire on them. “You shouldn’t be alone with these guys. They could be dangerous.”

The adrenaline rush fading, Amy was suddenly overcome with the sheer joy of being alive. She laughed with tears still falling from her eyes and squeezed his hand. “My hero.”

But Josh didn’t return the laugh. That’s when she knew she loved him. Any other man would have bullied her into telling him the truth—just so he could play the hero and go after the crazed villain with knife. Not Josh. He’d wait until she was ready to tell him. And she would, eventually. But not now. It was still too real.

“It looks worse than it was.” She tried to sound casual. “I’m a klutz. I tripped over the flamingo and fell over the counter. The hearts are very fragile—and valuable. I...can’t afford to lose any of them. Bu I’m okay now, but I…think I need to go home for a little while.” It took her two tries to get out of the chair.

He frowned, but he didn’t press the issue as she left him to lock the back door and grab her purse, calling over her shoulder, “Thanks for offering to help, Josh, but there’s really no need. Sandy and I can put it all back together tomorrow. Didn’t you say you were going out with someone?”

“No, I didn’t say that,” he answered when she came back to lock the front door. “I said there was someone I wanted to ask out. But as long as

I'm here, why not let me show you something spectacular that might perk you up after your..fall."

He stepped aside for her to exit first and lock the door. "It's over here," he said, taking her hand and leading her to a bench along the boardwalk.

Perhaps there was something magical about Josh after all, Amy thought. In a matter of a few short hours, he'd found her precious treasure and saved her from being killed by a drugged teenager. And now, simply by taking her hand, he led her out of a nightmare into an orange and blue-tinted fantasy world where dolphins played around tourist pontoons in the calm waters of Naples Bay.

To mark the moment, she looked up at the old tower clock above the entrance of Tin City across the bay. *Six-fifteen. Sunset.* She looked at Josh's strong profile next to her and followed his gaze to the West.

He and the hundreds of people around them stood silent as one of God's daily miracles began. Josh's hand left Amy's to rest on her shoulder as the golden sun lowered to kiss the cool, dark waters of the Gulf of Mexico. The power of that touch exploded into orange flames that lit the clouds, and for two breathtaking minutes, fire and water consummated their forbidden love with a bright green flash before melting into each other.

For those two minutes, Josh's body sheltered Amy from the cooling breeze. "I never get tired of this," he whispered close to her ear. "When I was a kid my mother told me that when the sun flashes like a green creamcicle like this, and you make a wish, it will come true."

Amy smiled into dark eyes that still seemed to reflect the sunset. "So you don't believe in romance, but you believe in magic creamcicle flashes?"

His laugh was lost in the crowd's applause for the day's grand finale. "Maybe. Care to make a wish, just in case?"

She shook her head, tears blurring the lines of his handsome face. "It's not necessary."

Her head resting on his shoulder, they watched the butter-colored water flow out to sea and darken under orange and blue clouds that slowly turned to gray. As the warm day became a chilly evening and the tourists turned to their evening pursuits, Josh turned to Amy. "I know you want to clean up your mess in the store and you still have a couple hours until the mall closes, but do you think you could close up early? I know a great place where we can have a quiet dinner. It even has candles on the table. Very romantic." He smiled. "And maybe you'll tell me what really happened tonight."

It all seemed like a bad dream now and she didn't want to spoil the peace she'd felt during the sunset or the comfort she'd found in his arms. But there was so much to do before Sunday. "Oh, I don't know. What about that other woman you were asking about…"

Josh's warm lips on hers answered her question about his mystery woman and after he pulled away to wrap his BPS jacket around her shoulders, he held out his hand. "Tell you what. I'll stop in early tomorrow and help you and Sandy unpack the rest of those boxes so you're ready for your big heart party. C'mon. The Pink Flamingo has the best swordfish in town."

Amy's laugh carried above real police sirens shrilling across the bridge and she took his hand. "Okay. And if you do a good job, I'll tell you why I now love pink flamingos."

THE END

About the Author

Doris Lemcke

A native of Saginaw, Michigan Doris Lemcke has published two Historical romances, *Passion's Secret* and *Passion's Spirit.* The first two books in the *Passion's Legacy* series are available at www.thewildrosepress.com and www.Amazon.com. Continuing the theme of family secrets that haunt future generations, Doris currently has a contemporary General Fiction novel awaiting publication. *Legacy of Lies* is set in contemporary Detroit and Michigan's Upper Peninsula in the early Twentieth Century.

https://www.facebook.com/pages/Doris-Lemcke/177898622282712

Love At First Flight

Mariah Lynne

I turned just as my office door burst open. Josh, my exotic bird assistant, bolted in flushed and out of breath. Frazzled, he pushed his yellow blond hair straight up making him look like he had just been struck by lightning. Pacing back and forth like an agitated gorilla, he spoke like he couldn't give me his news fast enough.

"It's Ferdinand. A volunteer Seabie put him in Flamingo Lagoon. Why? I don't know. I told the new guy that bird wasn't ready for prime time but he decided to listen to his iPod instead of me."

"What's the problem, then? Just use the net and get him out of there," I replied wondering why all the panicked behavior.

"It's not that simple. A tourist leaned over the fence and dropped his camera near the edge of the lagoon. Ferdie did not like what he saw and began to beat the camera with his beak. He wouldn't stop. The rest of the crowd moved in closer to take photos. I couldn't get through to him!"

I became so angry I couldn't speak. I shot up from my desk chair, grabbed my long pole with the big net and headed out my office door.

"Come on. You're coming with me right now. Didn't that idiot realize Ferdy's wings haven't been clipped? If he gets frightened by the crowd, he just might take off. Our only hope is that Ferdy doesn't know he can fly."

We jumped into my pink mini jeep and headed straight for Flamingo

Lagoon. I saw Ferdy first hand in the green blue water near the shore attacking the man's camera. By now, he'd attracted a good-sized crowd. What is it about cameras that drive this bird crazy?

I motioned Josh to follow. I needed help moving the crowd back. I carried the net and worked myself to the front. Better get this under control before man or bird gets hurt. I took a whistle out of my pocket and blew hoping to get everyone's attention. The chatter stopped

"Hi, everyone. May I please have your attention? My name is Marcy Moore. I am head ornithologist at Miami Seaquarium. We've experienced similar behavior from this young flamingo before. Everyone please remain calm and step back from the lagoon. I am a wildlife expert trained to take control of the bird."

Breathing a sigh of relief, I watched Josh walk the small crowd back from the large pond. Once they pulled back, I saw the incredibly bold camera owner walk right through the low red flowering hedges to the edge of the lagoon. He squatted trying to reach for his camera. Some older flamingos circled Ferdy for protection. I had to get that crazy guy of there.

"Sir, please step back slowly. Don't scare the flamingos. I can't guarantee your safety if you don't."

"I don't care about my safety. How about my $1000 camera? What do I do about that?"

I signaled for Josh to come and get him. Josh grabbed the man's arm and pulled him out of the water. I looked at Ferdinand. He still nipped at that blasted camera.

What's this? That pesky pelican that follows Ferdy around like a puppy just landed next to him. If that pelican picks up that camera and swallows it, I'll really have big problems. How will I ever explain that to the powers that be?

I moved in slow and easy getting as close to Ferdy as possible. The pelican kept a close watch on me before wading near the young flamingo. I had to catch Ferdy. I raised my net slowly. I could tell by his stare that sneaky Ferdinand was observing me with one eye. I felt like the Crocodile Hunter taking slow deliberate steps so as not to scare off my prey.

Then it happened. Right there in front of my eyes. I couldn't believe it. That pelican swam over and nudged Ferdinand out of the lagoon and into a running start. I knew what that meant. Even though he'd never flown before, he would have enough steam now to be airborne. *Yep. There he goes and that pain of a pelican is flying next to him.* I just held my head knowing what a headache this would be for me with park officials. I better get a head start and alert all the other Florida zoos, state parks and national parks.

I yelled for Josh as cameras clicked at the two mismatched friends in flight.

"Quick. Let's go. After I drop you back at my office, get on the radio and tell all the Seabies to go to the media room. Stat."

I drove to the media center while radioing for another assistant to help the man retrieve his camera. Once there, I found the volunteers had already assembled. I handed them each a list of media sources as well as the press releases to send to them.

"The Miami Seaquarium is looking for a runaway Flamingo. His name is Ferdinand and he is flying with a dangerous pelican. If you spot the pair, please do not approach. Call Marcy Moore chief ornithologist at the Seaquarium. 305-233-BIRD"

They faxed, e-mailed and called any and all news outlets in the state. It had been over an hour and those two crazy birds could be headed anywhere. I called park rangers in the Everglades (perish the thought), Sanibel's Ding Darling, park managers at The Tampa Zoo, Seaworld, The Naples Zoo, my list went on and on. I had to hurry before Ferdy landed and was scooped up by a hungry alligator or snake.

I always knew that pelican was a bad influence. Still in shock, I got in my Prius and drove out of the park hoping to get a visual but no such luck. I lost my appetite for dinner and found it difficult to sleep that night knowing the little guy's future rested in my hands. I mean what if he really did land in the Everglades loaded with gators and snakes? Oh, my poor Ferdinand.

I dragged myself to work the next morning. The main office didn't blame me but I blamed myself. I supervised the bird- feeding schedule as best I could. The feeding finished about ten. After which, I quickly raced back to my office hoping to catch any news regarding Ferdy's location. The intercom light on my desk came on as soon as I entered.

"Marcy, it's Jill. I swear we've had more possible sightings of Ferdy than NASA has of UFOs. I've been filtering the calls for you but this one sounds real. It's from a park ranger. Do you want to take the call?"

I perked up.

"Please, pass the call through to me."

I waited anxiously for my phone to ring. Bingo, there it goes. I answered so quickly I almost dropped the receiver.

"Head ornithologist Marcy Moore. How may I help you?"

A deep male voice answered. "This is Ranger Bradley North from Ding Darling on Sanibel Island. I need someone from your facility to come over here and get that menacing flamingo not to mention the pelican out of my park. ASAP. They're a nuisance to my eco-system."

I had to bite my lip. Here was a big brave park ranger who had to deal with alligators, panthers and the like upset by two fragile birds. I was so elated he found Ferdy, I decided to be polite.

"Ranger North, we appreciate your call. We're concerned about Ferdy's safety. He's young and has never lived in the wild. I'll be happy to come and get him, but what could he be doing that's so bad?

A brief moment of silence followed before I heard North's voice again.

"He landed in the pond where our Roseate Spoonbills mate and is cooing as if trying to make passes at Rosie, our most popular and beautiful spoonbill. He keeps walking over to her putting his head down next to hers while that nasty pelican stands guard. Your Ferdy and my Rosie are cooing oddly. It's spring and I know love is in the air, but not for your Ferdy and not in this air. Rosie's our star. She's a perfect specimen with offers for mates from the Jacksonville Zoo, Sea World, even Disney. It doesn't get any better than that. She will not bear mongrel birds for your amorous flamingo. I will keep them apart no matter what it takes. There will be no co- mingling of feathers. Got it? She's our prize."

Who does this guy think he's talking to? They can't co-mingle. They are different genus. He has to know that. I imagined he must be some stodgy old man with no life.

"And Ferdy is our treasure. Honestly, North, you must know they can't co-mingle. But if they could, Rosie would be hard pressed to find a better mate."

I hoped my answer would incite him. It did. He sure sounded angry.

"Now you listen to me, I don't want to hurt your flamingo or that nasty pelican but I have to keep them away from Rosie. We know they can't, but do they? Better not see her start to dance. Comprendo?"

"Si, señor. I'm on my way."

I hung up and yelled for Josh.

"Quick. Grab the flamingo cage and long net. Put them in the back of the pickup. Tell the park manager Ferdy is on Sanibel Island and I'm going to bring him home."

I jumped in the truck, started the motor and left on a mission of mercy to save young Ferdy from that mean park ranger.

Since it was off-season, it didn't take me long to reach Ding Darling, a little over two and one half hours. The more I thought about that ranger, the angrier I became. I muttered nasty things about North as I drove, like he must have been deprived a fun childhood and never went to his prom. I stopped working myself into a frenzy once I drove over the Sanibel causeway. What a spectacular view! The turquoise waters of the Gulf of Mexico melted into the deep blue waters of the back- bay. I made a quick stop to use the facilities at a gas station after refilling my tank for the ride home. Driving down the tree lined main road of the island, I spotted the sign for the park. I turned in and informed the ranger at the entrance I was there to meet North. She already knew I was coming.

"Ranger North will meet you a half mile down the main road on the right side."

I thanked her before making my way through this amazing stretch of natural beauty. All the different species of birds made it hard to focus on where I was going. It didn't take long before I spotted a brown ranger truck off to one side of the road. I pulled up in front of it and parked. I got out in search of fussy old Ranger Rick, but all my eyes could see was a tall muscular ranger with a pair of binoculars. He was looking at something past the brush.

I was sure he couldn't be North, too young, but maybe I should ask how to find North.

"Excuse me. Can you tell me where I might find Ranger North? I'm

Marcy Moore from the Seaquarium and have a meeting with him."

The ranger put the binoculars down and turned to look at me with the most amazing green eyes. I'd left in such a rush I don't know if I even combed my hair. I tried to straighten myself perspiring a bit. Hopefully something he wouldn't notice.

"The Miami Seaquarium. Who else would have hot pink trucks? You sounded feisty enough to be a redhead. I'm North."

I pushed my auburn hair out of my eyes hoping to improve my disheveled appearance.

He smiled. Why did he have to be so gorgeous? Not exactly who I imagined. I really wanted to hate this guy.

"Nice to meet you, too, Marcy. I have to admit you're not what I expected."

"You're not either. Thought you were older. Now let's get down to business. Where's my Ferdy?"

North walked closer and handed me his binoculars.

"Here. Look through the brush over there. I'll show you what your bird Casanova is doing. Stand over there and you'll see the whole thing."

I took his binoculars and walked over to where he was standing when I arrived. North walked behind me adjusting my stance and putting his arm around my shoulder to hold the binoculars in the exact position. Be still my heart. I looked out but couldn't help myself. I started to laugh.

"Look at my little Ferdy. He's all grown up and smitten. How cute is that! Ferdy wobbles like a love- crazed teen. Oh look he's rubbing Rosie's neck with his beak and she's making a noise. What a hoot!"

North looked puzzled.

"Hoot is for owls."

I lowered my binoculars.

What a nerd but a hunky one at that.

"I know that. I was just making a silly joke. Now tell me how I get out to where Ferdy is."

North looked at me and grinned like a Cheshire cat.

"The old fashioned way. We walk. You're probably not used to mud working on asphalt all day. Besides, I can't let you out there alone. We do have some gators and a big old croc on the premises. We're not allowed to carry guns but I have a pole and am trained to spot them."

He walked back to his truck and removed a thick pole from the back as well as a big net.

"Okay. Get your net and cage ready to catch that flamingo. When you are ready, follow me. Walk in my footsteps if you can."

I turned and went back to retrieve my equipment.

What did I do wrong? Why do I have to trudge through all this mushy marsh with gators no less? Ferdy, the things I do for you.

I looked at North. He saw my cage.

"Wait. I need a few more minutes to get a cage from the back of my truck for Rosie. Right now, we've got our eyes on the lovebirds, but after you retrieve Ferdy, I don't want to leave Rosie out there alone. She's too precious to be a gator's lunch. I need to move her back to her flock where the lovebirds met."

Wow, this guy is really dedicated. I'm impressed.

"No problem. It's only one thirty. I have plenty of time to get back to Miami."

North looked at me with those eyes.

"If we can do this quickly, I'd be happy to give you a personal tour of our park."

What breathing female could refuse? Of course I said yes.

"I'm the head ornithologist. I'm not on a schedule since this is a rescue. I'd love to stay."

North nodded.

"Great. Now's let's go get them."

He led the way through the marsh. Of course he had on rubber boots. My sneakers squeaked all the way. I followed close lugging the big birdcage and the net. As we approached, that pesky pelican started squawking a warning but I was too quick for my Casanova swooping the net down over him before gently pushing him into his cage. Rosie squawked, startled. North caught her off guard and caged her as well. The pelican flew over us all the way back to the road. I kept ducking in case he decided to bombard us with droppings. I put Ferdinand in the back of my truck. North put Rosie's cage on the back of his.

"Marcy, I'm going to move Ferdy to my truck. If I'm going to give you a tour, we shouldn't leave either of them behind."

After loading Ferdy's cage on the back of his truck, he told me to "Hop in."

The park tour was amazing, but so was North. He knew so much about the birds, the fauna, and the animals. He stopped to show me a prairie warbler, its bright yellow chest feathers gleaming in the sunlight. We drove further to find a green heron with rusty orange, green and brown feathers, ready to pounce on an unsuspecting fish as a little blue heron watched. A snowy egret, its soft white feathers moving in the gentile breeze, walked nearby. Brad impressed me. He was not just another pretty face.

We stopped at a look out point and talked shop the whole time we were there. We liked the same books, the same research journals, and had the same major in college, biology. I admitted that before I was offered the job in Miami, I thought about a job in a lab. Then it happened.

North put his arm around me.

"Please Marcy, call me Brad."

I was more than happy to do just that. Brad told me that he received his biology degree from the University of Michigan. He moved to Sanibel to be close to his parents who had retired there. When he started work at Ding Darling, he admitted it wasn't his dream job, but said he would not change jobs now for any reason. I told him I felt exactly the same way. Working outdoors with live species was incredibly rewarding.

Brad took off his ranger cap. He had the kind of curly brown hair I wanted to run my fingers through.

"I really had a great time with you today. It's hard to find someone with our same interests. We've been talking for over two hours. Didn't feel like that long. Anyway, our friends in the back are very quiet. What do you say we give them some water and take them down to the beach for a picnic? We can carry them in their cages. I'm sure any tourists or locals on the beach would love seeing them up close."

Wow! Did he just ask me out on a ranger date? I responded so fast I'm not sure I got all the words out in the right order.

"A picnic? Sounds like fun. I haven't been on one in years. Yes. Ferdy and I will stay."

Brad nodded and put his cap back on.

"Good. We'll go back to the station and grab water, a cooler of shrimp for them and a blanket for us. If you need to freshen up there's a washroom inside."

By this time, the washroom sounded real good to me.

Once back at the station, I made a dash for the washroom. Good thing I stuck some makeup and a hairbrush in my purse. I tried as hard as I could to make myself as presentable as possible. Brad got the bird grub as he called it before going into the back room.

No fair, he changed into shorts and a golf shirt.

Brad walked outside and loaded the cooler on the back of his truck.

"OK, Marcy we're ready to roll whenever you are."

I got in the passenger side. We drove to a small island grocery store. Brad went in and after about fifteen minutes came out with a large paper bag. He looked proud of himself.

"We're all set for a great picnic. I'll drive to a beach access where it will be easy for me to deal with the cages."

He turned the truck around before heading down a tree-lined side street.

"I'll grab the lovebirds. I'm putting you in charge of the blanket, the grocery bag, and the small cooler. Pick a nice spot for us. Who knows? You may get lucky and see one of our famous Sanibel sunsets."

I took the blanket and supplies from the truck and walked down to the beach. I hoped to find a spot with a gorgeous view of the water not too far from where we parked. I did just that. The water was so calm, so clear. I could see dolphins feeding nearby. I spread the blanket placing our bag in the center. A beautiful location, Brad found it easy to carry the cages there. He put them down in the sand next to us. Using gloves and plastic tongs, Brad pulled out their grub from a small cooler and fed them. Rosie and Ferdy had developed quite an appetite. Hungry, they eagerly gobbled down the shrimp. I looked over my shoulder to see that pesky brown and white pelican hovering nearby. Brad threw him a fish from that same cooler. We both laughed.

"I snuck in a couple of fish for him. I do owe him. You know Marcy, without that pelican, we never would have met."

Brad threw him another fish before removing his cotton gloves and grabbing the hand sanitizer.

"We are now ready to eat."

He opened the bag taking out two paper plates with two packets of plastic utensils. He placed a box of fried chicken, a small packet of sliced cheese, some grapes, and a container of cole slaw on the blanket. I looked at him.

"This is really nice. Thank you. I haven't relaxed like this in I don't know how long."

Brad nodded.

"We both work too hard. That's easy to do when you love your work. Wish I could have taken you out for a nice dinner but we have our charges to watch out for."

He whipped out two bottles of cold sarsaparilla.

"I'd rather this was a bottle of champagne, but I know you have a two hour drive. I'll owe you one."

"Owe me one," sounded pretty good to me.

We ate and drank and talked and laughed. Time got away from us. I saw a group of people chatting loudly as they walked down to the beach holding tropical drinks.

I quipped, "Looks like a party!"

"Just locals. It's almost time for our Sanibel sunset. If we're lucky, we'll see the green flash. Some say it brings luck."

"The green flash? I thought he was a comic book character."

Brad chuckled.

"No silly. When the sun hits the water, a flash of green light follows. The green flash. We're famous for it."

I stood up not wanting to miss a second of it. Brad did as well putting his arm around me. I was excited, pointing to the water.

"There goes the sun. Look. It's the green flash."

Everyone clapped.

Rosie and Ferdy cooed.

Brad hugged me and looked into my eyes.

"I'm glad you came. I coo for you."

He leaned in and kissed me. I was so happy I grabbed him by the shoulders and returned his kiss. The locals now clapped for us! Embarrassed? I guess, but sad that this amazing day had to end.

Brad sighed. "I guess this is where I have to take you and Ferdy back to your truck."

I responded, "I guess."

We drove back to the park to where I left my truck. Brad loaded Ferdy in the back before kissing me on the forehead. He slipped a piece of paper into my hand.

"Here's my e-mail. Send me a note telling me how you and Ferdy are and I'll answer. You know what they say about rangers. We always keep our word. Now, please be careful driving home."

I grabbed him by the shoulders and planted a long lingering kiss on his lips. At first he was surprised, but since he didn't pull away, I'm sure he enjoyed it.

"I promise Ferdy and I will stay in touch."

He smiled. "Good. I hope so. Now, follow me out to the main gate."

I jumped in my truck and followed him to the gate. Brad unlocked the gate so Ferdy and I could begin our drive home. All the way back, I kept thinking about what a wonderful day we had and how I'd like to spend more time with Brad. Ferdy cooed loudly in the back perhaps thinking about Rosie.

After a few days back at work, I noticed Ferdy was listless and refused to eat. I kept him in my office and put him on a vitamin drip but didn't know what else I could do for him. The park vet couldn't find anything wrong with him.

I decided to send Brad an e-mail asking for any ideas that might help Ferdy.

"Hi Brad,

I'm fine but Ferdy isn't well. He won't eat and has lost interest in everything. Any suggestions? Thank you again for such a wonderful day. I'll never forget the green flash. Marcy"

He must have been online because he answered right away.

"Hi Marcy,

"Rosie won't eat either. Maybe they miss each other and should have a reunion, Brad."

A reunion? How wonderful for Ferdy not to mention me.

I too responded quickly.

"Just name the date and time. We'll be there."

I looked at my inbox. Another e-mail from Brad.

"We'll come to you. Is tomorrow afternoon around one o'clock good? It's my day off. It'll be great to see the both of you but please keep that pelican at bay."

I responded.

"I'll do my very best but that bird is persistent. Please come. Ferdy and I will be happy to see you."

Tomorrow couldn't come soon enough for me. My heart raced when I heard a truck pull up next to my office. Ferdy lifted his head. He could hear Rosie's call. After a quick knock, Brad came in with the caged Rosie.

He stared into my eyes. "Hey" is all that came out of my mouth.

He put Rosie's cage next to Ferdy's.

"Hope this helps both of them. I know seeing you helps me."

Ferdy and Rosie picked right up cooing to each other.

Brad smiled when he heard short tapping noises at my office window. We looked over to see that pesky pelican trying as hard as he could to be a part of our reunion.

"Guess it's not a good idea to keep these two lovebirds apart. It's not good to keep us apart either. Since you left, I couldn't stop thinking about you."

All I could say was, "Me either".

Brad laughed. "I guess weekly visits are in order."

I nodded "Yes" before leaning in for a kiss.

THE END

About the Author

Mariah Lynne

Ever dream of traveling through time? Mariah Lynne does. She writes stories that take her readers along on exciting journeys. Travel to distant times and beautiful places with strong-willed independent heroines whose memorable tales will entertain with twisted plots that often dabble in the paranormal. Both of her novellas, THE LOVE GYPSY ((The Wild Rose Press) and THE DUCHESS' NECKLACE (Taliesin Publishing) fit that description to a T.

A Graduate of Syracuse University, Mariah lives on a beautiful Florida Gulf Coast Island where she wrote weekly entertainment columns for two island newspapers. She loves where she lives and makes Southwest Florida take center stage in her stories. When she is not writing, she enjoys swimming, traveling and spending time with her husband and dolphin hunting dog, Max. She is a member of The Southwest Florida Romance Writers and Romance Writers of America. To learn more about Mariah and her time travel adventures, visit her at

www.MariahLynne.com
https://www.facebook.com/pages/Mariah-Lynne/295721153858612
Twitter:@MariahLynne1

Gulf Coast Heaven

A. Y. Stratton

Ariel Campbell stood on the balcony six stories above the beach. "Listen to that surf!" She watched the waves roll in, spill across the path where the beach walkers trod, and glide out again. "Let's go, everyone! That's the Gulf of Mexico down there, and we're missing this beautiful day. Jenny? Where are you?"

"Bleaching my roots. Will you please bring me my robe?"

Ariel grabbed the pink robe off the chair and followed her sister's voice to the bathroom doorway. "Here. I'm going down right now. You can catch up."

Jenny Campbell, about to become Mrs. Timothy Layton Junior, squinted at a smudge of bleach on her temple. "Don't forget to cover yourself with sunscreen. I don't want my maid of honor to show up at my wedding with a pizza face."

"You'll never forget that day, will you?"

Jenny's laughter echoed off the bathroom walls. "Mom told you to stay home, but no, you had to be the talk of my high school graduation. Remember the jerk in my class who called you "Purple Prune" when you got so sunburned at the Lakefront during Summerfest? What was his name?"

Ariel shrugged. "All I remember is I had a crush on him for a while."

"No, way, Ariel. He was six years older."

"I always had crushes on your classmates, Jenny. Of course they never ever noticed me. I was pitiful. Stop laughing. It was not funny!"

"I'm sorry. I felt really sorry for you."

"Thanks a lot. Wait. Robby, that was his name. About a week after your graduation, I ran into him at the mall and actually got the courage to say hi. The guy with him asked Robby if I was the purple prune. I wanted to die." Ariel sighed. "I wanted to disappear."

Jenny rolled her eyes. "Well, you turned out all right. Wish I looked that good in a bikini. All the guys will be checking you out today."

"Thanks, Jenny. I promise not to get sunburned before the wedding." She turned and hugged her sister. "I am so excited for you and Tim. Everything is going be perfect. "Hey, if Mom needs me, tell her I'll do her errands as soon as I get back."

"Wait, Ariel." Jenny frowned. "I'm expecting a package. Would you mind checking at the desk?"

"Sure. What is it?"

"Table decorations. I found the cutest vases for our color scheme, white with pink stripes. They were supposed to be here yesterday, and the florist is having a fit."

Ariel paused at the door. "Pink, of course."

"Of course," Jenny said with a grin. "Even Tim liked them."

The phone rang and Jenny dashed for it. Ariel heard her sister gasp and start to blubber. "They lost them?" Jenny said. "That's impossible. All of them?"

When their mother burst from her bedroom and dashed to Jenny, Ariel escaped, hoping the crisis would be solved by the time she returned.

* * * *

"Excellent!" Derek stood on the patio of the tenth floor condo, inhaling the salt air. "Look at the parade of women on the beach, nothing but deep tans and deep cleavage!"

"Grow up, Derek!" Rob dragged his duffle into the living room and left it next to the couch. "Something's missing here. This room has a TV, a bar, and two couches. Do they both turn into beds? Nope. Just one does." He swung around. "Where's the other bedroom?"

Dave slumped into the nearest couch. "It must be through that door. Pretty nice place, eh? And it's hot out there. Think it's too hot for golf?"

"Swim first, then golf? Great idea, coming here, Rob." Derek unzipped his bag. "Bathing suit right on top." He stripped and pulled on his trunks. "What are we waiting for?"

Rob tried one of the doors which turned out to be a closet. He spun around with a piece of paper in his hand and frowned. "Where're the other bedrooms?"

Derek turned away from the window. "What do you mean?"

Rob threw up his hands. "I can't believe it. This is it, a one-room condo." He squinted. "We were hooked by false advertising. Sure, it sleeps four, four people eager for close companionship." He gritted his teeth. "So here's the deal: the lowest two scores on the golf course sleep on the couches. Other guys get the floor."

Derek shook his head. "Wait, Rob, let's put this to a vote. It's hot. We need to cool off before golf. The water awaits. All in favor?"

Rob was outvoted.

* * * *

Still worrying about the centerpieces, Ariel strode through the lobby, out the revolving door and down the garden steps. Their mom would find something to substitute for the missing vases. She always managed to save the day.

The Gulf of Mexico sparkled in the afternoon sun. Seagulls and pelicans swooped and swirled. Children's screams faded in the gentle wind. When her clogs sank into the soft sand, Ariel stopped and inhaled. No more dry wintry winds. No more frigid nights. For the next few days she'd be parked right there on the beach, in the warm sun, or floating in the Gulf, as if she was… As if she was what? As if she was head of the advertising department, instead of the groveling assistant. As if someone was madly in love with her, grinning at her the way her sister's fiancé did when they held hands.

Ariel strolled around the giant L-shaped pool twice before she found an empty lounge chair. She spread her towel, dropped her bag, and headed for the water. Not the pool. She dived into the Gulf of Mexico, feeling the water slip across her back. She sank back and let the waves swirl around her like a silky blanket. Gulls and pelicans soared above. A cloud appeared and vanished. The day was divine.

The thunk of a volley ball got her attention. Ever since high school, she'd loved the game. Every year the coach would tell her she was too short for the game. And every year she proved the coach wrong. She tried to stand up and realized she'd drifted so far from shore that she had to swim in. The volleyball game had just begun. Four guys were pulling off their shirts, looking like hotshots hoping for an audience. She smiled. She'd probably have to bully her way into the game, but she didn't mind the challenge. Dripping wet, she strode past them to her lounge chair, dried off, pulled on her baseball cap, and slogged through the sand again right up to the tall guy who was about to serve..

"Mind if I join you?" All four of them froze and frowned at her.

The tall guy who happened to have quite a nice body spun the ball on the end of his finger and grinned. "You play volleyball?"

"Varsity in college. And you?" He looked familiar. Had she seen him somewhere before?

His eyebrows slid up. "You played volleyball in college? Okay." He shrugged. "You're on my team, then, but I warn you, this is high stakes. The team that loses pays for one night's stay at the hotel."

"Great idea!" She reached to shake his hand, and then hesitated. If she lost, she'd have to borrow the money. She grinned. Her team always won.

The guy nodded. "You're on. I'm Rob, that's Derek, Dave and Jake. And you are…"

"Rob?" Ariel pointed at him. "Hey, I remember you. You're from Milwaukee, right?"

"Right." He bit his lip.

"You were in my sister's class in high school."

"Maybe." Rob frowned at her. "Who's your sister?"

"Jenny Campbell." She watched Rob's double take.

One of the other guys laughed out loud. "*The* Jenny Campbell? Rob remembers her really well."

"Oh, he does?" Ariel asked. "And why would that be?"

Rob looked as if he hadn't heard any of that exchange. "We dated a couple of times."

"Yeah. More than that." Ariel laughed. "I used to spy on you when you were parked in our driveway. And you embarrassed me at your graduation."

That got a big laugh.

"I embarrassed you, huh?" Rob tossed the volleyball into the air and caught it. "Hey, are we going to play volleyball or are we gonna talk all day?"

* * * *

Rob was thinking the woman was a surprisingly good volleyball player, considering she was no more than five feet six. With a nice body. Weird how she remembered him. So she was Jenny's sister. He sure remembered Jenny. But the sister didn't ring any bells at all. Maybe she'd changed a lot since high school. In all the right places. Ariel was an odd name. Did he ever know a girl named Ariel? And what had he done to embarrass her?

The play went back and forth, with the men beating her to the ball. She'd probably get bored and quit. Big surprise. When she finally got her turn to serve, she won every point, spiked a winning shot, and dug out a bunch of others. She was fast, aggressive. She even chased one that was obviously going out and leaped for it, sending it deep. Their opponents didn't expect it and let it drop. Rob gave her a thumbs-up and a pat on the back.

The next few points were quick and brutal. Their side was solid at the net, but five deep shots forced them back. Rob called a huddle and explained his new strategy. The two men would play net, with Ariel covering the back. The next serve came right at her. She sprang for it. So did Rob. They landed hard, face down in the sand.

"Sorry about that. You okay?" Rob reached for the woman's hand. She stood up and then bent over holding her nose. Blood gushed down her lip and chin. "Holy crap!" he yelled. "I hope your nose isn't broken." He helped her sit up and waved at the guys. "Hey, bring a towel, quick!" He bent down to get a look at her face. "I'm sorry, Ariel." She wasn't speaking, just moaning something about her sister. "And ice, guys. Get some ice!"

"I'm okay," she said pinching her nose. He held her hand tightly as she tried to stand in the soft sand. Blood trickled down her neck.

When they reached the walkway he pulled off his T-shirt and handed it to her. "Here. Press that against your nose and keep your head down. Look at the ground.. I'll walk you to one of those lounge chairs."

"Thanks," she said, sounding like she was about to cry.

Rob had his share of bashed noses. They hurt like hell. He led her to a row of empty chairs. "Here, lie down, and keep looking down, pinching your nose. I'll be right back." She was beautiful, even with tears in her eyes; even with blood streaming down her chin, neck, into her—bikini top. Really beautiful.

Ariel couldn't hear, couldn't think. The shattering pain consumed her. She hugged the T-shirt to her nose, choking back tears. Rob disappeared for a few minutes and returned with a bag of ice. He stared at her for a second and backed away.

"You'll be fine, you know?" He licked his lips and breathed hard. "Once the swelling goes down, you'll have some bruises, but I don't think it's broken."

"My sister is going to kill me." She crumpled onto the lounge chair and started to moan.

"What can I do?"

"You can tell my sister I won't be able to be in her wedding."

"Oh, crap! When's the wedding?"

"This afternoon."

He sat down on the lounge chair next to her and reached for her hand. "I'll be the messenger of the bad news, if you want. Uh-oh, was that the wrong thing to say? I mean, please, don't cry any more. People are staring at us. They think I beat you up." He was trying to make her smile. It wasn't working. "When you're ready, I'll go with you to see your mom."

"No need. Here she comes." Ariel pointed to an older woman striding onto the beach and waving at them.

* * * *

Jenny marched over to the living room couch to hand Ariel another ice pack and kissed her on the forehead. "Well, little sis, look at it this way—you got Mom off *my* back—just like the old days, when I'd come in late, and you would bale me out by doing something worse."

"It hurts to laugh. Jenny, I am so sorry. I've ruined your wedding."

Jenny shook her head. "That's ridiculous. So what if you walk down the aisle with a little bump on your nose? You know Mom will cover it with makeup. And anyway, everyone will be looking at me, rather than my gorgeous sister."

When Ariel began to cry again, Jenny pulled her into a hug. "Why are you crying now?"

"Because you're so sweet to me. Tell me some good news… did you finally get the table decorations?"

"We'll see."

"What do you mean?"

Jenny took a deep breath. "The decorations arrived in Naples, all right—Naples, Louisiana."

Ariel waited for her sister to explode. But she didn't. She was amazingly calm. "I'm impressed with you, Jenny."

"For what?"

"For being so nice when things are going wrong, for being so reassuring. I thought you'd kill me."

"I might have killed the florist," Jenny said with an evil squint, "And I'm definitely going to kill Sam."

"Sam? Is he one of the groomsmen?"

"Yes, Tim's best man. They were roommates at Northwestern. Handsome guy, but oh, so forgetful. Sam, who, get this… forgot his I.D., missed his plane and might or might not get here until six o'clock." By the time Jenny finished the sentence, her face was bright red.

"He'll miss the wedding. Oh, dear."

Jenny nodded. "It was bad enough that we had to send Daddy out to locate table decorations that will match our color scheme, but now Mom wants to find someone to fill that tux hanging over the door." Jenny crossed her arms and frowned. "Do you know anyone who's tall and muscular and happens to be staying in this hotel?"

"Cousin Jimmy?" Ariel said. "Oh, he's too short. How about one of the bridesmaid's husbands? Chuck's too skinny. Oh, wait. No!" She grimaced. "Never mind. He'd never do it."

Jenny squinted at her. “Who would never do it?”

“You remember Rob, the guy who was in your class,” Ariel said, “The one who embarrassed me when I got all sunburned?”

“Yes, I do.” Jenny covered her mouth and giggled.

“He’s the guy I was playing volleyball with today. Thanks to him I have a broken nose. He owes us.”

“Robby Carlson is in this hotel? How does he look? Is he still in shape? I’ll call him. Now.” Jenny headed for the hotel phone and lifted the receiver. “It’s worth a try. This could be very interesting.” Jenny chuckled as she lifted the phone. “Crazy, but interesting.”

Rob was standing on the high dive platform, preparing to win the competition between him and the guy they met on the beach, when he heard his name over the speaker system and almost had a heart attack. Had his credit card bounced? Did someone die? He did a lousy double flip, swam to the side, pulled himself out of the water and jogged to the pool guard who directed him to a phone. He listened to the message and was relieved and then baffled.

Jenny Campbell, a high school classmate whom he remembered very well, babbled on about her sister, Ariel. And Ariel turns out to be Ariel Campbell, the volleyball player with the bashed-in nose. The nose that he bashed in, accidentally, of course, but nevertheless. Nevertheless a disaster. And then there was something about an usher who had missed his plane and was going to miss the wedding, and something about a tuxedo that might fit him.

“Wait a minute!” He interrupted her breathless flow. “Exactly what do you want me to do?”

“Here, I’ll let Ariel explain it. I am all flustered.”

Well, he’d be glad to talk to Ariel. She might make sense. “Fine. Put her on.”

“Hi, Rob.”

Her voice sounded soft on the phone. She’d been in his thoughts ever since the incident. Correction—ever since he saw her in that bikini. “Hi, Ariel. Has the swelling gone down?” He heard her sigh.

“A little.”

“That’s good. Your sister sounded, uh, pretty frantic,” he said. “I was afraid you were in the hospital. What’s going on?”

"One of the groomsmen can't come to the wedding, which is in two hours."

"Really? Whoa. That's too bad. Wait, does she really want *me* to fill his place?"

"Yes."

"Okay, why would anyone want a stranger in their wedding?" Would he ever get that golf game in? Or would this whole day be a disaster?

"There are five bridesmaids plus me, and there are five groomsmen, plus the best man. Even, see? But now there's only four groomsmen.

"Why me?" Rob asked, hoping he'd nix the idea in favor of golf. "There has to be someone on the guest list who would fill in."

"That's the trouble, Rob." Ariel hoped she sounded urgent, but not desperate. "No one we know is big enough to fit into the absent groomsman's tuxedo."

Rob laughed. "It's the Cinderella story in reverse. If I can fit into the tuxedo, I get to be in the wedding?"

"That's the deal." She laughed with him, relieved that he hadn't told her she was crazy.

"What do you think? I mean, it's okay if you are busy with your friends. We'd understand.—I mean it's awkward…"

"Where do I go to try it on?"

"Uh, here. We have a suite on the top floor."

"Want me to come up right now?"

"That would be great, before my sister has another meltdown." Rob's chuckle made her stomach unclench.

"I'll take a quick shower. What's the room number?"

The guys were huddled in front of the TV watching basketball, when Rob marched into their miniature room. In his hand was the hanger holding the tuxedo gear. No one looked up.

"You won't believe where I just was," he said. No one responded. "Hey!" Rob bellowed. "I have news." Still no reaction. So he stood in front of the TV until they all started grumbling at him. "I won't be with you guys tonight."

Only Derek turned and frowned. "What happened to a golf game? And what about going to the Everglades Room to watch the game on the giant screen? Are you sick? Wait, did you go shopping?"

"I have to be an usher in a wedding." Rob saluted Derek and hung the clothes up in the closet. "Jenny's wedding."

"Who's Jenny?"

"Ariel's sister."

"Ariel, the girl with the bloody nose?"

Rob nodded. "One of the groomsmen is a no show, so she asked me."

"Who asked you? Oh, I get it." Derek squinted. "Hey, guys, listen up: pretty boy Rob volunteered to help sweet-looking Ariel, the victim of the volleyball collision, by serving as an usher in a wedding." He turned and wrinkled his nose. "Rob, nobody normal volunteers to be in a monkey suit when he could be in a bar watching basketball. Even if the woman has a body like Ariel. Nobody."

By the time Rob found the Green Terrace where the photos were about to be taken, the photographer was already lining up the groomsmen. "Hurry, gentlemen," the man said, as he adjusted his camera. "We want to get the sunset in the perfect angle. Over here, sir, yes, you," he pointed to Rob, "You're limping. Are you okay, sir?"

"Not really, thanks for asking. I'm wearing a pair of shoes two sizes too small."

An older woman, the mother of the bride, he assumed, turned to him and pinned a pink flower on his lapel. "You look very nice, young man. We are grateful that you agreed to help out this evening." She brushed a speck of something of his shoulder and moved to the next guy.

The bridesmaids arrived, circling and chatting with the groomsmen. One pointed at Rob and nodded. He had never seen so many pink dresses in one place. And pink shoes and pink bouquets, even pink necklaces. He obeyed someone's order to get in the back row right behind the groom, and the guy turned to face him.

"Hey, I'm Timothy, Tim to everybody. You are one heck of good man to do this voluntarily."

"Thanks." Rob extricated his hand from the firm handshake. "Have you met the bride's sister? She's very persuasive."

One of the groomsmen laughed loudly. "Did she bribe you?"

Rob laughed. "She did."

"With what?" The other two groomsmen elbowed each other.

"She promised to marry me if I did this. Pretty good deal, eh?"

"Very funny," Tim said. "Really, did they offer to pay you?"

He grinned. "Nope. So far my only reward is a bunch of blisters from these shoes. Where are the bride and the sister?"

"Hiding out so we don't see each other before the wedding. We have to move into the bar now, to make way for their turn with the photographer. Come on, I'll buy you a drink."

* * * *

"I saw him," Jenny said, grabbing Ariel's hand with her sweaty one.

"Who, Timothy? Jenny, that's bad luck."

"No, I saw Rob. Ariel, he was good looking in high school, but now, wow!"

"Yes, he looks good in a tux." Ariel knew he would.

"Hey, he's coming this way, looking for you, I suppose. Yoo-hoo, Robby, come here and tell us why you're limping."

He didn't answer Jenny, didn't even glance at her, but kept walking right up to Ariel and reached for her hand. "Hi. You feeling better?" His voice was soft. "Your nose looks fine."

"Thanks," she said. "The ice really helped. And by the way, you look really good in the tux. It fits you perfectly. What's wrong with your foot?"

"What? Oh, my foot. These shoes don't fit."

"They're Dad's. He's the only one who thought to pack two pairs of dress shoes. Sorry about that. You get to take them off when we get to the beach anyway."

"Really? That's great. Why?"

"Because it's too hard to walk on the sand, especially in heels. Everyone, even the guests, leave their shoes on the patio before they walk to the seats."

Rob sighed. "That's a relief. Can I leave them off while we're dancing?"

"While we're dancing? Oh, you mean after the ceremony?" Thinking about dancing with him sent heat up Ariel's neck.

He faced her and took her other hand. "You have a nice family,

Ariel, really friendly. Your sister's fiancé seems like a good guy."

If he didn't stop staring at her, she was going to have to sit down to catch her breath. Luckily, the photographer called the bridesmaids to gather around the bride. "I have to go over there."

"I'll wait here for you."

All that attention from Rob was making her crazy. He acted as if he really wanted to be her date. Well, of course—he must be feeling awkward. He didn't know anyone else to talk to.

Ariel had never seen a more beautiful setting. The beach looked like a movie set. The sun was low, an orange glow floating over the horizon. Wisps of clouds scudded southward. Pelicans circled and careened, breaking the glimmering surface of the sea and swooping up again. Rows of chairs were set in a semi-circle on the beach, facing the spectacle. On each chair a pink bow waved in the gentle breeze. Elegantly dressed guests filled the chairs. Moments after piano music echoed from speakers set up near the podium, she saw two young boys look up from the sand castle they were building and dash across the sand to spy on the action.

Rob and one of the groom's sisters were the first two down the aisle. Ariel and the Best Man were last. She turned to face the minister, her throat so dry she couldn't swallow, and saw Rob grinning at her. He looked wonderful. For a minute she forgot about her sister on her special day and imagined what it would be like to dance with Rob, with his arms around her, his cheek next to hers. She hardly knew him, but she knew she wanted him. And he wanted her.

The ceremony was just right. Perfect music. Short, thoughtful comments from the minister. Everything went smoothly, until the bride made her entrance to the tent. The guests were silent, settled in their chairs, waiting for the bridal couple's first dance. The band was playing a waltz. Jenny entered the tent hugging her new husband to her side and gasped. "What are those things on all the tables?" Her eyes scanned the crowd for her father.

The bridesmaids giggled first, and then the laughter spread to the groomsmen and finally everyone in the tent was laughing.

Her father stood, silenced the band with a wave of his hand, and lifted the microphone. "I did my very best, Jenny dear." He bowed. "You ordered pink and I found pink."

"Oh, Daddy, thank you!" The bride hugged her husband's arm. "Pink flamingos. They're even better than the centerpieces I chose. The whole room looks like a kid's birthday party."

She smothered her father in a hug. Still clinging to Jenny's hand, he turned to the crowd. "There's one flamingo for every guest, so please don't leave the party without your bird. I bought every pink flamingo in Florida!"

On the beach again, hours later, Ariel and Rob watched the moon and its shimmering ribbons of light.

"Are you chilly, Ariel? Here, let me give you my coat."

She snuggled into it, absorbing the warmth from his body, inhaling his male scent. "It was a wonderful wedding, wasn't it?"

"Yes." He slipped his arm around her waist. "Wonderful."

"Thanks again for helping out."

"You don't need to thank me, Ariel. I had a great time."

The silence grew. They were alone. "I'm sorry it's over," Ariel said.

"Are you going to stay a couple more days?" he asked.

Ariel sighed. "I wasn't planning to. How about you?"

"We're here for a week."

"Hmm, you're staying a week with all your buddies?"

"Yep." He turned her around and kissed her on the lips, lightly, being careful about her nose. "I'm glad we met, Ariel."

She slid her arms around his neck and kissed him back. "Me too. You're nicer than you were when you were in high school, when I had a big crush on you."

"You're kidding, right? Did I know about that crush?"

"Of course not. You made fun of me, after I got a really bad sunburn." She sighed.

"I did that? Why would I do that? Wait, were you the kid who followed me around all the time? "

She nodded. "I was a brat."

He pulled away and shook his head. "You're, um, not a brat now. And you grew up beautiful, and um, really, what should I say?" He brushed a lock of her hair off her forehead. "Really beautiful."

She giggled until he laughed into her ear, tickling her with his breath and holding her close. They danced cheek to cheek, her arms around his neck, both of them humming the last song the band had played, an old favorite her father had requested, "I'll See You in My Dreams."

"I don't want this to end." He kissed her forehead. "Any chance you can change your plans?"

What should she say? Don't think. Don't analyze. Just do what you really want to do. "I have some vacation time. I could mention the injury to my nose." She leaned her head against his cheek. "You think your buddies would miss you if we spent the rest of the week together, playing volleyball and swimming, and um, getting to know each other?"

A low rumble burst from his chest. "They'll be glad to get me out of the way. I annoy them, boss them, belittle them, and beat them in every sport." His whisper tickled her ear. "And now they have plenty of toys to play with."

"What toys?"

"Your father's flamingos, of course. I guarantee those guys will make up an event involving the diving board and flamingos. Or flamingo volleyball. Maybe flamingo foot races. Besides, I have some work to do. Did I mention I'm a free-lance journalist? I decided my topic this week is Florida's wedding industry. You can help with my research."

THE END

About the Author

A. Y. Stratton

A. Y. Stratton grew up in Glenview, Illinois, and Elm Grove, Wisconsin. By the time she was 14, she was determined to write stories like Ellery Queen, Mary Roberts Rinehart and Agatha Christie.

While her children were young, she submitted short stories to magazines and newspapers and received rejection slips. A.Y. jumped at the chance when a friend asked her to write cover stories for an ad publication. Next she begged her way into free-lancing for a string of community newspapers, which led to her own bi-weekly column.

After A. Y. joined Romance Writers of America, she concentrated on writing on romantic mysteries. In September of 2009, The Wild Rose Press published *Buried Heart*, a romantic suspense tale involving an uptight public relations agent, an archaeology professor and a Mayan Codex dating back before the invasion of Cortez.

Buried Secrets, Stratton's romantic mystery released in November, 2013, begins when a man and a woman break into the same house and on the same wintery night and witness a murder. It is available in paperback and digital.

Tickled Pink

Diana Welker

The snowbirds exit from Southwest Florida meant fewer employees, so today Rayanna Ladd expected to lose her job. The last-in-first-out theory.

Six months ago, the owner of the hair boutique she'd managed announced bankruptcy. Today she expected her current employer, Ms. Penelope Penrod, to announce her dismissal due to the usual drop in seasonal business.

After a final spritz of spray to her long dark curls, she inspected her hot-pink manicured finger and toenails. She surveyed her overall appearance in the slightly cracked mirror on the back of her bedroom door. Turning in a complete circle, she scrutinized her white slacks, neon pink shirt, and her bright rose sandals. Perfect.

The upside of her pending unemployment meant she wouldn't be required to wear the salon's official pink flamingo color. Even though the color showcased her walnut eyes and olive complexion she swore she would never own anything pink again.

No pink in her future.

A quick survey of her immaculate, tiny bedroom assured her of the order she must maintain in her ten year old son, Jason's, life. An inspection of her son's bedroom and their living/kitchen area revealed nothing lying about.

Her verbally abusive ex-husband accused her of being a neat-freak because he refused to accept their only child's mild form of Asperger Syndrome. Chaos turned Jason into a demon. Neatness and calm soothed him. She, too, placed a premium on cleanliness and order.

Tickled Pink

A glance at Jason's black Kit-Cat clock confirmed she needed to hurry. The drive from Bonita Springs to Naples took forty minutes on a good day and leaving now would give her a ten minute cushion. In the operation of the spa, Ms. Penelope deemed punctuality as necessary as water.

The traffic reporter on Channel Two announced an accident at the corner of Tamiami Trail and Pine Ridge Road, a couple blocks north of her destination. The detour would negate her extra time. He added a warning that the police would be monitoring Interstate 75 between Corkscrew and Pine Ridge Road. No heavy footed driving this morning. Her tight budget didn't include extra money for speeding tickets. She could barely afford Jason's weekly Saturday night splurge at New York Pizza and Pasta.

Rayanna clicked off the TV, grabbed her keys, and headed for her blue Honda Civic. When she'd explained to Jason that she'd brought him home from the hospital in this car, he'd included weekly washing "his" car as a favorite activity…another weapon for her ex-husband's neat-freak accusations. But he'd dropped out of Jason's life immediately after the divorce three years ago. His abandonment had caused monumental problems and Jason's therapist despaired over his adjustment. Over the past several months they'd witnessed dramatic improvement. She maintained a secure atmosphere to keep him from backsliding.

During the drive, she planned what she'd say to Ms. Penelope and her co-workers. She hoped to maintain contact with everyone except Claudia, her I'm-always-number-one former friend.

No good came from thinking of her ex or Claudia, she realized, when the flashing lights behind her indicated a state trooper. Darn it. Only a half mile to her exit. So close. Easing to the shoulder, she stopped, rolled down the window, and waited for the officer.

"Good morning, sir," she stated in a non-panic she didn't feel. Late and a ticket. She gave the officer a tight smile.

He bent low. "Good morning. License and registration, please. Do you know why I stopped you?"

"I didn't pay attention to my speed." She unfastened her seat belt and reached into the glove compartment for her registration. "Much to my regret," she whispered.

He chuckled.

She retrieved her license from her flamingo-embossed salon bag and handed him both documents.

He said nothing as he checked her paper work. "Just a moment, please." He returned to his car.

She drummed her fingers on the steering wheel and looked at the car clock. Eight fifty five. A hard swallow helped fight the tears of frustration. Tears signaled weakness, an emotion she couldn't afford any more than the looming ticket.

The officer returned. "Ms. Ladd, you were four miles over, but I stopped you because your brake lights aren't working. Please see to that *ASAP*."

"Thank you, sir. I'll take care of it today."

"Good. And just a reminder." He tapped her license. "Your driver's license expires next month."

"Again, thank you." As she pulled away her relief turned to worry. What would the impending repairs cost?

One space remained in the employee parking area. Braced for a verbal reprimand and dismissal, she entered the employee's back door and headed for Ms. Penelope's office, decorated to rival a room in Versailles. Three pink walls, one featuring a huge oil painting of the flamingos at Hialeah Park, and a white one with a bank of ceiling to floor windows casting morning light on the birds. The white and gilded classic French executive furniture sat on pink carpet.

Ten folding chairs, nine of which were occupied, formed a semi-circle in front of the desk. Surprisingly, Ms. Penelope's white leather chair remained empty. The weekly meetings always began precisely at nine o'clock and the flamingo etched glass doors opened exactly one hour later.

Seated in the chair nearest the desk, Claudia leaned forward. A frown laced her enhanced, blonde eyebrows.

"You're late and so is Ms. Penelope. Were you two together?" Her hard voice matched the malice in her eyes. "In all my years here, I've never known Ms. Penelope to socialize outside of business. What are you up to?"

During her first few months at the salon, Claudia welcomed her, but as Rayanna's cliental grew Claudia's friendship cooled. When Rayanna took first place in the hair color competition at a trade show in March, their friendship ceased. Since her win, Claudia watched Rayanna's every move and criticism poured forth over the tiniest infraction. She suspected Claudia in last month's disappearance of her first place certificate and trophy.

Ignoring her, Rayanna placed her bag underneath the chair next to Eugene.

A scowling Ms. Penelope, dressed in a rose sheath with gold jewelry accents, rushed into the room. Seating herself, ram rod straight, she folded her hands and laid them on her desk. "Good morning, staff. We've much to cover. Unfortunately, I ended up directly behind a stupid driver who caused an accident on Tamiami Trail and it took forever to clear away." Annoyance laced each word.

Claudia leaned out and turned a smug smile toward Rayanna before looking at their boss.

"I'm certain that's the reason for Rayanna's lateness. She must have been behind you, but how did she arrive just minutes ahead of you?"

Her employer's auburn brows shot up. Her hazel eyes narrowed. "Were you caught in that mess?"

"A mess is an accurate description of this morning's commute." Rayanna believed in straight forward speech, but today spinning the truth seemed warranted. She would wrestle with her conscious later; after she secured her letter of recommendation.

Claudia started to interject, but Ms. Penelope pointedly glanced at the brass carriage clock and cut her off.

"We've wasted enough time. I want to get through our agenda." She handed Claudia ten copies to pass around.

Rayanna's name appeared after the first bullet point.

Ms. Penelope met her gaze. "Rayanna, congratulations. I'm proud to announce you've proven yourself these past six months with an exceptional client growth, and today you are officially a permanent member of our staff." She gave Rayanna a rare smile. "Your expertise boosted our client list. Plus, your award enhances our salon's image."

Her boss leaned deep into her chair. She interlaced her fingers and a brilliant smile lit up her countenance. "I received a call last week from a local freelance writer who wants to do an article about our salon with emphasis on Rayanna's recent win. This is not *can,* but *will* boost our image and give us an edge over the Golden Oasis." She unfolded her hands, sat forward, and absently reached for her pen. Tapping it on the blotter, she continued. "My goal is to topple them from the top of the Readers Choice Awards. We will be voted number one this coming year."

She straightened and made individual eye contact. "Whoever played that prank of removing Rayanna's certificate and trophy, return it before the interview."

Eugene broke the ensuring silence. "Wow. Congrats Rayanna."

Speechless, Rayanna glanced at her co-workers. A few girls sported wide grins and thumbs up. Relief overwhelmed her. The down side—no escaping pink.

Claudia scowled. "Whatever."

Her co-worker's sarcastic tone and warning lifted the fog of shock. "Ms. Penelope, thank you. I promise to give you one hundred percent."

"I wouldn't have made this offer if I believed otherwise." Ms.

Penelope tapped her agenda and wrapped up their meeting. The Elite Pink Flamingo opened on time.

Four days later, Ms. Penelope summoned Rayanna to the office. An open package sat in the middle of her desk. Inside, her certificate and trophy lay in a jumbled heap. Lifting the certificate from the meager packing revealed the broken pieces of frame and glass. A black marker had obliterated her name but the trophy, double wrapped, remained in perfect condition.

Ms. Penelope removed the mutilated certificate from Rayanna's trembling fingers. Her voice hardened. "If I ever find out who is responsible, I'll fire them."

"Thank you." With bravado she didn't feel, Rayanna held up the trophy. "This will be enough."

"For now. I'll contact the contest sponsor and see if they will provide a replacement. I'm relieved to have the trophy unharmed. Our interviewer will be here Thursday at eight-thirty."

Sometimes Rayanna wondered if her employer remembered she had a son. Two days—she just hoped her neighbor would be able to see Jason off to school. Upon her move into their apartment, Mrs. Beeson, better known as Aunt B, offered to help with Jason. With Aunt B's patience and experience as a long time school teacher, she and Jason bonded. Now Jason considered her part of his extremely small family.

Gathering up the certificate and trophy, Rayanna began returning them to the box.

Ms. Penelope stayed her hand. "Take the trophy and place it between the two large flamingos on the shelf behind the register. Leave the certificate with me."

The salon's arrangement contained an open airy welcome/reception space surrounded on three sides with small private styling rooms. Each room had a wide door so the stylist could see out. The fourth smaller area, located near the back, was designated for haircuts.

When she returned to the entry area with the trophy, her co-workers grinned and high fived her…everyone except Claudia, who'd taken off for a dental appointment.

* * * *

Rayanna's happiness topped the charts. Since the publication of her interview three weeks ago and with some added advertising, her bookings overflowed. For the first time since her divorce, she didn't fall asleep figuring out how to stretch her earnings.

Eugene, whom she'd been mentoring in color, thanked her constantly for the increased traffic. Through it all, Claudia remained sullen and silent.

Aunt B and Jason had informed her this morning that they would meet her, after work, at New York Pizza and Pasta for her birthday celebration. With a plumper paycheck, she planned to have a glass of wine. A birthday gift to herself.

This afternoon she had one more appointment, a haircut, with a difficult three year old and her more than difficult mother. It would take about an hour. Their initial appointment had included the mother but she'd called in yesterday cancelling her highlighting. That left her two hours before closing and she doubted, on an unusually hot Saturday afternoon, a walk-in would stroll through the door.

She'd hoped to leave early but no way that would happen. Claudia, already working on an intricate hair extension for a society matron, would close. Ms. Penelope left Claudia, their master stylist, in charge during her absence. Rayanna wouldn't give Claudia the satisfaction of denying her an early departure.

The mother and daughter tag team entered. Looking past them, she noticed a shabbily dressed, long haired, ill-kept bearded man wandering past the window. She couldn't be certain, but she thought she'd seen him yesterday sitting on the bench across the street. His odd actions had caught her attention when he made eye contact and then swiftly lifted the newspaper intent on the contents. Perhaps she had seen him at St Matthew's House homeless shelter where she and Jason helped serve holiday meals.

Dismissing the man, she turned her attention to the mother and daughter. "Good afternoon, Princess," Rayanna said to the youngster as she squatted down to meet her. Straightening she greeted her mother also. She returned her attention to the young girl. "Are you having a fun day?"

"No!" she exclaimed as she stamped her foot, crossed her stick thin arms over her beautiful designer outfit, and gazed hard into Rayanna's eyes. "My mother won't let me have ice cream after I'm done."

The impeccable groomed mother gave an inpatient huff. "Now darling, I explained to you about ice cream making you fat."

Rayanna held her tongue, but barely. Rayanna felt certain this woman, model thin and dressed in designer clothes, lived by the motto that you can never be too rich or too thin. A three year old shouldn't have to worry about such things.

She turned to the child. "With your mother's permission, I have an animal sticker book and it will be your salon gift."

Rayanna escorted them to the cutting area. "Would you like a sticker book?"

"Well…it isn't as good as ice cream, but I suppose." She flounced into the chair, faced the full length gilded mirror, and Rayanna attached the pink cape. "Can I have it now?"

"Why don't we wait until we finish? That way we won't get any hair on the stickers."

She twisted in the chair to face Rayanna. "Well, I won't get any hair on it, but you might."

"Perhaps." Rayanna gave her a tight smile. "Let's get started shall we?"

Her mother explained the exact haircut she expected. With eagle eyes she monitored each snip of her daughter's blonde curls. After much discussion, the mother announced satisfaction.

Before she could change her mind, Rayanna removed the cape and produced the book.

"Here are the stickers I promised. I hope you enjoy them."

The child examined the book apparently appeased. "Thank you."

"You're welcome, Princess."

The receptionist had already left so Rayanna finished the business transaction and ushered them to the door. "Thank you for visiting today."

As they exited, she saw the ragtag man leave the bench.

Making a mental note of her closing tasks, she turned toward her station. A rush of sticky air surrounded her as the door whooshed open.

Him! The man on the bench stood just inside the door arrayed in all of his scruffiness with a newspaper secured under his arm.

Their eyes met. His, an earnest plea. Hers, a question. She knew hers clearly stated, *what are you doing here?* She couldn't read his. But the jolt she received studying his large blue-gray eyes caused a shiver in spite of the intense heat they radiated. Heat in his eyes? Not likely. Heat of the day…yes. The shiver? Probably worry about what he's up to.

They spoke over each other. "May I help you?" Rayanna asked.

"Could I speak to you?" he inquired.

In the silence, while each waited for the other, Claudia and her client emitted loud gasps. Ignoring them, she inhaled a deep breath, caught a faint hint of his body odor, smiled her professional smile, and called forth the same calm she'd exhibited with the officer last month.

"May I help you?"

His gaze on the floor, he shoved his hands into his frayed pockets, huddled into himself, and took a step back. The folded newspaper remained tucked under his arm.

She instinctively knew he needed some kind of help. He wasn't here to harm them. Instead of her business smile, she gave him a wide grin. She reached out and touched his grimy sleeve.

"You asked to speak to me. How may I help?"

His head jerked up and met her gaze again. Those pleading eyes would melt a steel tempered heart. She had a marshmallow one. Her ex used to laugh and call her a real sucker. He might be right in this case.

"I..." He straightened to his full six-feet height, threw back his shoulders, which with a few good meals would be wide, and smiled. Another degree of heat surrounded her. No man ever affected her like this. Not wanting any of these emotions, especially from an untidy and unemployed person, she pulled her professional shield around her and waited.

He set his jaw. Determination laced his eyes. "I came here today to see if you would consent to a bargain to help me get a job."

Claudia stepped from her room. "Rayanna, if he is a personal friend, you need to take this outside." Her acid tone would dissolve gold.

"I'll handle this, Claudia" she whispered. "Please, return to your client."

Claudia shot them a killer look before returning, all smiles, to her customer.

She refocused her attention. "Please continue."

"Rayanna!"

Claudia laid down her rattail comb, but her patron shook her head, patted her arm, and in a low voice said something. Claudia, with a glare that would singe the devil, picked up her comb and continued working.

He shifted his attention between her and Claudia. "I don't want to cause you any trouble."

Ignoring Claudia, she kept her attention on him. "You won't." She could only hope. "If you want employment here, you'll need to talk to Ms. Penelope. She'll be in the salon on Monday."

The rumble of baritone laughter filled the salon and for the first time since entering, he relaxed. "No, I'm not seeking employment here." He glanced around at the Italian pink and adobe white walls, the rose marble counters, and flamingo mosaic floor and gave another heartfelt chuckle. "Please, let me explain."

This man intrigued her. The need to help him overrode her common sense. "Come back to my station. We'll talk there."

Weariness filled his eyes, but he followed her to the last station in the cutting area.

At the back of the room Ms. Penelope kept a delicate pink wooden chair, used for any unexpected overflow. She grabbed it, placed it beside her styling chair, and waved her hand indicating he should sit. His incredulous glance at the pink thing made her smile as he settled in.

"Are you certain you won't get into trouble," he asked as he laid the

Wall Street Journal across his lap.

"I'm certain." She crossed her ankles. As a child, she'd crossed her fingers, when she hedged the truth. "Now tell me about this bargain and the job."

He leaned back, removed the paper, and began tapping out a soft rhythm against his leg.

"It's no secret that I'm down on my luck. However, I haven't always been a hobo and I don't intend to remain one. I've secured a job interview." He held up the newspaper. "Listed in here. I have all the qualification and I've worked with the person conducting the interview. He assured me the position is mine. But obviously not in this state."

He stood up, reached into his pocket, and produced a worn grimy pouch. Reaching in, he pulled out an elegant thin gold wrist watch and with the care a mother would give a new born, held it up for her inspection "This is the only possession I have left." He resettled himself. "I would like you to give me an executive makeover. I'll leave this as payment, but I want your promise to hold it until I'm able to redeem it."

Before she answered, she needed to think this through. "Why didn't you take the watch to a pawn shop?"

Rayanna thought of the ramifications of accepting his proposal. No, he'd said bargain. The word proposal and this man didn't fit well for her. Surely, Ms. Penelope wouldn't object if *she* paid the salon for her work. She'd cashed her paycheck last night, so she had enough to cover the charges, but there would be no frills tonight or the next several weeks.

"I did. Told me only the gold case had value, and it didn't weigh a pittance. They offered me twenty five dollars. Twenty five dollars!" He ran his fingers through his dingy hair. "What am I to do with that?"

She couldn't endanger her job, but no one could object to helping out another human being could they? Doing the right thing was never wrong was it? A quote by Mother Teresa on a small plaque given to her son popped into her mind. It read, *Help one person at a time and always start with the person nearest you.* He qualified. Mind made up, she listened.

"Yesterday I sat on the bench across the street trying to figure out what to do. I recognized you from St. Matthews." He gave her another of those melting smiles. "You and your son are so upbeat. Never any pity. After seeing you yesterday, I decided to approach you for help."

Uncrossing her feet, she stood up. "I accept your terms. You're right. What can you do with twenty five dollars?" *Oh yes, have pizza with your son at his favorite restaurant.*

He extended his hand. "Thank you. By the way, I'm Gabriel Brock. Please, call me Gabe."

She shook his hand to seal the deal. "Pleased to meet you. I'm Rayanna. Let's get started, shall we?"

She reached for the pink cape. He took a step back. Laughing, she hunted around, found a black one, and held it up. "Better?"

His eyes sparkled. "Much."

For the next two hours she worked her magic. Shampoo, cut, styling, eyebrow trim, shave, and a manicure. She learned that he'd once held a vice-president's position with a New York based well-known failed financial institution, had lost his house and car, his wife and kids, and lastly, his self-respect. He explained that with every interview he'd either been suspected of helping cook the books, which he had not, or the interview ended with his favorite phase.

"You're over qualified for the position."

She finished his manicure, the last step of his makeover. His back had been to the mirror most of the time. "That's everything, I believe. Did I miss anything?"

"It's more than I anticipated. I've done all the talking Rayanna, and you've done all the work."

"We could cover my life in a minute or less. Yours has been much more, ummm, interesting." She stood, pushed the table aside, and inspected her work literally from the top of his head to the tips of his fingers. "Ready to see the results?"

A twinkle appeared in those soul searching eyes, and a wide grin accented a hidden dimple in his left cheek. He had the features of a Viking god.

She removed the cape, drew in a deep breath, and turned the chair. The sparkle turned to shock as he squinted and leaned into the mirror. His brow rose to meet his gray-touched onyx hair. Water swam in his eyes and he coughed. Clearing his throat, he met her eye to eye in the mirror. He held her immobile. Needing to break the strange bond, she shook out the cape.

"I don't recognize me," he whispered.

"Well, let's hope your old co-worker does."

He barked a deep laugh. "Be assured, I'll remind him." He removed the tattered bag, gently took her hand, placed it in her palm, and folded her fingers over it. Warmth fused their fingers.

"I value this watch above all else, but at this moment its value is diminished by your kindness and talent."

Never so glad she only cried when frustrated, she broke the contact, but not their intense gaze. "I promise to keep this safe. And I wish you the best on your interview." She needed to get her emotions under control. Breaking eye contact, she turned and headed toward the entrance. He trailed a few steps behind. As they moved down the row of mirrors, she saw him glance into each of them, disbelief showing in his every reflection.

The door loomed ahead, and she stopped a few feet short. She extended her hand and marveled at the gentle strength of his handshake. “Good Luck.”

“Thank you. I assure you I’ll return for my watch.” He swept his hands down the front of him. “And much better dressed, too.” He gave her a saucy salute and left.

Not one to pry into another’s business, she wondered where he would find clothes. She suspected one of the men at St. Matthews would assist him. He’d taken the first step.

Claudia and her patron stepped into the entry area. The matron approached and nodded her head toward the door. “He came in a bum and left a movie star…reminded me of a younger Harrison Ford. My dear, I can’t believe the talent you possess. They should call you Wonder Woman.”

Claudia gave Rayanna an I’ll-deal-with-you-later glare.

Rayanna turned her to attention to the matron. “Thank you.”

She moved behind the register, set her purse on the counter, placed the watch inside the zippered pocket, and removed money from her wallet. “Would you both witness that I paid the salon for each of the services I preformed?”

“Of course we will.” She turned expecting Claudia to concur.

Rayanna rang the transaction, made certain they saw the exact amount, and placed the payment in the register.

“This is highly unusual.” Claudia shook of her head. “I’m not certain Ms. Penelope will approve.”

The matron looked between them. “Well, if you think this young lady will get into any trouble, I’ll pay for it.”

“Oh no!” Claudia replied in a horrified voice.

Rayanna backed up Claudia. “That won’t be necessary. He left collateral and assured me he would return with payment.”

Satisfied, the matron left.

Claudia stomped to the door, locked it, and turned on Rayanna. “What did that tramp really want and whatever possessed you to allow him in here?” Towering over her, Claudia started walking Rayanna backward. “I always knew you had no class and this proves it.”

Rayanna stopped. “First of all Claudia, it isn’t any of your business. But if you must know, he has an interview for an investment broker position, but he couldn’t interview looking like that.”

“Investment broker? Really? Are you freaking nuts? He’s probably going to scam some old woman out of her life savings."

Rayanna threw her hands in the air. "You might be right. I've always thought the only difference between the two is one's legal and one's not." She headed to her cutting station. "I'm going to clean up and get out of here."

Claudia grabbed her arm and spun her around. "I guarantee you'll be sorry for all this."

"Claudia. Let. Go." She jerked her arm out of a wrestler's grip. "This is between Ms. Penelope and me. She'll understand." The conviction in her voice didn't match the uncertainty in her heart.

The clean-up took longer than she thought causing her to be a few minutes late for her "date." A bouquet of balloons and a small decorated cake set in the middle of the table. Eugene sat at the table with Aunt B and Jason. Over the last six months, Eugene had run into them when he picked up carry-out. Lately, he started coming in ahead of his pick-up time to visit with her son.

Jason spied her. "Surprise, Mom! Come and look what Aunt B and Eugene did. It's a party for you."

Stunned, she approached the table, stooped down and buzzed Aunt B with a kiss on the cheek and then repeated the kiss with an embarrassed Eugene. Jason didn't like public affection, so she refrained. "Thank you all so much. I had no idea. The best part of my day, believe me."

The little party cheered her, but she worried. As they left, she snagged Eugene and related the afternoon events.

"Oh, Rayanna, why did you do it?" He held up his right hand. "I know why you did it and I agree, but you may have to do some hard talking with Ms. Penelope."

"I plan to be in early on Monday to explain."

"Good Luck."

Rayanna left early Monday, but as she pulled into the parking area she saw her boss's car parked next to Claudia's. Not a good start. She composed her thoughts, entered the building, and walked directly to the office. "Good morning, Ms. Penelope. Claudia. How are you?"

Claudia smirked.

Ms. Penelope wasted no time on pleasantries. "Is the story Claudia told me about that bum true?"

Being defensive wouldn't help. "He is a long time unemployed man, assured of a job, but wouldn't have gotten it without help. I did the right thing and Ms. Penelope, I paid the salon."

"Damaging the reputation of this salon, especially in the presence of Claudia's client, is not the right thing!"

Her malicious tone rocked Rayanna. "Even Claudia's patron offered to pay. She…"

"Paying isn't the issue here. Lack of judgment is. You may perform whatever charity you wish on your own time, but not here. You're fired." Rising she started to the door. "I'll escort you to get your personal items. You'll never work here again."

The triumphant grin on Claudia's face said it all.

In spite of these two, Rayanna knew she'd done the right thing and that knowledge allowed her to make a dignified and silent exit.

The upside—no pink. Ever Again.

* * * *

Finding snowflakes outside her door in July would be easier than finding employment off season in Florida. Last night Aunt B had asked for a makeover. Rayanna felt certain Aunt B wanted to lift her spirits and it worked.

Approaching the checkout counter at Beauty Alliance, she saw a friend she'd graduated with at the Hair Design Institute.

"Beth, it's good to see you." Her diminutive friend hadn't changed. In school everyone thought they were sisters. "I thought you went to New York."

"I did, but didn't care for the big city pace. I'm a bone deep Florida cracker." She shifted her purse to her other shoulder and sat her purchases on the counter. "Are you working here in Naples?"

"I'm unemployed. Been to every salon from Ft Myers to Everglade City, but no luck. You wouldn't happen to know of anything."

"Sorry, I don't." She paused, head tilted to one side." But, if you don't have any prospects, I have a proposition for you. Just a minute." The sales girl collected for her purchases.

Rayanna paid for her few items and followed her outside.

Beth set her bags on the sidewalk. "I'm working at Shell Point Retirement Community but I have an opportunity to travel to Italy for a month. I've been looking for a good operator to take my place. If you'd take over for me, I could go. I'll give you my wages for the month and the tips are really, really good. I think you'd do extremely well. What do you think? You'd start in two weeks."

Her unemployment didn't allow for a single extra. When she told Jason she needed to cut corners on her budget, he brought her a circle of colored paper and told her to try it. He loved statistics, graphs, and math.

Indecision washed over her. If she took this, she wouldn't have time to job hunt, but this would keep her here for six weeks. Maybe something would open up. The thought of having to move Jason terrified her.

Besides, she didn't know how to get in touch with Gabe. The day after losing her job, she'd gone by the shelter but no one had seen him. She'd left word with the person in charge to call her if Gabe returned.

A big disappointment to be certain, but she couldn't decide if she'd lost faith in him or something entirely different. And she could use the money he owed her.

Beth indicated tips would be good. Maybe good enough for a renewed trip for pizza. "I'll do it."

"Fantastic! Bummed out didn't begin to cover my disappointment when I thought I'd be unable to go." She held Rayanna in a bear hug, released her, dug around in her purse, and held up her business card. "Call me the first of next week and we'll work out the details. I hate to rush, but I need to get back." Retrieving her packages, she started to her car. She turned and called back. "I can't thank you enough."

Rayanna came in a couple of days before Beth left to familiarize herself with the shop.

She loved the clientele, especially a spunky lady, nicknamed Bird, who had owned a beauty shop as she put it, "before the creation of light." Bird wanted all the details of Rayanna's employment at the Elite Pink Flamingo. She informed Rayanna that in her day a clean shop and the latest gossip spelled success. They didn't need all that fancy stuff.

The four weeks flew by.

Beth hadn't unstated the tips and Rayanna wanted to leave a thank you gift. She decided on a gift card at Beauty Alliance.

The same sales associate who'd helped her before stood by the register. "Hi, I need a gift card."

"Certainly." She began processing the card. "Didn't I hear you're looking for a job?"

Rayanna's heart beat escalated. "Yes, do you know of something?"

"The Golden Oasis will have an opening next week, but you can't tell anyone where you heard it. My roommate is giving her notice there next Friday."

"I'm on it. If I get the position, I'll buy you dinner."

"Just remember, you can't tell anyone where you heard about it."

"I won't. Promise."

Rayanna left the store, stopped by the Golden Oasis, and caught the manager between appointments. He recognized her from the newspaper article and without being aware he would be losing an employee, hired her. She started Tuesday. Before getting into her car she did a little happy dance.

On Monday Rayanna decided to volunteer at St. Matthew's House for lunch hoping to see someone who knew Gabe. Two people did, but neither had seen him. On most occasions serving at the shelter brought joy, but disappointment filled her time. He'd left a deep impression, and she couldn't shake the memories of him.

The Golden Oasis manager advertised color specials with Rayanna, and her clientele flocked to her new location. For the next several weeks, they related various false stories about her abrupt departure, including her supposed move out of state. Each time someone mentioned her moving, the worry of Gabe not finding her surfaced. She would keep checking back at St Matthews.

Yesterday, one client said Claudia insinuated Rayanna had been fired for stealing. Between appointments Rayanna contacted her manager. He told her not to worry. He'd heard the same thing, and after contacting Ms. Penelope, she verified that Rayanna had paid for the services. Not able to let it go, she called Eugene asking him to meet her Saturday night at the pizza parlor.

Her last appointment on Saturday canceled, so she picked up Jason and headed for the restaurant. He quickly claimed his favorite table. Her hungry son wanted to order the pizza just as soon as their drinks were delivered so it would be ready when Eugene arrived. Jason did things in an orderly way. Drinks, pizza, check when he finished the last bite. And no paper napkins. Only cloth which she carried in her large canvas carry-all.

Rummaging through her bag for their napkins, she said, "Let's order our root beer and I'll call him to make certain he isn't working late. Okay?"

"Eugene is already here." Jason pointed to the door. "But, I think he's with someone. Do you know him?" he whispered. Jason starting rubbing his forefinger and thumb together. He didn't do well around strangers. Eugene, a whopping grin on his face, waved to Jason.

She gasped. A stab of excitement speared through her. The sight of Gabe, impeccably dressed, a hesitant step behind Eugene made her fumble her bag. The contents tumbled to the floor.

Gabe brushed past Eugene, bent, and started retrieving her items while Eugene went directly to Jason and distracted him with some kind of gift. She needed to reassure Jason, but she also need to get her stuff off the floor. Frustration spawned the tears she despised. "I'm so clumsy," she whispered swiping them away.

His questioning eyes focused on hers. "I hope those are tears of happiness to see me and not tears of hoping-never-to-see-me-again."

Deja vu flooded her. A girlish giggle escaped. "I'm extremely happy and relieved to see you. I only cry and giggle when frustrated."

"I decree them happy tears so no need for frustration." He rose and handed over her bag. "You're back together." His gaze locked with hers for an intense few seconds.

Eugene, standing close to her son's chair, cleared his throat. "Gabe, I'd like you to meet Rayanna's son, Jason."

"Pleased to meet you, Jason. On our way here, Eugene told me you can recite all the stats for each one of the Tampa Bay Ray's players."

Jason lowered his eyes and fanned a pack of new baseball cards. She suspected Eugene brought the cards to ease Jason meeting Gabe.

Rayanna prayed he knew about her son's Asperger's. Gabe reached into his pocket and handed Jason a small Ray's watch with a nylon wrist band. "Your mom has been keeping my special watch safe for me and I brought this hoping it might become special to you."

Startled, Jason hunched his shoulders and stared at the floor. He clutched his cards but didn't say anything.

She knelt. "Jason, it's true. Gabe left me his special watch for safe keeping and he wants to give you one that might become special to you. Would you like that?"

He bobbed his head in affirmation. "Mom, we haven't ordered drinks. We should have ordered drinks."

"Our waitress is right here and we'll do that. We'll take our seats, order drinks, then the pizza, and you can show me your cards and try on your new watch."

Eugene and Rayanna took their usual seat flanking Jason. Gabe, laying the watch on the table, took the chair across from her son. After placing their order and getting their drinks, Jason began reciting all the stats for his new cards. Gabe listened attentively.

"Jason, I'm very impressed. During the last three months, I've been in St Louis training for a new job involving figures," Gabe said. "I enjoy numbers a great deal."

Jason looked over the table at Gabe. "I like math. I help Mom with our budget. Can I look at the watch?"

Gabe complied.

Her son examined it. "I like it. It has all the numbers. I like numbers."

"Jason, did you thank both Eugene and Gabe for your gifts?"

He took the cards in one hand and held the watch in his other one. "Thank you for my gifts. I like them."

The waitress arrived with their pizza. As they ate, Gabe explained that he'd come back to visit his grandmother, whom he hadn't seen in five or six years, and to retrieve the watch she'd given him upon his graduation from the Wharton School of Business.

He turned to Rayanna. "When I arrived yesterday, I went directly to The Elite Pink Flamingo. They informed you'd left and they didn't have contact information. I couldn't believe it." He glanced at Eugene. "He chased me down outside, asked me to meet him, and over dinner last night told me everything." He reached over and took her free hand. The heat of his touch seared her. Gabe laid his other hand on top of hers. "I'm so sorry for what happened."

"The situation with Claudia had become intolerable so it did work out for the best." Reluctantly, she withdrew her hand. "I have your watch at our apartment. How do you want me to get it to you?"

"I'll follow you home, if that's okay. I have an afternoon flight tomorrow so I'm meeting Grandmother in the morning."

Their waitress arrived and handed Rayanna the check.

"Oh, here let me get that," Gabe said as he reached for it.

"No! Mom always pays. That's the way we do it," Jason replied emphatically.

Resigned, Gabe agreed.

Rayanna laid her hand back on Gabe's. "It's no problem. We're going directly home."

On their way home, Jason inspected his watch and cards. "Mom, I like the numbers on the watch. I like Gabe, too. He doesn't make me feel different."

Rayanna's heart jumped a beat. Jason liked so few people upon first meeting. It proved Gabe's goodness. Then it hit her. Gabe wouldn't be in their lives after tonight. She must help Jason understand.

"Gabe is a very good man but he doesn't live here, so we won't be seeing him anymore."

Jason nodded. "I know. He lives at the St. Louis Cardinals." For the remainder of their trip Jason recited the stats for each of the Cardinal players.

Gabe parked beside her and followed them into the living room/kitchen. "Oh, I love the cat clock."

"It's mine," Jason said. "Mom told me her mom gave it to me on my first birthday. I like it."

"Gabe, please have a seat. I'll get your watch."

"Mom, it's time for *The Sandlot*."

"Yes, Jason, it is."

Rayanna started the movie, disappeared into her bedroom, and returned with the watch.

Gabe sat watching the movie with Jason. They resembled a father and son enjoying family time. Squelching that thought, she turned to Gabe. "Here it is just as you gave it to me."

He laughed. "Not exactly like I gave it to you. You washed the pouch."

Rayanna dropped her head and burst out laughing also. "Well, yes, I guess I did."

He placed the watch on his wrist and shoved the pouch into his left pants pocket. Reaching into his right one, he withdrew a bank envelope containing her payment. "Rayanna…"

"You two are talking too much," Jason informed them. "Mom,

aren't you going to watch with me."

As he handed over the envelope, he gave Rayanna an imploring look then turned to Jason. "Would it be alright if I stay and watch too? It's more fun being here with both of you than returning to my hotel room. And if your mom agrees, I'll treat you both to ice cream at the DQ. There's one open until ten on Tamiami Trail."

Jason remained silent for a few moments. "I would like that. I like hot fudge sundaes.

"Hot fudge it is young man."

Gabe kept his promise of ice cream.

Rayanna felt giddy. Licking the last of the hot fudge from her spoon, she couldn't help remembering Charles Dickens's, *It was the best of times; it was the worst of times.* The time to say good bye loomed. "This is late for us and we need to be going." She extended her hand and Gabe accepted with alacrity. His fingers enfolded hers and she wanted to hang on to *now* forever. "Thank you for a delightful evening. I wish you the best in your new life."

He didn't release her hand. "Thank-you is a two way street. Thank you not only for your help, but also for the great evening." Letting go, he took out his new wallet, removed three business cards and handed her one. "I hope we can stay in touch. I'd like you to call me." He removed a pen from his crisp shirt pocket and flipped over the second one. He pinned her with a gaze as soft as a caress. "And, I'd like to call you also."

Excitement zinged through her. "Now that sounds like a plan." Rayanna laser seared his face into her memory.

Tomorrow she would shop for a new phone…something with unlimited calling and texting. She gave him her cell number and the number of the Golden Oasis. Her temperamental employer wouldn't allow personal calls, but because of Jason, he'd allow the receptionist to take a message.

Gabe turned to Jason, scraping hot fudge from the side of his dish, and held out the last card. "I hope you, too, will call me."

Jason put his spoon in his dish and examined the card. "I don't have a phone, but I'll use Mom's. I don't need the card. I'll remember the numbers."

"I look forward to talking to you, Jason." He stood, came around the table, bent down, and planted a gentle kiss on her cheek. "And you too, Rayanna. Thank you again. And I am sorry about your job, but not one bit sorry I met you."

Before she could react, he gave her a snappy salute and disappeared.

They shouldn't have sat next to the entrance. If they'd been in the back, she'd have had more time to memorize him.

He called Sunday night to let them know he had made it back safely.

* * * *

For the next three months they talked and texted at least three to four times a week. Jason bonded with Gabe over the phone and Jason's therapist, who didn't think phone bonding possible, finally agreed. The ramifications of Gabe dropping out of their lives worried the doctor. A worry she shared for more than one reason.

Her feelings grew deeper with each conversation. The last couple of weeks his warm baritone voice whispering, "*Good night, sweetness,*" filled her with an intense yearning. Was it possible to fall in love long distance? Did he have the same feelings…the same longings?

Last week Eugene suggested Jason might enjoy Skyping with Gabe. Jason's therapist agreed. With the season in full swing, business continued to increase. Two weeks ago she'd decided to take their advice and give Jason a laptop, an early Christmas present. Six weeks early to be exact. She suspected seeing Gabe, even electronically, would be an early present for her too.

Under Eugene's expert tutelage, Jason excelled in all things computer. After dinner tonight, they would hold their first Skype session with Gabe.

Both excited and nervous she restyled her hair while Jason set up the computer. "Mom, Gabe's on screen and he wants you to come here. He has something to tell both of us."

She chided herself for dressing for a video date. With one last fluff of her curls, she leaned into the camera. "Hi, Gabe. Can you see and hear us?"

"I can. This is great."

"I couldn't agree more," Rayanna said. She couldn't tear her gaze from his face.

Jason nodded his head.

Gabe moved closer the camera. "I have news. I'm coming to Naples for Thanksgiving and hoped to see you guys over the long weekend.

What kind of plans do you have?"

Jason answered. "I always serve rolls at St Matthew's on Thanksgiving. Maybe you can help us."

Jason knew nothing of Gabe's background. Rayanna jumped in. "Are you coming to spend Thanksgiving with your grandmother?"

"Yes, I am. But Jason, if I hadn't promised to have dinner with Grandmother, I would've helped. I'd like to help on Christmas Day."

His gaze traveled to Rayanna. "But back to your plans for Thanksgiving."

"After we finish at St. Matthews, Jason and I come back here and share dinner with Aunt B. Would you like to come by for some dessert?" Rayanna held her breath like a teenager hoping for a date with the football captain.

"Would that be pumpkin pie with ice cream?"

"Yes." Both she and Jason answered at the same time.

"It's a date. I'm sorry, but I have to cut tonight short. I have a dinner meeting with a client and she called a short time ago to move the time up. Talk to you later and see you soon."

She'd gone to bed but the anticipation of seeing Gabe and a nagging worry about his dinner with a female had her so revved up she couldn't sleep. She prayed nothing would interfere with his trip. And that he felt the same about her as she felt about him.

And what if he didn't?

Her cell phone chimed. A text from Gabe. "Urgent. Need to Skype."

Despair swamped her. She just knew he couldn't come. Probably had a better offer in St. Louis. That woman probably invited him to meet her family.

She'd been fooling herself.

With trembling fingers she found the computer and jiggled it awake. After a few attempts she got the program up.

And there he was. So handsome and… his eyes raking over her face and dropping lower to the tops of her… "Yikes! Don't look. I forgot you can see me in my nightgown." She clutched at the lace edges of her V neck gown. She felt the heat of her blush every bit as much as the heat in his eyes. Those smoldering flames shot hot desire straight to her soul.

His velvet laugh burrowed deep in the pit of her stomach "Oh, Rayanna. I wanted to see your beautiful face before going to sleep, but this is so much better than I ever imagined."

"But your text said urgent. What's urgent?"

"Seeing you before I went to sleep."

Rayanna couldn't believe it. "Are you serious?" Her heart lurched. "Really?" Her voice softened. "You truly just wanted to see me before going to bed."

"No. I *needed* to see you. To see your face when I wished you a good night. He winked, gave her a two finger salute, pressed his fingers to his lips, and blew her a kiss. "Good night, sweetness."

Her screen went blank.

He didn't return her call or text until the following night.

The days melted like ice in August and soon Thanksgiving had arrived. She could hardly believe he would be here any minute. The remnants of their turkey dinner cleared, Rayanna placed the homemade pie in the center of her kitchen table along with colorful fall plastic plates and the forks and spoons wrapped in cloth napkins. Jason had inveigled Aunt B into playing a game of chess.

Even though she expected the doorbell, she jumped and dropped the knife she'd been about to place beside the pie. She snatched it up, threw it in the sink, and with a nervous, indrawn, breath opened the door.

"Hi, sweetness." Gabe handed her a dozen pink roses. "For you."

Their fingers met and the warmth she remembered arrowed straight to her toes. Unable to suppress her laugh, she took them and buried her nose in one. He knew how she felt about pink. "Oh Gabe, these are beautiful in spite of their color. Come on in. I'll get these into water."

Jason called from the living room. "Gabe, come watch me capture Aunt B."

"Coming." He gently kissed her cheek, bent close to her ear and whispered, "These roses match your blush. And I live for the day to see up close and personal that same blush in that same gown."

She burned pink as she turned her lips into the palm of his hand and placed a light kiss in the center. "Thank you."

"Ah, Rayanna."

Jason interrupted. "Gabe, are you coming?

His tender expression again sent those desire-arrows downward. "We *are* going to continue this conversation later." He turned and made the very short trip to join Jason.

Never having received flowers, she rummaged around and decided on a tall juice pitcher. She buried her face in the bouquet to memorize its sweet scent and interspersed the baby's breath and roses. She carefully folded the green paper. Silly but she would save it. She placed the roses in the center of their pass-through and joined the group.

Jason challenged Gabe to an engaging chess game, followed, thankfully, by rave reviews for her brandy pumpkin pie.

Gabe handed her his crumb-free plate. "I'll never be able to have another Thanksgiving with plain pie. This sets a new tradition." Something unspoken passed between them.

Jason wanted one more game before his ten o'clock bedtime. Aunt B departed. After announcing they'd each won one game, Jason went off to his room leaving Gabe and Rayanna alone for the first time.

She crossed the room. He stood and gathered her into his arms. "Rayanna, this has been the best evening I've had in years." He pulled her deeper into his embrace and gently kissed her.

Wrapping her arms around him, she deepened the kiss, but then pulled back. She wanted this. Oh, how she wanted this, but she needed to think of Jason. Before she said anything Gabe released her.

"Rayanna, I'd like for you to meet my grandmother tomorrow. I'm taking her to the Green Flash Restaurant on Captiva for dinner. Would you join us? I mentioned it to Aunt B and Jason during our first chess game and he agreed to stay with Aunt B. I assured him we would do Saturday night pizza."

"I won't be finished until three. I could be ready by four."

His grinned widened. "That's perfect. I'll pick you up at four." He kissed her hard, gave his signature salute, and disappeared through the door.

Sleep eluded Rayanna as she thought about their relationship. About the possible problems relating to Jason. By three o'clock the next afternoon, she didn't have a solution, but even if she had the excitement of spending time alone with Gabe overrode everything.

He looked like a native dressed in a light blue shirt and tan Dockers.

"What are you laughing about?" he asked as he helped her into the car.

"We look like we are going steady." She pointed to her tan Dockers and blue blouse.

"You say that like it is a bad thing." His penetrating gaze seared her.

She drew in a deep breath. "We do need to talk."

"Yes, we do. And I'm starting with Jason." He explained how, after meeting Jason, he had read all the material available on Asperger's, talked and spent time around the son of a co-worker with the same diagnosis.

As he parked on a strip of white sandy beach, she realized that during the trip he'd relieved her fears concerning her son. She felt entirely comfortable with Gabe in Jason's life no matter how their relationship evolved.

He helped her out of the car, bent down, kissed her, and caught her hand. "Come on, Rayanna, let's walk. I love the gulf."

She inhaled the scent of salt water and watched the sun lowering. She loved the beach at this time of the evening. A few others strolled along the sand picking up shells. Her heartbeat outpaced the lapping waves.

"Rayanna, I've done all the talking, but I find myself at a loss for words now." He wrapped his arms around her shoulders and pulled her to him, leaning his forehead against hers. "I've fallen in love with you." He gave her a quick kiss. "And I want to marry you." His sweet, gentle kiss deepened. She greedily drank it in and returned it with a passion new to her.

"Is that a yes?" he whispered in her ear.

"I think I fell in love with you when you gave me that first salute." She planted a return kiss. "That's a yes." As they broke apart, she looked beyond his shoulder. Her breath caught at the perfect lavender, pink and gold sunset.

"Gabe, look at the sunset. It's breathtaking." Shared love turned her world suddenly brighter. Happier.

"It's not as beautiful as you. He gave her a lingering kiss. "Or this moment. But I agree, it's magnificent… and a reminder. As delightful as stealing kisses from my fiancée is, we need to pick up Grandmother at Shell Point." He kissed her again. "She's a stickler for punctuality."

She waited in the car. Only a few minutes passed before she spied Gabe escorting Bird, the spunky retired beautician she'd met a few months ago.

Gabe opened the car door. "Rayanna, I'd like you to meet my Grandmother. I understand you know her."

Grinning, Rayanna turned toward the back seat. "It's so good to see you again. But I'm having trouble believing you're Gabe's grandmother."

Bird's eyes sparkled. "I've anticipated this surprise all day."

"You're a delightful surprise, but I can't believe Gabe didn't tell me about you?

"I asked him not too. It would've spoiled my plans."

Rayanna turned to Gabe as he pulled out. "Do you always listen to your grandmother?"

Gabe's eyes twinkled. "No always, but this *is* priceless."

Their table overlooked the water. When the waiter arrived, Bird ordered champagne. "Rayanna, I've a little story for you."

Watching Rayanna, she settled into the cushioned rattan chair. She nodded toward Gabe. "My only grandson went missing for six years and I despaired of ever finding him. A few months ago my oldest friend's daughter, who's known Gabe since childhood, had a hair extension done by Claudia at The Elite Pink Flamingo. She spotted Gabe there and rushed to tell me everything.

"Later, she returned to relate Penelope's mistreatment of you. I can't tell you how broken hearted I was, or how elated when you showed up at Shell Point."

"You knew I'd helped Gabe?"

"Yes, dear."

The waiter arrived with the champagne. "Please leave it chill for a few more minutes," Gabe instructed.

Bird continued. "If you remember, I questioned you about all aspects of the business."

Rayanna nodded. "I remember."

"Well, I started the Pink Flamingo." She raised her hand to keep from being interrupted. "On our fifth anniversary, my husband, my daughter, and I drove over to the Hialeah Race Track. He won the trifecta and gave me the winnings to open my own place. Our daughter, Gabe's mother, talked about the pink flamingos all the way home. She wanted her own. Intending to pass the business to her, I named it so she would always have her own flamingo. Since her death, I've hired mangers. Before retiring to Shell Point, I put the business in trust for Gabe. I suspect Gabe picked the salon because of his mother and me."

Gabe interlaced his fingers with Rayanna's. "I believed it an omen when I saw you at St. Matthews and then saw you walking into the shop once owned by my family. Sorry, Grandmother, I have a hard time believing I now own it."

"You do and I hope your first decision is to fire that despicable Claudia and Penelope."

Rayanna sucked in her breath. "Oh Gabe, that's not necessary."

"Yes it is." Firmness laced his words. "But I'll wait until we're married." His grin reached his eyes. "After I fire them, I'll need a new manager. Would you be interested?"

He released her hand, motioned for the waiter, and requested the bubbly be served.

While the waiter poured, Bird leaned forward. "Yes is the right answer, Rayanna."

"Oh… yes. Of course. Yes!"

Gabe lifted his glass for a toast. "To the two women I love and to our upcoming marriage."

Bird and Rayanna drank deeply.

Gabe, reached into his pants pocket, pulled out the clean tattered pouch that once held his watch. He drew out a beautiful flamingo designed pink gold ring pave` set with pink and white diamonds. "Rayanna, this ring was Grandmother's thirtieth anniversary gift. She hopes you'll like it as your engagement ring, but if not…"

Droplets trailed down her cheeks. "I love it." She *could* cry happy tears.

Bird held up her glass. “Gabe and Rayanna, congratulation, I’m just tickled pink.”

Gabe slipped the ring on Rayanna’s finger.

“I’m tickled pink, too.” Rayanna laughed at the irony of it. “Pink is my new favorite color.”

THE END

About the Author

Diana Welker

When Diana Welker learned her dream of becoming a writer/photographer for National Geographic would not be coming to fruition, she embarked upon a career, for the next thirty years, in the glittering world of jewels and gemology. After retirement, those old dreams resurfaced. She entered the world of words by combining freelance writing/photography for a regional magazine with writing romantic fiction.

www.dianawelker.com
https://www.facebook.com/diana.welker